"My world is differe
Sarah."

Something in his voice drew her gaze to his. "I'm not like other humans." His hand flattened on hers with more force. "But I'll fight to my death to protect you."

For the first time in years, Sarah trusted someone at their word. She looked into Max's tormented hazel eyes, and she let herself be lost. Lost to him, to the moment, to the whirlwind of emotions taking hold of her.

"I believe you," she whispered. Max felt the brush of Sarah's lips on his and it was all he could do to remain still, to hold back. But he had to hold back. Had to. Attached to him, mated to him, she would not be protected. She would share his destiny, his potential hell.

"Sarah…"

She pressed a finger to his lips. "Don't talk. I need you, Max. Make love to me."

Books by Lisa Renee Jones

Silhouette Nocturne

*The Beast Within #28
*Beast of Desire #36
*Beast of Darkness #43

*Knights of White

LISA RENEE JONES

is an author of paranormal and contemporary romance. Having previously lived in Austin, Texas, Lisa has recently moved to New York. Before becoming a writer, Lisa worked as a corporate executive, often taking the red-eye flight out of town and flying home just in time to make a Little League ball game. Her award-winning company, LRJ Staffing Services, had offices in Texas and Nashville. Lisa was recognized by *Entrepreneur* magazine in 1998 as the proprietor of one of the top-ten growing businesses owned by women.

Now Lisa has the joy of filling her days with the stories playing in her head, turning them into novels she hopes you enjoy!

You can visit her at www.lisareneejones.com.

BEAST OF DARKNESS

LISA RENEE JONES

Silhouette® Books

n o c t u r n e™

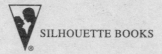 SILHOUETTE BOOKS

ISBN-13: 978-0-373-61790-6
ISBN-10:   0-373-61790-9

BEAST OF DARKNESS

www.silhouettenocturne.com

Printed in U.S.A.

Dear Reader,

One of the things I enjoy so much about writing
THE KNIGHTS OF WHITE is the message
throughout the series of good conquering evil.
And while the battles fought by these knights might
require swords, they also require the same things we
all need each time we face obstacles in our lives—the
courage to risk failure balanced by determination
not to fail.

Beast of Darkness is a story of sacrifice, pain, love and
faith. By the end of this book, you will know there
are new dimensions to the role the Knights of White
will play in the war against evil. The characters in
Beast of Darkness took me on a roller-coaster ride
of danger and emotions that kept me on the edge
of my seat as I wrote. There were times when the
battles exploded with excitement, when I feared the
outcome for some of the characters. Every time I sit
down to write a story in THE KNIGHTS OF WHITE
series, I am amazed at where the characters take me.
Each story has felt so different; each has been an
adventure I've enjoyed exploring immensely. I hope
you feel the same and enjoy *Beast of Darkness!*

Lisa Renee Jones

To DH for the supernatural marathon week of television, videos and books that helped me work through my plot points! And thanks to Jordan Summers for coming up with the name of my ghost town. The name sparked ideas and took my imagination in all kinds of new directions!

Prologue

He'd broken a rule and now he would pay a price. It was as simple as that. Max had taken the life of a human. His reasons didn't matter.

Pulling his Harley to a halt in front of Jaguar Ranch's west-end training studio, he killed the engine, prepared to face the consequences of his actions. His gaze lifted beyond the wooded terrain, taking in the barely visible main house. To its right was a cluster of extra housing where the Knights in training lived. This was home to The Knights of White. And for a short time he had felt he might finally have found his place here, as well. But he'd been wrong.

Dismounting his bike, Max sauntered toward the studio entrance, boots scraping the dirt-and-gravel path, apprehension working him inside out.

He took some comfort in knowing his actions had

saved a woman's life—and not just any woman. He'd saved the mate of one of his fellow Knights. A mate who had healed the stain of the beast inside that Knight.

But regardless of the reasons for his actions, he'd broken a sacred vow by taking a human life. And for that, he would face consequences. Though Max knew this, even accepted it, he was no more at ease as he stepped inside the air-conditioned studio. He shut the door with a thud that was unintended, that screamed of finality. Of hard actions to come. But then, he didn't expect leniency. Max knew how close to the darkness he walked. Four hundred years of battling the stain on his soul had worn him down.

Max felt the lightly padded floor beneath his feet, barely noticing the weapons lining the walls, weapons that were used in the war against the demon Beasts they fought, the Darkland Beasts. The lights were off; meditation candles flickered in each of the room's four corners.

Max's attention focused on the two men standing in the center of the room. He approached them, in awe of the dominating figures they both were, how similar in so many ways. Long, dark hair touched each of their shoulders, powerful bodies spoke of warriors, of Knights. But more than anything, an inner strength radiated from them both.

Max offered Jag, the leader of The Knights of White, a nod. Dressed in jeans and a T-shirt as Max himself was, Jag used his role as horse rancher to disguise his true role as demon hunter.

Though Max was centuries older than Jag, Max respected him no less. For Jag had brought hope to the Knights—even to Max. Jag had been the first to find a mate, to prove that the right woman could tame the beast in all of them. And he'd replaced the leader Max had once known, a leader who'd turned to the darkness inside himself, who'd become a Beast, turning away from the Knights. A leader who had forced his men into hiding to avoid death by his swords.

But Max's attention didn't linger on Jag. His gaze strayed to the man dressed all in white, standing beside him, to Salvador—the one who'd created him. The one who could end his existence with a mere wave of a hand.

Max met the light green stare of his maker with directness. If he were to fall this day, he would do it bravely; he would do it with his head held high. And he felt the touch of those eyes as if they moved inside him, as if they reached to the depths of his soul. Perhaps they did. Perhaps that moment, that look, exposed the truth in him: that Max was so near the darkness, he could almost taste evil with each breath he drew.

Long seconds passed before Salvador spoke. "Leave us," he said softly to Jag.

Jag hesitated. "Without Max's help, we would have lost Jessica. And without Jessica, I have no doubt Des would have succumbed to his inner beast."

Max's chest tightened at the protective gesture from Jag, regret biting at his gut. He'd been alone so very long. Finally, he'd felt a sense of belonging at Jaguar Ranch, and now it was in jeopardy.

But that realization didn't change the facts. He had to live with what he had done. Max knew all too well that he couldn't turn back time. Crossing his arms in front of his chest, he widened his stance. "I'm prepared to face the consequences of my actions."

Jag stepped forward then, pausing to lay a hand on Max's shoulder. "Peace be with you, my friend." And with those words, he departed.

Somehow, Max doubted peace would find him anytime soon. The heavy silence between Salvador and him certainly set his imagination to work, taunting him with the possible punishments he might face.

The sound of the door shutting, of Jag's exit, echoed in the room. Then, and only then, did Salvador speak. "You've been a Knight for how long?"

Max supplied the answer they both already knew. "Three hundred and seventy-one years."

"You've faced much in that time. Made tough choices."

"Yes," Max agreed.

"Fought the darkness and won when others failed. Devoted yourself to protecting humanity."

"Yes."

"Yet you chose to take a human life." It wasn't a question. "Why?"

Max squeezed his eyes shut. He'd dreaded this moment, hated what he had to admit. He forced his gaze to meet Salvador's. "I remember the human charging at Jessica with a knife. I tried to save her, but I saw the blade go into her side. I grabbed him and...I don't remember anything until he was on the ground. Dead."

Salvador studied him, his stare intense, potent. "So you have no idea why you killed him? Or even if it could have been avoided?"

"No." He shook his head, his throat dry. "But I cannot lie. I know I felt fury. And darkness. I was lost to what I felt."

Salvador raised his hand and a sword flew off the wall and into his hand. "On your knees, my son."

Max did as he was told without hesitation, his heart pounding wildly against his chest, his eyes cast to the ground in disgrace. He knew death by beheading would follow and he did not fear it. To take a Knight's head was one of the only two ways to kill him. But he wanted the end to be quick. He wanted this to be over.

"Choose now," Salvador said, the blade touching Max's shoulder. "Choose life…" Metal brushed the other shoulder. "Or choose death."

The words shocked Max and his eyes lifted to Salvador. He could barely conceive of what he was hearing. Was he being given another chance? "I don't understand."

"It's a simple question," Salvador proclaimed. "Life…or death?"

Indeed, it was a simple question. Max didn't want to fail the Knights, to fail his duty. And death meant failure. "Life. I choose life."

"You are certain?" The blade swung upward, above Salvador's shoulder, before slicing through the air. It drew to a halt a whisper from Max's neck. "One sharp movement and you can find the darkness you claim to embrace."

"Life," Max whispered. Though he tried to yell, his voice simply wouldn't come out. "I choose life."

Salvador pulled the blade away from Max's neck and tossed it in the air. It disappeared as if it had never existed. "To your feet, Knight." Somehow Max obeyed, his knees weak. Once he was standing, Salvador stood toe to toe with him. "You will be sent to a place few know of, a place where you will face a great test. There you will need every gift your centuries of life have given you."

Max's response was instant. "I will not fail."

"Make no mistake. This test will push you to your limits. It will force you to face your greatest fears. And you must face this test on your own, my son." He held out his hand to Max. "But you will not face it alone. You are never alone."

Max understood. He knew the Knights were always there for him. He knew Salvador was, as well.

He accepted his creator's hand and repeated his prior words. "I will not fail."

Chapter 1

Destination: Nowhere, Texas. A town with a strange name and no location on the map. Now, that little Nowhere town had managed to scare up stories of real supernatural troubles. Or so the town sheriff seemed to believe, which was exactly why Sarah Meyers and her team were headed that direction. They investigated the paranormal events, the unexplainable and often scary things most thought to be fiction.

Sitting in the passenger seat of the van, Sarah eyed the flatland around them, not a sign of life in sight. She glanced at Edward, a research assistant and friend, who manned the steering wheel on most occasions. He was their driver and electronics expert. "They don't call it Nowhere for nothing," she commented.

He grunted his agreement, which was about all Sarah expected from him. A big black man with the brains of a genius and the sense of humor of a rag doll, he didn't waste words. When he chose to speak, his words either had real value, or they were meant to annoy Cathy, who rode in the backseat for that specific reason. The two had a love-hate relationship, to say the least. At times, Sarah's ability to mediate Edward and Cathy's tiffs successfully felt like more of a gift than her ability to receive communications from spirits.

"What is a five-letter word for a breakfast?" Cathy asked, her voice laced with an Alabama accent despite graduating from the University of Texas. Cathy had an affinity for magic and crossword puzzles. The magic part of that equation had turned her into their field expert.

Edward flicked a look over his shoulder to offer a word choice. "Pizza."

Sarah smiled, not having to see Cathy to know she was rolling those big brown eyes, her brown bob bouncing around her head. Hunting spirits and demons who had nocturnal preferences demanded erratic hours, but it also bred a love of junk food—pizza being Sarah's favorite anytime snack.

Feeling a bit mischievous after the long hours trapped in the van, Sarah decided to aid Edward's efforts to tease Cathy. "I have to agree with Edward on this one. Pizza is—" Her words cut off as pain splintered through her head. "Oh." She moaned and grabbed her head, lacing her fingers through her long blond locks as she prayed the pain would ease.

Suddenly she was in the middle of one of her visions, a spirit communicating with her by making her relive an experience from the past. She was inside an unfamiliar car, seeing through the eyes of the female driver. She reached for the dash, but in her mind, it was the steering wheel. She had become the spirit that was guiding her.

Approaching an upcoming bridge, the rain pounding on the windshield, visibility near zero, she was nervous about the bad conditions, but the butterflies in her stomach were excitement not fear. Eagerness to get home, to celebrate her one-year wedding anniversary, dictated her mood. The special gift for her man waited in the backseat, adding an extra thrill. She couldn't wait to see his face when he opened the big box.

The radio screeched, a terrible sound that bit through her eardrums. She reached forward to turn it off, glancing down for only a moment, but it was a moment too long. Her heart lurched at the sight of an animal in the road—a big black dog of some sort. No. It was too big for a dog, but the rain made it hard to tell.

She honked as she approached but it didn't move; it didn't even seem to hear the sound. And she was close now, unprepared for its stubborn stance. Her foot slammed down on the brakes, pumping them to no avail. The brakes gave her nothing, they wouldn't work.

Her stomach was in her chest as she jerked the wheel to the right to miss the animal, relieved when she didn't make contact. But when she tried to right herself, the car was going too fast. The front bumper hit the bridge's edge with a jolt that shook her teeth. The second before everything went black, she called out to the one she loved. Allen!

Sarah snapped back into reality with a gasp of air, yanking herself to a full sitting position to ensure she wasn't in the water.

"Easy, easy," Edward said, grabbing her arm as if he were afraid she might need stabilizing.

"Are you okay?" Cathy asked, concern in her voice. "I swear, I will never get used to this happening to you. It scares the hell out of me."

"I'm fine," Sarah said, and she was. She had lived with these visions since her teen years just as her mother had before her, and hers before her.

Reality slid slowly into place as Sarah noted they'd pulled over in front of the very bridge she'd had a vision of. She reached for the door and got out. Walking to the edge of the bridge, she noted the skid marks and shivered despite the hot summer day, hugging herself.

Edward and Cathy appeared by her side, but they didn't say anything. They'd been around long enough to know she needed to process and think. Sarah stood there for what could have been seconds, minutes, or much longer.

When she finally turned away from the bridge, she spoke. "A woman was murdered on this bridge."

"How?" Cathy and Edward asked at once.

"Black magic," Sarah answered, knowing the impact the two words would have on her friends, knowing they understood the implications. If there was one thing the three of them knew, it was what kind of trouble the dark arts could bring. Thanks to the university's support and plenty of grant money, they'd seen far too many bad things in their time together. Whatever was going on in Nowhere, Texas, had the kind of roots that festered into hell far too fast for comfort.

Sarah and her team pulled to a stop in front of the two-story town inn, the one recommended by the sheriff when he'd requested her presence. In a small town of three thousand, the 1800s Victorian-style house was the closest thing to a motel they possessed.

"Well, this is quaint," Cathy said. "So far the town looks more fairy tale than nightmare."

"Apparently, it normally is," Sarah commented, reaching for the door and shoving it open. She'd been hunting the supernatural since she was twelve, tagging along with her parents before their deaths. They'd died at the hand of a friend who was possessed by a demon. Sarah knew better than to underestimate a situation because it "looked" safe. Nothing had been safe since their deaths. "Let's size up the place before we haul our equipment inside."

Ten steps led them up to a porch that covered the front of the house. Cushioned chairs and couches sat in various positions, welcoming people to sit down and relax. Several wind chimes dangled from the roof, lifting with the wind. The scent of rain was in the air.

Edward held the door open for Sarah, and she entered the house, her boots scraping against the hardwood floor. To her right was a small dining area where several people mingled around a table, sharing coffee, and to her left, a lounge area with a fireplace and winding stairwell—all part of the inn's cozy allure.

Sarah walked up to the desk directly in front of her and pumped her finger on the bell. A woman came down the stairs mumbling as she rushed forward. "All right, already. I'm coming."

The gruff response took Sarah by surprise, and she turned to see if Edward and Cathy shared her reaction, only to find them arguing, their voices low but laced with heaviness. A flutter of unease touched her stomach. The sheriff had spoken of odd, violent behavior in the townspeople.

"Ringing the bell once was enough," the fiftysome-thing woman said, as she shoved her glasses on her face and slammed the guest book down. "Impatience will get you in trouble, Miss."

In a different situation, Sarah would point out that she had rung the bell only once. Not this time. Not in this situation. "Sorry for any inconvenience," Sarah said. "I should have reservations for three rooms under Meyers."

Before the woman could answer, two men came down the stairs exchanging heated words. One of the patrons in the dining area stood up and shoved his chair to the ground, yelling at the person he'd been speaking pleas-antly to. The woman behind the counter screamed and took off toward them, as if intending to interfere. Sarah turned to find little five-foot Cathy poking a finger at Edward's chest, fearless of his towering six-three frame.

The door to the inn opened, and her eyes went wide at the unexpected sight of the man filling the entrance. Dressed in jeans and a leather jacket—that had to be hot considering the Texas summer, but damn he wore it well—he towered well above six feet tall; his shoulders nearly reached the width of the entry. His hazel eyes melted into hers for all of two seconds before he moved.

Next thing she knew, she was lying on her back, the hot leather-clad man on top of her. A knife zoomed past her and planted into the wall next to her head.

"You okay?" her stranger asked, near her ear.

"Yes," she mouthed, unable to find her voice. As

okay as she could be with insanity and his rock-hard body surrounding her. Not to mention, the weapon she felt pressed against her leg. And it wasn't the kind meant for pleasure. Whoever this stranger was, he came armed and ready to fight. If he lost control like the rest of them, they could all kiss their tomorrows goodbye.

But he wasn't out of control that she could see. And it seemed they were two sane people, alone in a crowd that seemed to be losing their minds.

A crashing sound put them both into action. He eyed the counter and in silent agreement, they scrambled behind it, taking shelter. They both settled with their backs against the solid surface, waiting for what came next.

But nothing happened. "Do you hear that?" Sarah whispered.

He frowned and rotated to face the counter, squatting beside her, listening. The sound of nothingness filled the air. Complete, utter quiet had taken over where chaos had ruled.

"Let's hope this is a good sign," he said, as he eased upward to check out the situation. But Sarah had a feeling this was only the beginning. The beginning of what?—that was the question.

Max eased from his squatting position, analyzing the reason for the sudden silence. He knew he'd been sent to Nowhere, Texas, as part of a test. The ultimate test that would decide if his soul was worth saving. And as he peered from behind the desk, taking in the sight before him, he had no doubt that the test was not only already in full-blown effect, it was going to be hell.

Scrubbing his jaw, he watched as the faces of the inn's guests filled with bemusement, as if they had been zapped back to reality and struggled for their memories. They had no idea they'd just damn near killed one another.

In his four hundred years of living, three hundred and seventy of it had been spent fighting demon foot soldiers and protecting unknowing humans. He'd stuck to his own kind, The Knights of White; he had no clue what to do with a bunch of humans who'd clearly lost their marbles. But how ironic that he was here, dealing with them now, considering he'd gotten in trouble for killing a human— albeit an evil human, but it still broke the rules.

Beside him, the gorgeous blonde, who had his gut tightening and his heart pounding, peered out from behind the counter. "They don't know what they did, do they?"

"It doesn't appear so," he commented, discreetly inhaling another whiff of her jasmine-scented perfume. He cut her a curious glance. "Why is it you weren't affected?"

She narrowed her eyes on him. "I could ask you the same."

He laughed at that, watching her walk toward a petite brunette and a big black man. She had spunk, this one. Max felt an unnatural desire take hold, to pull her back by his side, to kiss her until she told him what he wanted to know.

There was something deep inside him that seemed to respond to this woman, seemed to call out to him. No woman had ever drawn such an instant reaction. The kind of reaction he'd heard spoken of as a sign of mating. But then, that seemed unlikely. He was inches from being destined for hell. He would not be rewarded with a mate.

Then again, this was the ultimate test he was living, a test that would push him to his limits. Perhaps, facing his mate and being strong enough to walk away, selfless enough to put her needs first, was part of that test. To claim her would mean locking her to him eternally. She would share his destiny, which was uncertain at best.

Of course, there was one other option. She could also be part of some sort of demon trick or manipulation. He couldn't be too cautious at this point.

Max decided whatever her role in this test—and she had one, of that he was certain—he had better keep her close. He stepped forward and joined her and her friends. "How is everyone?" he asked. "No serious injuries, I hope?"

The blond, would-be mate, would-be trickster answered. She had a soft, sweet voice that danced along his nerve endings with sensual results.

"Thankfully, they seem to be fine," she said, her gaze on him, a probing look in her sea green eyes. "They don't remember any of it, though." She paused and studied him. Something in her probing stare gave him the impression she was looking for a reason to distrust him. "I'm Sarah Meyers, by the way." She motioned to her friends. "This is my research team, Cathy Wilburt and Edward Marshall."

He inclined his head at the introductions. "I'm Max," he announced, not willing to give a last name. He hadn't used one in centuries. His past was his past.

"Nice to meet you, Max," Sarah said, offering her hand.

Max steeled himself for the impact as he reached out to accept Sarah's hand. The minute their palms connected, molten heat shot up his arm. Shock darted across her face, and he knew that she, too, felt what he did. Discreetly, he cleared his throat, withdrawing his hand with regret. "What kind of research do you do?"

Before Sarah could answer, a murmur of concerned voices filled the room as it grew darker inside; the sunlight was no longer shining through the windows. Rain began to beat fiercely on the roof. Someone flipped on several lights as both Max and Sarah looked outside, to the storm that was stealing the attention of the other patrons.

"What the hell?" Max said, half to himself, his voice low. The rain was black. A thick, greasy-looking black.

To get a closer look, Sarah stepped to the window. At the same moment, Max moved, as well, claiming a position beside her. Their shoulders brushed, and for a moment Max felt as if they were one. Neither moved, neither stepped away from the other.

After several seconds, she glanced at him. "Do you believe in supernatural experiences?" she asked.

Max drew in a breath and let it out. "Yes," he said, eyeing the darkness outside the window, the sun having disappeared.

Sarah shivered and hugged herself. "Something evil has come to this town."

Max feared she was right. He knew evil in an intimate way. Long ago, a Darkland Beast had bitten him, turned him into a demon, his soul lost. Though he'd been given back that soul, saved to fight evil, he'd felt that sinister reality—still felt it—inside him. He still possessed the primal side that the Beast had created. Yet nothing he had felt, past or present, nothing he had experienced, came close to the sinister feeling that crawled through the air this day.

Whatever caused that rain, whatever caused the humans to lose control, was evil personified. And Max knew he had to destroy it.

Before it destroyed him, and everyone around him.

Chapter 2

The lights flashed and then went out; the inn was cast, once again, into dark shadows. The room grew silent, the people inside transfixed by the sight of the black rain.

Max and Sarah remained side by side, arms touching, watching the oily-looking substance pound into puddles on the ground. Sarah's presence beside him drew unfamiliar feelings. A desire to keep her close and safe. The way she lingered near him, allowing their physical connection—the touch of two strangers—seemed to indicate that the invisible bond between them was growing without effort, growing from simple exposure to one another.

It was Edward who broke the silence. From behind Max and Sarah, his deep, gravelly voice filled the air. "Shouldn't we call the sheriff?"

Sarah responded by turning to the woman behind the counter. "Can you get him on the phone?" she asked.

Max's eyes remained transfixed on that cursed black rain one more second before he glanced at Sarah, wondering what kind of evil was going to try to thwart his ability to claim his mate. If she were his mate, he reminded himself. She could be part of a trick.

"I doubt the sheriff can help with this," he pointed out.

"Unfortunately, there's truth to that," she said. "That's why he called my team to assist. But he still needs to know what just went on here."

"Phone's down," the front-desk clerk called out, concern lacing her now friendly voice. Gone was the grumpy, gray-haired woman who'd yelled at Sarah, replaced by a sweet woman with fear in her eyes. "Computer, too."

Reaching for his cell, Max checked for service. "Nothing." Max held up the screen for her to see the no-service notation.

"Damn," Sarah murmured.

"I'd say we should get our equipment," Edward said, "but it's outside. And frankly, I don't want any part of that junk falling from the sky."

Cathy interjected, "If they can log our reservations manually, we can get checked into our rooms. Then we'll be ready to set up when it stops."

"If it stops," Edward muttered bad-naturedly, a snort following his words.

Cathy nudged him. "Be positive for once."

"Yes," Sarah said. "Be positive. And grab me a room key, too, please."

Max wondered what equipment they were referring to. "You said the sheriff requested your presence?" he asked, as Edward and Cathy moved out of hearing range.

"Right. Apparently there had been some strange things happening before the rain." His brow lifted in question and she responded, "As in supernatural things." She hesitated and then added, "We're paranormal investigators." She dropped the words into the air with emphasis, much like dropping a bomb. Then she waited, studying him closely, giving him a second to reply. When he didn't, she asked, "No smart remarks? No rolled eyes?"

"I was actually thinking the sheriff was a pretty smart guy," Max commented. "Because whatever is going on here isn't of this world."

"I'm amazed to hear that you believe in the supernatural," she said, surprise in her voice. "Most people either don't believe, or won't admit they do for fear of looking silly."

He eyed the black rain flowing by the bucketful, hard and fast. "If I didn't believe before this storm, I would now."

"There are all kinds of scientific explanations for black rain," she inserted.

"And we both know they'd all be bull crap," he quickly countered.

"Yes," Sarah said, amusement lacing her words as she repeated his statement. "They would, indeed, be 'bull crap.'" She sobered quickly, as her gaze scanned the room. Around them people murmured concerns, fear in their voices. "And clearly these people know that."

"It's in everyone's best interests that we figure out what's going on," Max asserted. "How about I lend you a hand with your investigation? I'll go grab that equipment of yours. And while I'm at it, I'll get my laptop computer. It's got a hell of a battery, and I'm not half-bad with research."

"Aren't you worried about that rain?"

"I've been chin deep in all kinds of sh—er, junk in my lifetime. A little black water isn't going to make me melt."

"You don't think it can hurt you," Sarah said, and it wasn't a question. A hint of suspicion laced her words. "Just like you weren't affected by whatever made everyone start acting weird. Why is that?"

She didn't trust him and he didn't blame her. But he couldn't afford to trust her, either. Not with everything he had on the line. A fool he was not. Sarah could be part of his test. He countered with a reminder. "I believe I asked you that question a few minutes ago and you avoided it."

She seemed to hesitate. "Yes. I guess I did." She paused, and then admitted, "I'm a medium. As in I communicate with the spirit world. Have been since I was about twelve. I assume it must offer me some sort of mental shield."

Interesting. So, she wasn't like everyone else here any more than he was. That supported his theory that she was his mate, the light to his darkness.

A frown dipped her brows. "No comment?"

Max smiled, resisting the urge to reach out and brush his fingers down her ivory cheek. "You want me to say I don't believe you, don't you?"

They stared at each other for several seconds, her eyes searching his. She was seeking something in his gaze, something he didn't understand. But he wanted to. He wanted to understand everything about this woman.

Her lashes fluttered and she turned to the window, her

fingers spreading on the panel. "People don't understand what I am."

The statement, the emotion attached to her words, took him off guard. He felt pain that wasn't his own. He felt her pain. It was as if they were one, bound without the actual mating ritual.

"This isn't my first supernatural experience," Max confessed, wanting her to know she had found acceptance in him. "In fact, I have a few talents of my own." *Like immortality,* he added silently. Unless someone sliced off his head or bled him dry, he wasn't going anywhere. He could feel pain, he could even get hurt, but he'd heal.

Her head whipped around, body tensing, her attention fixed on him. "Meaning what?"

"You investigate what can't be seen, Sarah," he said, shoving aside his jacket enough to expose several weapons. "I hunt things you don't *want* to see. Things, I can promise you, most people don't want to even know exist. Let's just hope you don't see them for yourself, though I fear you might. Something is telling me our two worlds have come to a crossroads. We need to figure out what we're facing before it finds us."

Confusion flashed on her face. "I feel the same thing. It's…unusual."

He continued, "Time is what matters right now. We need to figure out what this rain means before something else happens. If that equipment of yours will help, I need to go get it." Max held out his hand. "Keys?"

"Okay," she said, "but I'm not done asking questions. Not even close. If I consider working with you—and I'm not saying I am—I need to understand who and *what* you are."

He inclined his head. "Understood."

She gave him a probing inspection, seeming to gauge his words. Apparently accepting his reply, at least for the time being, she gave him her back, walking over to the front desk where Edward and Cathy were busy with check-in. She whispered to her friends. After a moment, Edward and Cathy twisted around and looked at Max as if he were insane.

A long, hard stare later, Edward reached into his pocket and tossed the keys to Max. "It's your death wish, man."

Max caught the keys and smiled. "They don't call me Wild Thing for nothing," he commented dryly.

Sarah stared at Max, ignoring his joke. She wasn't buying into his nonchalant attitude about the rain. He might have some sort of "gift" as she did, but she was pretty darn certain he was aware he was taking a risk. There was no telling what effect that rain could have on what it touched.

The idea of Max risking his safety bothered her. Not that he couldn't take care of himself. Still, for some reason, she fought the urge to insist he not do this. She also knew herself well enough to know her feelings were a bit over the top. She had to assume her emotions were getting mixed up with those of the female spirit making contact. It was clear this spirit worried for her husband. That could happen. At times, she felt the spirits so intensely, they almost became her.

The fact that she was attracted to Max probably aided her sensitivity to the spirit's emotions. This wasn't the time or place to be distracted by a man, not to mention her libido, but she couldn't seem to turn off her attraction to him.

Suddenly, she realized she was not only still staring at Max, he was staring back. She swallowed, feeling the heat of his hazel eyes all the way to her toes. Something about him got to her in a big way. A way that defied the circumstances, which were quite serious. People's lives could be on the line, she reminded herself.

She drew her spine stiff and delicately cleared her throat, afraid she wouldn't find her voice otherwise. "At least take an umbrella," she suggested, needing some semblance of comfort that he had protection.

The front-desk clerk was quick to assist. "I'll get you one, and we have a carport 'round back. Pull around there and you can unload under the shelter."

Max looked as if he would refuse, which wasn't okay with Sarah. When his gaze found hers, she made sure he saw the determination in her expression. He sighed with resignation and walked to the desk.

The front-desk clerk headed toward a closet as an elderly man approached the desk. He placed several lit candles on it as he called to the clerk. "Hold up, honey," he said, and eyed the rest of them, but she didn't listen. She grabbed an umbrella before returning to the counter. The man lowered his voice. "You're the people the sheriff called in from that Austin University?"

"Yes," Sarah said. "That's us."

"I hope you got answers that don't require fancy equipment 'cause nothing's working. Not even battery-powered."

Sarah grimaced with that news. "No need to risk the rain for equipment that doesn't work."

The man's lips thinned, his expression grim. "I don't want to scare the guests, but we got us big trouble here in Nowhere, Texas. We got us a ghost or a demon or something evil like that."

The clerk swatted his arm, and he shot her a mad look. "You know it's true, Helen," he said. "Tell 'em."

"Actually," Cathy said, doing one of the things she did well—calming people's fears. "There's a long list of scientific explanations."

"Name one," the man said.

Cathy was quick to respond, drawing them into conversation, Edward assisting her. He never showed his cranky side to the public, saving it for Cathy and Sarah.

Thankful for the escape Cathy had offered her, and concerned about the newest developments, Sarah motioned to Max. Discreetly, they moved away from the group. "Look," she said softly, the sense of unity she felt with this man like that of a longtime friend, not a virtual stranger. "If you have any idea what we are dealing with, please tell me now. Don't avoid my questions. Who called you here and why?"

Max hesitated and Sarah narrowed her eyes on him. She wanted to know about this man. About why he was here and what made him different from everyone else here. Because he was different and they both knew it.

As much as her instincts said he was worthy of her trust, her past history told her to be concerned. She'd learned the hard way with her parents' death that, in the world of demon hunting, trust could lead to destruction. She wouldn't give Max, or anyone, her blind trust, ever again. "Did the sheriff call you?" Sarah asked, pressing Max for answers when he offered none.

"The sheriff didn't call me. I work for a covert operation called in under extreme circumstances. I'm told where to go and I show up—sometimes, like now, with very little information. All I know for certain is that my boss is selective about what I deal with. I wouldn't be here if the situation wasn't bad. Real bad."

Sarah wanted to press for more details. Turning her attention to the view outside the window, she processed what she'd just been told. He'd basically admitted to hunting the supernatural, just as she did. Only he hunted a different breed. Perhaps those who bore fangs?

Without looking at him, she said, "I know you aren't telling me everything there is to tell." She cast him a sideways look. "Since we're the only two people who seem unaffected by what's going on, it appears we might have to work together. I can't do that if I don't trust you. I can't trust you if you talk in code. I need to know who sent you and why."

Several people walked past them and Max hesitated. "Now isn't the time or place for unveiling deep, dark secrets."

She drew a labored breath, her chest expanding with effort. He was right, of course. And her instincts told her to trust this man. For now. "Fine." She narrowed her gaze. "But soon."

"Fair enough," he agreed.

Sarah considered her next move. The best thing they could do now was to start researching. That meant interviews, since they were cut off from technology. "As much as I don't want to go out in that mess," she admitted, referring to the weather, "I need to talk to the sheriff and get some answers. I need to do something productive while we wait for our equipment to work again."

"I'm all for that," Max inserted. "It beats the hell out of standing here in the dark, waiting for some invisible bomb to explode."

"Yeah, it does," she said, searching his face, surprised at how accurately he described what she felt, and how in tune they were with each other. How in their own world. These people around them were scared, her team included, but no one else seemed to sense the ticking clock that she and Max did. "I'll get that umbrella."

She started to turn away and his voice called her back. "Stay here where it's safe. I'll go and bring the sheriff back."

It was a gentleman's offer, and she appreciated it. She just couldn't accept. "I don't know if I'd call here, or anywhere in this town, safe," she said, not one to worry about her own safety, anyway. Risk was part of this job, as she suspected he knew from his own work. Demon hunters made bad lovers; they were always knocking on death's door. "Besides. I'm not the type to sit and wait."

"I'd feel better if you stayed," he said.

"I wouldn't." She gave him a smile. "But thank you, anyway."

"What if I insist?"

"I'll go anyway, and you can't stop me," she said sternly, turning away with decisiveness this time, and as expected, facing an argument with her staff over her decision to go out in the storm. But they knew what Max was starting to learn. She made her own choices.

Sarah returned to Max's side with an umbrella and a few supplies. "Ready?"

He gave her a nod and pulled the door open. They stepped outside, the wind gushing with sudden force as if it were warning them to turn back into the inn.

Sarah was about to step off the porch when Max grabbed her arm. "Not until I do a test."

She rolled her eyes. "Macho is so not appealing."

"Humor me," he said, and started to hold his hand out.

Instinctively, she yanked it back. His brow arched. "Sorry," she said. "That water just looks so damn evil."

"But you want to go out in it," he said flatly. "I told you I can go and get the sheriff."

"I'm going," she said, her voice firm.

"You're very stubborn," he declared.

"Yep," she said. "I am."

"Then I guess we better try my test again," he suggested as he eased her fingers from around his wrist, which she was holding tighter than she realized.

She crossed her arms in front of her chest so she wouldn't be tempted to grab him again. "If you insist."

"I do," he said quickly.

She held her breath as he reached into the rain. The dirty-looking substance ran over his skin, through his fingers, splattering on his leather jacket. But nothing more happened. No pain. No insanity. No demon possession. Not that she could tell, anyway.

Sarah let the air slide from her lungs. "Thank God."

Still, he held his hand under the water, apparently not quite satisfied it was safe. It was hard for Sarah to shake the fear of demon possession after watching a demon take over a friend and turn him into a killer. A killer who had murdered her parents. The thought had her studying Max with renewed concern.

Yet she was attracted to Max in a way she didn't remember ever being attracted to any other man—in a way that went beyond his physical beauty. She thought she'd shut off that part of herself when she'd lost her parents—the part that connected beyond the surface, that allowed emotion to flare—but somehow Max had slipped under her guard. And she couldn't help but wonder how and why.

She drank in the vision he made, his face so full of character, full of strength. A dimpled chin. A long scar across his right brow. She wondered how he got it. Would he tell her if she asked?

He was different from anyone else she'd met, she concluded. Could she actually have found someone who she didn't have to fear would be possessed by a demon? Did she dare hope?

She stiffened. That was a dangerous thought that would only lead her to destruction. She couldn't let down her guard. "You still feel okay, right?" she asked, needing that verbal confirmation.

"Same as I always do," he said, shaking the water from his hand. He popped the umbrella open and offered her his arm. "Shall we?"

The air around them crackled with menace, and Sarah gratefully slipped her hand beneath his elbow, welcoming the warmth and security of that deliciously muscled, well-armed body. A strange thing for her. She preferred to stand alone, not depending on anyone.

She prayed that the feelings that urged her to trust Max were genuine. She prayed she wasn't being lured into some dangerous charade by some evil spirit.

But deep in her core she felt Max was part of her

journey in this town. He felt familiar in some odd way. And her gut said they were headed for a fight, and it was going to require both of them to win.

Something was here, around them, near them. She could almost feel it watching. Something that could strike at any minute. She didn't know much about Max. Nor did she know what she would face in the next minute, the next hour. Only that danger seemed to surround them, to blanket them in warning.

Determination formed in Sarah. She didn't like defeat. She didn't like allowing things to spin out of control. She was going to learn Max's secrets, to dig beneath the surface of the sexy stranger who'd pulled her under some sort of seductive spell. And she was going to find out the source of evil in this town and what killed that woman on that bridge. Sarah couldn't turn back time and prevent that woman's death, but she could help her rest in peace. And she could stop anyone else from dying the same way.

Chapter 3

Demon Prince Vars fed on human desires and emotions, created each person's personal destruction by delving into their innermost thoughts and feelings. Until he was cut off from his connection to the earthly realm, imprisoned in the Underworld beneath a magical barrier created by the Archangel Raphael. For centuries, he had been without his powers, weak and pathetic.

That had all changed when Kate and Allen Walker had chosen the land above his hell hole, his prison, as the place to build their home. Their presence had delivered to him the power to find escape, had allowed Vars to create a tiny hole in the magical barrier of his prison and begin controlling their lives.

Vars stepped to the top of a boulder, the highest point inside the confines of his prison, and looked down at the fiery caverns he would soon depart. Satisfaction filled him. Everything was going as planned. Stage one had been Kate's death, which had led to Allen's interest in the dark arts and his study of black magic. An amateur at his craft, Allen had accepted the mental push Vars had given him, and foolishly tried to subordinate demons as his servants, demanding they resurrect his wife. All part of Vars's plan, of course.

Unknowingly, Allen evoked the most powerful of Vars's demon legions, Vars having guided him to their names. When Allen found the demons too weak to do his bidding, he attempted to send them back to hell, but he was too inexperienced to succeed. Instead, Allen had set them free to roam the earthly planes, to aid Vars's efforts at escape. But escape for Vars would not be as simple as it had been for the lesser demons who reported to him. To break the binding spell of an archangel, Vars would require a source of great magical energy. A source Allen would now bring to him.

When Allen became brave enough to call on him, Vars would promise him his wife, in return for a few little favors and a blood oath of service. Once he had that oath, he would be powerful enough to contact the Underworld. Most importantly, he could contact Cain, the king who oversaw the Darkland Beasts. Cain hated Raphael and his army of Knights even more than Vars did. He would aid Vars's escape, and together they would crush all that Raphael valued. They would crush humanity.

Vars laughed. Yes. Allen would deliver all of this to him and more, in exchange for a promise of his wife's return. Not that Vars had ever kept a promise in all his centuries of existence.

* * *

Power flowed through Allen as he stepped to the edge of the magical circle drawn in the center of his living-room floor. Candles flickered at four points outside the circle's boundaries. He drew a breath, claiming his magic, feeling it flow through the long black robe he wore and the sheathed black dagger he clutched in his right hand.

Each time he used his craft, he grew stronger, more capable of mastering his skills. A rush of adrenaline poured through him as he thought of what was to come, what would happen when he stepped inside that circle. He'd come to crave this high magic that was delivered to him; he devoured the feeling of ultimate control it offered, and he hated himself for that.

Deep down he knew Kate would hate it, too, that she would not approve of his touching the dark arts. But he had tried her way, turning to the church, praying for her return. All they'd offered him was a promise that the pain would ease. That Kate would always be in his heart if not by his side. He refused to accept a promise that left him without his wife.

Besides, he knew his Kate. She would want to be with him. She knew how much he needed her. She was all he had, all the love he'd ever experienced. After a life of foster homes and loneliness, she had brought him joy. The church wanted him to forget, but damn it, he didn't want to forget. He would *not* forget.

His hand tightened on the dagger, his jaw clenching. This path he'd chosen had been for one purpose and one purpose only: to get his wife back. Kate would understand why he had to do this.

New resolve formed and he stepped inside the circle. Tonight, he would evoke an upper-level demon, the one that lesser demons had called "Vars." And he was ready. He could feel the tingling of electricity dance along his nerve endings, the surge of his own energy rippling through his veins, charging the air.

He unsheathed the dagger and sliced his hand, dropping the blade to the ground as he let the blood trickle from his skin to the floor. In a low voice, he began the evocation spell, willing Vars to show himself. Evil crackled in the air almost instantly; the hair on the back of Allen's neck stood on end. Fire flickered within the triangle, and Allen felt the heat as if he were on fire, but still he chanted, still he continued. He had to do this. He had to get his Kate back. A vague shape within the fire began to take solid form.

"I command the demon known as Vars to show himself!" Allen shouted.

The man, or rather demon, that appeared in the center of the triangle stood a good six feet five, his long black hair in a braid that disappeared between broad shoulder blades. He wore a black shirt and pants and boots that covered his calves.

The demon lifted his hand, fingers pointing at Allen. Suddenly, Allen's legs gave out on him, and he fell to his knees. The demon closed his hand into a tight fist, and Allen felt his chest tighten, as if the demon were squeezing the breath out of him. Fear shot through Allen's body. The precious control he'd reveled in moments before now gone. The lesser demons he'd summoned had not wielded this kind of power.

"Prince Vars is my name," the demon said. "Address me with respect or do not dare address me at all."

The invisible grip Vars held on Allen's chest disappeared, he gulped for air. Desperate to escape, Allen tried to get to his feet, but his legs were still frozen in place, as if they were glued to the hardwood floor.

"Those who serve me, bow to me," Vars bellowed.

No! Allen screamed the word in his mind, silently beginning a spell meant to subordinate the demon.

Vars laughed. "You cannot control one such as me, Allen," he said, making it clear he knew Allen's name and what he was attempting to do. "I am royalty in the Underworld, one of the great powers. You will bow to me or you will not get what you seek." His lips twisted sardonically. "You do want your precious Kate back, do you not?"

"Yes!" Allen said, too anxiously. He could not help himself, could not contain his urgency. "I want my Kate back."

Vars tilted his head and studied Allen. "I can help you, but only when I have my freedom. I am bound beneath the earth, my powers bound with me. Free me and you shall have your wife."

"How?"

"I will guide you, human." Vars pointed at the dagger and it flew through the air into his hand. He sliced his hand and black liquid poured from his palm. "Vow a blood oath and give yourself to me. Within our blood, I will be connected to you. I will lead you on your path. A path that will deliver you to your wife."

Allen pushed to his feet, free to move now. He didn't hesitate, determined to find his way to Kate. A second later, he stood on the edge of the triangle and extended his bloodied hand across the line. Vars grabbed his palm, pressing it to his own.

The instant their blood mingled, a current of electricity dashed through Allen's body. He felt numb, shaken, scared. He cried out. The pain, the pain was too much... and then it was just gone.

In its place, he felt calmness, peace; a sense of magnificent energy flowed through him. In his head, he heard Vars speak the name of three great sorcerers. *Bring me their souls, and I will give you Kate.*

Allen smiled, knowing he would not fail, aware he now wielded great magic, borne of his connection to Prince Vars. Yes. He would deliver those souls, and he would have his Kate.

Chapter 4

Max and Sarah didn't speak as they walked toward the sheriff's office, both watchful, the edginess they shared as evident as the puddles of ominous black rain splashing around their feet, its mere existence seeming to scream with silent threat. But there was a connection between them that didn't need words, an understanding that what they faced would be faced together. Not to mention a charge of awareness, of attraction, that seemed to heat his arm where her hand rested.

In Sarah, Max found a brave, feisty female; she was bold and uncompromising about being different, about being a medium. A woman who accepted his admission about hunting the supernatural. He had no doubt she had questions about who and what he was; yet, she had still accepted him. She even wanted to trust him, though she was fighting that desire. If she were, indeed, his mate, she would instinctively trust him. But she had baggage of some sort telling her those feelings were wrong. He could feel it in her, feel the worry, the hesitation.

Still, there was something surreal about finding a mate in this time of judgment for himself, a time that might well forge his demise.

He shoved that thought aside as the sheriff's office came into view, noting the pitch-black interior. "It looks as if no one is home," he commented. "If the entire town broke out in rage like the hotel occupants did, I imagine they're out trying to clean up the aftermath."

"Either that or they don't have any candles," Sarah said, indicating her bag. "Glad we brought our own."

They took the stairs and found cover from the rain beneath a small overhang. The meager space demanded they stay close, bodies touching. Which is where Max wanted Sarah, anyway—close and safe.

He dropped the umbrella to the ground beside the stairs as Sarah tried the locked door and then knocked. No one came to the door, no one called out in response. "We still have to go in," Sarah said. "He was expecting me. It seems logical he'd have a file with notes to hand over."

He slanted her a sideways look. "Are you asking me to break into the sheriff's office?"

She didn't look even mildly ashamed of her request. "Desperate times require desperate actions."

A smile touched his lips at that and he reached into his pocket, withdrawing a small leather case he kept there for just this type of situation. In about sixty seconds, Max had the lock popped.

"Impressive," Sarah commented. "Not sure I want to know where you learned that."

"You never know when a skill might save a life," he said, thinking of the many things he'd encountered in the four hundred years he'd lived. "I like to be prepared." Besides being a fairly capable locksmith, Max could hack into just about anything electronic in existence, a skill he'd put to use for the Knights on more than one occasion.

He shoved open the door and surveyed the interior, before letting Sarah enter. Max's instincts reached well beyond that of a normal human, and they told him the building contained no threats, but caution dictated he do a walk-through just to be safe.

Once Sarah was inside the lobby, he locked the door to keep out unannounced visitors. He turned around to find himself almost toe to toe with Sarah, her gaze locking with his. The setting was dark and intimate, the attraction between them hot and heavy. The desire to claim Sarah, to possess her, burned him inside out. Flaring to life without warning, threatening his control. This was like nothing he'd ever experienced before. The primal side of him, the part touched by a Darkland Beast, a demon, cared nothing about time and place, about danger. It simply wanted Sarah.

"It's very dark in here," she murmured, her voice washing over the rawness of his nerve endings and calming him a bit. Ironic how one woman could cause the same rawness that she could calm.

Before he could stop himself, he reached up and caught a soft strand of her hair between his fingers, the desire to touch her too intense to resist. Her eyes widened with surprise, and he saw the flash of uncertainty in her gaze. As if she wanted to pull away but couldn't. Damn, how he could relate to that feeling. This woman was going to be his undoing if he wasn't careful. If she knew how much he burned to taste her, to feel her softness against his body, she'd likely run for cover.

Her soft scent lifted in the air, insinuating into his nostrils, and Max felt his willpower sliding away. He knew he had to distance himself. "Stay by the door while I have a look around," he said, but he didn't move. He was too transfixed in the awareness between them, by that desire to taste her that wouldn't let go.

Her teeth scraped her bottom lip as if she were thinking the same thing. The action drew his gaze, tempting him further, pushing him to take what he wanted. The beast clawed and pressed, devouring his willpower.

"You might want a candle," she suggested, reaching for her bag.

Her words helped jar him back to reality. "I don't," he said a bit abruptly, as he reached for the control he'd been about to lose. He turned away from her, starting his inspection of the office.

As for the candle she'd offered, the truth was that his night vision was as good as his day vision. And staring into those deep-green eyes of Sarah's was driving him insane with want, a feeling he shook off, reminding himself of the need for a clear level head, ready for battle. Ready to protect Sarah and defeat an enemy.

That thought helped him step into duty mode. It didn't take long for him to finish his scan of the few small offices he found and confirm the building was secure. On the way back to the lobby, he grabbed a roll of paper towels from the bathroom in case Sarah wanted to clean off a little.

* * *

Sarah was grateful for a few minutes alone as Max inspected the offices. Her emotions were reeling as she lit the four candles she brought with them from the inn. She'd wanted Max to kiss her. Wanted it in such a desperate way, she'd darn near grabbed him and pulled his mouth to hers. This was so not like her. Not one bit. She didn't get distracted from her work. Didn't get close to people, especially not strangers, not men. But something about Max had her twisted up with need. Had her wanting things she'd long ago decided her work made impossible.

Before she had time to analyze her feelings, Max was back. "We're good," he said, stopping in front of her. "I need to check out the computers and see if I can get anything working." He was close. So close she could feel the heat of his body. She reached for the paper towels in his hand, needing a distraction, a reason to avoid eye contact.

"Thank you," she said, taking a step backward to give herself some distance from Max and then busying herself cleaning her boots. "I'm getting mud everywhere."

"I'm sure the sheriff will understand."

She tossed the dirty towels in the trash. Her hands went to her hips, and she blew hair out of her eyes. "It's strange he's not here. And what about his staff? Where are they?"

Max leaned on the desk, casting his ruggedly handsome features in candlelight. "Based on what I saw as I looked around, there's only one deputy. I assume there's a secretary. And if the violence that broke out at the inn occurred all over town, maybe someone got hurt. If so, I'm sure they had their hands full with the aftermath."

"Good point," Sarah said, agreeing. "And since no one seems to remember what happened, I'm sure there's a lot of confusion." She paused, thinking a moment. "I wonder if the sheriff even knows what happened."

"I'd venture to say he is as confused as everyone else, and still trying to deal with any chaos caused by today's events. Everyone but you and me were affected at the inn."

"Everyone but you and me," she repeated, feeling torn about that similarity between them. Should she be relieved or suspicious to find someone else who couldn't be touched by this thing—whatever it was?

Abruptly, he pushed off the desk again, but not before she saw a flash of understanding in his gaze. He knew she wanted answers and he wasn't ready to give them. "Let's check out the sheriff's office," he said. With those words, he turned away, shutting her down before she could begin questioning him.

Sarah grabbed a candle and followed him; but she wasn't letting him off the hook. Because she was going to demand they clear the air, that he start talking. Feeling this kind of intense attraction to someone she didn't know made her vulnerable. She didn't like vulnerable. Despised it, in fact.

She took a step forward, when a sudden awareness of a spiritual presence took hold—it was the woman from the car accident. Sarah forgot Max, focusing on the connection to the spirit, trying to understand any message that might be sent to her. What Sarah felt in that moment was urgency, an urgency to find out more about that car accident. Driven for answers, she headed toward the back offices.

Max had already grabbed several stacks of files and was setting them up on top of a table in the break area. She set her candle down, as well. "Are these all the case files?"

"From what I can tell," he said. "But I'm going to check the deputy's office. Anything particular you need?"

She sat down at the table and reached for a file. "Yes, and this would be so much easier if the sheriff were here. He could find what I'm looking for right away, I'm sure. It's a car accident on the bridge leading into town. It's somehow related to what's going on."

He leaned a shoulder on the doorjamb. "What's the name?"

She shook her head. "I only know the husband's name. Allen. And before you ask, I know this sounds crazy, but I had a vision as we drove across that bridge. Sometimes that happens. The spirit wants me to know something, and it makes me relive the event."

"Relive the event?" he asked, his voice holding surprise. "What exactly does that mean?"

"One minute I was talking with Cathy and Edward. The next I was transported into that woman's car, living through her crash." She paused and let out a heavy breath. "And her death."

"Holy shit," Max murmured, stunned. "How often does that kind of thing happen to you?"

"Not often," she assured him, "but the experience isn't something you get used to. It's a bit like how I've heard seizures described. I completely zone out. Everything around me disappears."

"What if you were driving, or doing something dangerous when that happened? You could be killed."

She shrugged. "I don't think the spirits are trying to

kill me. Just communicating. My mother had the same thing, and it never happened at a time when she could get hurt. And, like I said, that type of experience is rare. Usually I just hear whispers in my head, and I have to decipher their meaning. Or I have a vivid dream. Often I dream about a case before I'm officially involved. That's what happened with this town. I dreamt about it and the next morning the sheriff called."

"Okay," he said, scrubbing his jaw, obviously thinking aloud. "Let me get this straight. You dreamt about this town. You had a vision of the car accident." He cast her an inquisitive look. "Are we thinking the woman who died on that bridge is haunting this town?"

A couple of files flew off the table onto the floor and a book pounded down on top of them. Max pushed off the doorframe. "What the—?"

"She's here, and no, she's not the one causing havoc." She smiled. "And obviously, she doesn't like that you suggested otherwise. She wants to help us."

Max mumbled to himself and then motioned toward the stuff on the floor. "The woman from the bridge did this?" Sarah nodded. "And I suppose she thinks it's funny to throw things around like that? To try to spook someone?" He didn't wait for an answer. "Tell her I'm not laughing," Max said, bending down to grab the files. He paused to glance up at her. "That is, if you can talk to her. Can you? Obviously she can communicate with you."

"It's a one-way conversation. They do all the talking," Sarah said. "I just listen."

Still kneeling by the fallen items, Max balanced his weight on his heels, hands on his muscular thighs. "How do you know she isn't tricking you? What if she *is* the one doing all of this?"

"She's not tricking me," she said. "I can't explain it, but I get a real sense for who these spirits are. Especially when I am in one of those visions. This woman is worried about her husband. He's involved. We need to find out who he is and talk to him."

Max grabbed the files and the book from the floor and then joined Sarah at the table, setting the materials down in front of him. "Okay then. You trust her, I trust her. "Maybe this spirit was telling us something by throwing these specific items on the floor." He reached for the book. "This is the town history. I'll read through it and look for anything that might help. Maybe a myth or a legend of some sort. Usually there is some distorted truth to those things. Maybe something about that bridge." He inclined his chin to indicate the files. "Hopefully, one of those is your car accident."

Sarah blinked with surprise. She simply couldn't get over how easily Max accepted her world. "The way spirits talk to me doesn't freak you out at all, does it?"

"Macho guys like me don't get freaked out," he said, smiling as he referred to what she'd called him earlier at the inn. But as quickly as that smile had appeared, his expression turned serious. "I accept easily what others don't, because I've seen a lot of things, Sarah. A lot of them ugly. Things you might not want to know about."

She did want to know. Had to know, in fact. But before she could say as much, a sound at the front of the office had her pushing to her feet.

Already standing, gun in hand, Max said, "Stay

here." He didn't wait for a response, rounding the corner, gun stiff-armed in front of his body.

Max entered the lobby just as a big burly cowboy in
uniform charged through the door, a 9 mm pistol in his
hand. Though Max had no doubt this was the sheriff, he
also didn't know what the man's state of mind was.

"Put the weapon down, son," the sheriff ordered. "No
reason anyone has to be hurt."

"Normally, Sheriff," Max drawled cautiously, "I'd be
happy to comply. You are wearing a badge and all. But
forgive me if I'm cautious. We haven't exactly been received by a welcoming party."

"Who is *we?*" the sheriff asked.

Sarah appeared beside Max, carrying a lighted candle. "Sarah Meyers, Sheriff Jenson. And this is Max."

A flicker of recognition sparked in the sheriff's eyes.
"I was expecting you, Ms. Meyers. Will you be kind
enough to tell *Max* it's not smart to draw a gun on the
sheriff, and it's downright stupid to do it in his own office?"

"Max," Sarah said, her hand touching his arm.

"Where's that deputy of yours?" Max asked, not
ready to lower his gun quite yet. After what he'd seen
back at that inn, he couldn't be cautious enough. *He*
wouldn't die from a bullet wound, but Sarah would.

"I'd like to know, too," the sheriff said. "But it appears we have no phones."

"Max, please," Sarah whispered. "Put down the gun."

Slowly, Max complied, easing his gun to his side,
finger still on the trigger. He stepped in front of Sarah
as he shoved the Glock into his holster, protecting her
with his body until he was sure she was safe.

"Now you," he ordered the sheriff, sidestepping as Sarah tried to get around him.

The lawman looked as if he might refuse, but after a second he blew out a breath and harnessed his gun. His finger slid over his long mustache and then tapped his cowboy hat back on his head. "I hope the two of you are really here to help, because we need it."

"We *are* here to help," Sarah said, casting Max an ir-ritated look, as he finally let her step to his side. Her gaze caught on the sheriff and then went past him, to the window. "The rain stopped."

"For now," Sheriff Jenson agreed. "Still cloudy as hell, though." He flipped the light switch. "And no power yet. No phones or Internet, either. Truck worked, though, and so did my flashlight. Hope that's a sign some of this has passed."

Sarah glanced at her wrist. "My watch is working again. From my best estimate, it rained a couple of hours at the most. I expected six hours of rain." Her throat bobbed as she swallowed hard, her eyes lifting and catching on Max's. "Today is June 6. The sixth month, the sixth day. I'm wondering if there is a third *six* we haven't identified."

"As in the sign of the devil?" Sheriff Jenson asked. "Just what are we dealing with here, Ms. Meyers?"

Devil. Demon who received power from the devil. Max didn't know the answer, but he'd seen plenty of bad stuff. He'd fought demon soldiers by the hundreds. Win-ning those battles had been a matter of raising a sword. A Darkland Beast died when its head was cut off. Max had a damn bad feeling this spirit stuff was a lot more complicated than that, a lot nastier. That Sarah appeared quite rattled didn't comfort his worries. This was familiar territory to her, and her obvious unease wasn't a good sign.

"Whatever it is," he assured her softly, "we'll beat it."

"Ms. Meyers?" Sheriff Jenson said, his tone more demanding this time. "What *are* we dealing with?"

"Call me Sarah, Sheriff," she said, turning to face him. "I don't know what we're dealing with yet, but things are looking really bad. I need some information and I need it fast. I had a vision about a car accident on that bridge coming into town. About a woman who died there. I need to see the case file." The sheriff's face noticeably paled.

Sarah studied him. "What is it, Sheriff?"

"I'm sorry," he said, obviously flustered. "I've never been a believer in ghosts and all the paranormal junk—"

Sarah interrupted him. "But you invited me here."

"Right," he said. "I'll be frank. I didn't want you to prove I had ghosts or spooks. I wanted a scientific explanation for all of this. Which brings me back to that car accident."

Max could tell Sarah wasn't pleased over the sheriff's admission. "What about it?" Max prodded.

Sheriff Jenson scrubbed his jaw again. "A woman died in that accident. Since then, her husband's behavior has become a bit of a concern to folks around here." He eyed Sarah. "The fact that you bring up the same incident is a bit disconcerting."

Sarah stiffened and Max remembered her words. She had claimed that the husband was involved in all of this. "What's wrong with the husband besides the obvious grief of losing his wife?" Sarah asked.

The sheriff held up his hands stop-sign fashion. "Before I go on, let me say this. Small towns breed superstitions and rumors." He motioned to the back room. "This is a long story. Why don't we go sit?"

Sarah and Max exchanged a look as they followed him back to the break room; they sat down on either side of him. There was no doubt Sarah was concerned. Max saw it in her eyes, in the tension in her body.

"Here's the thing," the sheriff said. "I've had reports that Allen has been acting a bit suspiciously for quite some time now. Long before the strange stuff started happening 'round town. So when it did, he was already on the town radar." Sarah and Max nodded their understanding, and he continued, "Since Kate died—that was his wife—Allen's been a real recluse. Before that, he was a real friendly guy. In church on Sundays. At all the town events. That kind of thing. But after Kate's death, he didn't show his face in town for months."

"That's understandable," Sarah commented. "That had to be a hard time for him."

"I agree," Sheriff Jenson offered quickly. "Allen and his wife grew up here together. For him to have a hard time with this was expected. The chatter didn't start until he ventured out again. He'd changed. Wouldn't make eye contact, wouldn't speak. Then, he bought some rather odd supplies, and the rumor mill split wide-open."

Sarah frowned. "What kind of supplies?"

"Candles, incense, knives. Some say he's messing with black magic. One of the neighbors' kids snuck onto the property and saw a big circle and triangle drawn on his living-room floor."

"That doesn't sound good," Max inserted, eyeing Sarah.

"It would be used for evoking spirits," Sarah confirmed, her eyes full of concern.

"The kid could be lying," Max offered.

Sheriff Jenson agreed. "That's what I thought but the parent pressed and I checked it out. I stopped by and visited Allen, and I didn't see anything. But then, he has a rug on the floor. I couldn't rightly lift it up."

Sarah sat back in her chair and drew a breath. "He wants to bring his wife back," she said softly.

The sheriff looked stunned. "Is that possible?"

Max's brow inched upward, surprised at Sarah's statement. But he wasn't a fool. He'd seen things. Lived some miracles himself. After being turned into a demon and saved by Salvador, he knew anything was possible.

"In theory," Sarah admitted, her lips thinning. "But we are talking black magic, which Cathy will know more about." She seemed to get lost in her thoughts a moment before she refocused on the sheriff. "Tell me everything you know about Allen and Kate."

The conversation continued and Sarah drilled the sheriff about every detail of that car accident on the bridge—and the events and people involved.

Max thumbed through the town history book as he listened, scanning for anything of importance. He had almost skipped a half torn-out page, when he paused to study the text. "Excuse me, Sheriff," Max interrupted, reading enough to know the page was important. "What can you tell me about this legend?" He slid the book toward the man. "Part of the story is missing."

Sheriff Jenson glanced at the page and sighed. "I'd have said it's an urban legend, but now, I don't know."

"What is it?" Sarah asked, grabbing the book to take a look.

"It's the legend of a powerful demon doing battle with an archangel," Sheriff Jenson explained. The minute he said *archangel,* Max went on alert. This might just be the piece that tied him to this town, the explanation of why Nowhere held his destiny. The sheriff continued, "The demon was defeated and sentenced to prison deep beneath the earth. That location is said to be directly below Nowhere, Texas."

"This makes sense," Sarah said quickly. "It's not uncommon to evoke the aid of a demon when using black magic. If an unskilled practitioner performs an evocation, the demon could easily take control of the human."

Max hardly heard her; he was focused on one thing. On a critical point that impacted his mission, his test. "Any idea which archangel?" Max asked.

The sheriff frowned. "Hmm. Michael. No. That's not it."

"Raphael?" Max prodded.

The sound of the front door opening filled the air. "Sheriff?" It was a female voice.

"That's Mrs. Carmillo," Sheriff Jenson said. "She lives alone. I imagine she's scared." He started to get up.

Max grabbed his arm, halting his departure. "Was it Raphael?"

The sheriff looked surprised at Max's urgency. "Yes. Yes, that sounds right."

Max let the man go, his mind racing with the implications of what he'd just learned. Now Max knew the connection between himself and Nowhere, Texas. Raphael. The archangel who had created The Knights of White had imprisoned the demon that Max was now destined to face in battle.

This was a demon so powerful, it had taken an archangel to defeat it. Max inhaled. Salvador would not have sent him here alone if this were more than he could handle. He could defeat this demon. Though, clearly, not with a sword. Salvador had said he'd need every life experience he had lived to do this.

Sarah's fingers brushed his hand, a soft touch that shook him to the core. "What is it, Max?"

Her question, her presence, somehow brought back Salvador's words. *You must face this on your own, but not alone.* Max's gaze lifted to Sarah's beautiful green eyes. Eyes that seemed to reach inside and touch his soul. He felt that connection, that moment, in every inch of his body. He knew now that Sarah was, indeed, his mate. Whatever evil was here, they were to face it together. And that evil was nothing like the Darkland Beasts. Nothing like the demons he knew how to slay with a sword. This evil used humans to do its deeds. Humans whom Max existed to protect.

Max was headed to war, and he had everything on the line. His future as a Knight of White. And his mate, Sarah. A mate he may well have found too late. A mate he could not claim. Because if he didn't pass this test, if he didn't save this town, he was doomed to eternity in the Underworld. And he wouldn't take Sarah with him.

Chapter 5

"Max," Sarah said, willing him to look at her and tell her what was going on. Something about that town legend had him rattled. In turn, it had her rattled. No, if she were honest with herself, the way Max made her feel had her rattled. There was a weird connection between them. Even now, she could feel his distress almost as if it were her own. That had only happened with spirits until now. "Max, please. Talk to me."

His gaze lifted, locking with hers, the look in those soulful hazel eyes grim, matching the feelings he'd somehow been feeding her. He opened his mouth to speak, but paused as the sound of raised voices filled the air, rising in volume with each passing second. "That doesn't sound good," he said, pushing to his feet, hand going to his weapon.

"I hope like heck you don't need that," Sarah said,

standing up, fearful they had another obstacle to conquer before they'd even begun to tackle the root problem they faced. "Please, Lord," she whispered. "Don't let it be another bout of craziness overtaking the town. We have enough to deal with without saving them from themselves."

Max started for the door. "Maybe the demon wants to keep us busy," he commented, more to himself than to her.

Reacting to his words, Sarah took a fast sidestep, intercepting him, her hand going to his arm. She ignored the jolt to her stomach the touch created and focused on more important matters than her overactive libido. "What about this archangel? What do you know that I don't?"

He stared down at her, his eyes dark, probing; his big body close; his scent, spicy and all too alluring. "We have a great deal to discuss, Sarah," he said softly.

Something in the way he said her name, the way he looked at her, said he referred to far more than demons and the troubles of this town. Her heart kicked into double time, heat rushing through her limbs. Good Lord, what was it about this man that got to her this way? She had a town to save, people to help.

"So talk," she said, her tone demanding by design. She would not let him see how much he affected her. Better yet, she would tune him out completely, at least on a personal level.

The sound of voices lifted in the air again, demanding attention. "Not now," he said. "We both know we need to deal with whatever is going on out there."

She hesitated and then forced herself to drop her hand from his arm. "Fine." Her lips pursed. "But I want answers, Max. I won't involve you in the investigation if you don't shoot straight with me."

He narrowed his gaze on her. "I know what you want, Sarah."

Though he spoke in a low, almost monotone voice, she could feel an undertone of heat rush through the words and then directly to her cheeks. Quickly, she turned away from him, hiding her reaction, taking the lead down the hallway—or trying to. Max quickly aligned himself next to her, and together they headed toward the source of the noise.

Still, as much as she needed space away from Max to consider why he impacted her as he did, she was also glad to have him by her side. As much of a loner as she considered herself, the idea of being the only person in this town unaffected by whatever was happening here was a bit daunting.

As they followed the sounds of chaos to the outer office, Sarah noted Max's hand on his gun, ready to draw it at the first sign of trouble. She couldn't blame him for being cautious after the way people had gone a bit whacko at the inn earlier. Fortunately, there was no rage and fighting this time and no need for a gun. Just a group of six or seven citizens assembled around the sheriff, all desperate for answers.

Sarah and Max looked at each other, pausing in the doorway as he eased his hand off the gun, the danger they'd feared clearly not present. In silent agreement, they stayed in the background, listening in on the conversation without interference.

A redheaded woman in her mid-to-late thirties

shivered and hugged herself. "I know it sounds crazy, but my doors flew open and shut by themselves."

"That could have been the wind," Sheriff Jenson argued, clearly trying to downplay the paranormal fears feeding the town's panic.

"Three times?" the woman challenged, her chin lifting defiantly. "I don't think so."

"My dog tried to attack me," an elderly man chimed in. "That dog has never so much as growled at me before today."

"It's that Allen Walker," another man said, running his hand over his bald head. Sarah and Max exchanged a quick look at that statement. The man continued, "He's working some kind of voodoo. If that black rain and absence of sunlight aren't proof, I don't know what is."

"He's right," the redhead said. "We've all been worried about Allen."

The bald man spoke again. "He came into the post office the other day to pick up a package, and I swear, his eyes were so black, there weren't any whites around them. It was pure evil I saw in those eyes."

"All right now," the sheriff said, irritated. "That's enough of this talk. We all want answers, and it's easy to look for someone to blame. But none of us need to go persecuting a man who isn't here to defend himself. Anyone who lost his wife, as Allen did, would act funny."

Another woman, with short dark hair and black-rimmed glasses, spoke up then. "You've been telling us that about Allen for a month now, Sheriff, but frankly it's not good enough anymore. We need to know we're safe. That our kids are safe."

A murmur of support for the woman's words filled

the room. "I'll talk to Allen," the sheriff conceded, "but I need all of you to go home and stay inside. We don't know if this rain is over."

The woman with the glasses spoke again. "We don't know anything about what's happening, do we, Sheriff?"

A few more minutes of conversational dodgeball continued, with the sheriff as the target, until finally the lobby was empty.

As the last person exited, Sheriff Jenson leaned against the door, rubbing his temples. "If I don't get some answers soon, I'm going to have a lynch mob on my hands," he said. "I told you. They're convinced Allen is behind this."

"They aren't the only ones. Sarah thinks he's involved, too. I think it's past time we pay Allen a visit."

"Agreed," Sarah said. "I need to go by the hotel and get Cathy and Edward on the way."

"Might be best if I drive out there and bring him into the station," the sheriff inserted, his voice holding authority.

Max beat Sarah to voicing an objection. "You don't even have your deputy and frankly, Sheriff," Max said, "dealing with the paranormal isn't exactly textbook law enforcement. You know that or you wouldn't have called Sarah in the first place."

"He's right, Sheriff," Sarah quickly agreed. "You called me here for a reason. My team is trained to handle this kind of situation. We've studied the paranormal for years and that includes black magic."

"Black magic," the sheriff said flatly. "That's twice now you've mentioned that. Is that what we think is causing all of this? Can black magic create this magnitude of events?"

"I can't say anything with certainty right now," she replied cautiously. "My point is simply that we must be prepared for anything."

The sheriff's lips thinned but he nodded his agreement. "I need to round up my deputy. I'll drop you by the inn and then swing by his house. It won't take more than a few minutes."

Sarah exhaled as she cast Max a frustrated look. They needed time alone to talk before going to see Allen. She would not go into a dangerous situation with him by her side without some answers. And if he didn't like it, she'd tell the sheriff to leave him behind. But as Sheriff Jenson started out the front door, she glanced in Max's direction, noting the way he watched her, the way he seemed to touch her without even moving, without making contact. And she knew…she was in big trouble.

She had no business lusting after a man who could be an enemy, a man she didn't know for certain was friend or foe. She just knew she wanted him in a bad way. A way that defied reason and kept her from thinking straight. She was smarter than this. She had to clear her head, to stop operating in a lust-filled haze—before it got her, or someone else, killed.

Chapter 6

On the short drive from the sheriff's office to the inn, Max rode in the backseat of the patrol car while Sarah sat in front. A good thing because Max needed to think through some things before she had time to question him. Time to think about things like what he was going to tell her about that legend, about how Raphael's connection indicated that his own involvement was far more profound than mere chance.

The answers weren't simple, considering he was partnering with Sarah and her team to some extent, and by doing so, possibly exposing the Knights and their secrets. Which simply wasn't done. If the Beasts thought a human was important to the Knights, or might hold information about the Knights, that human became a target.

By the time the car stopped in front of the inn and

Max got out, he'd settled on the details of a basic cover story about the Knights being a special-ops group. He hated lying to Sarah, especially since there could be a time when he had to face that lie. But this would earn him enough of Sarah's trust to stay close to her and her team and keep them safe. The rest he'd deal with later. Or never. He didn't know. His life might be headed to hell, and Sarah deserved better than he could offer. Maybe a lie and goodbye were all there could ever be.

And one kiss. He had to kiss her at least once. Damn, how he wanted to kiss her. Like he'd never wanted to kiss a woman before. Hell, the thought of kissing her got him hotter than having sex would with most other women. Of course, he knew why. Deep down inside, he needed no confirmation beyond what he felt. Sarah belonged to him. She was his mate.

The minute Sarah exited the car, she rushed toward the front of the inn where the van was sitting, its rear doors standing open. Max followed her, noticing that Cathy already stood at the rear, peering inside. Since Max had Edward's keys, he assumed they had a spare set.

"Everything okay?" Sarah asked, as she and Max stopped on either side of Cathy.

Cathy motioned to where Edward sat inside the van at an equipment panel. "We still can't get anything to work," Edward muttered, scrubbing his jaw.

"Elaborate setup you have there," Max observed.

"We landed a nice little grant last year," Sarah said.

"Must have been." Max noted the impressive equipment. What he wanted to look at was the circuit board in the computer, though. He'd snuck a peek at the computers in the sheriff's office right before they left; the boards had been fried. "I know my way around electronics. Mind if I take a look?"

Edward glanced up, his expression skeptical as he looked to Sarah for approval. "Yes. That's fine," she said. Though his expression carried disbelief at his boss's agreement, Edward climbed out of the van, apparently more than willingly, and motioned Max forward.

"Feel free," Edward said. "I damn sure can't get anything to work."

The sheriff pulled up just then and called out to Sarah. "I'll be right back," she said, and disappeared.

"I'm choking to death here. I'm going to hunt down a bottle of water," Edward said, excusing himself and leaving Max alone with Cathy.

Max settled into Edward's seat at the panel and began checking out various wires and connections.

"I'm impressed," Cathy said. "Sarah doesn't let anyone inside our group, but she seems to be letting you in. She even seems to be giving you her trust. I wonder why that is."

The hint of suspicion gave Max pause, and he glanced up at her. "I imagine the fact that I was the only person acting sane when the rest of you were trying to kill each other."

"Which makes me even more curious," she said. "Sarah is unique. She talks to dead people. I can see *her* having some weird immunity to all of this, but why are you immune?"

"What are you getting at?" Max asked, starting to get irritated and not one to sidestep an issue.

"I'm just wondering what your story is. Sarah doesn't trust easily. Frankly, I don't want to see her get burned."

His irritation disappeared as he realized Cathy was simply protecting Sarah. "I'm here to help, Cathy," he said, looking her in the eyes and hoping she saw his sincerity. "Nothing more. Nothing less. Help. There are things going on here I don't think any of us have faced before. We need to be united in this, so we can succeed."

Sarah rounded the back of the van with Edward, ending any further conversation between Max and Cathy. "The deputy is hanging back at the sheriff's office," Sarah explained. "Apparently, they are still getting lots of upset citizens there. So whenever we are ready, the sheriff is, too. He's inside juggling more questions and trying to make people feel safe."

"I need a few more minutes to check out the equipment," Max told her, glancing at Cathy and looking for some semblance of approval. She gave him a slow incline of her head, discreet, but definite.

"All right then," Sarah said to Max's request for more time. "I need to bring them up to speed on a few things, anyway."

Max went back to work as Sarah filled Edward and Cathy in on what had happened back at the sheriff's office, including the information about the town legend, her contact with the spirit and her belief that Allen was trying to bring his wife back to life.

"If he is, he's treading on dangerous territory," Cathy commented, her voice full of concern. Clearly, she was their expert on the subject. "The blackest of black magic."

"That's what I said, too," Sarah affirmed. "I was hoping you would know what would be involved."

Cathy considered that a moment. "There are several ways, none of them good."

Max looked up at that, his gaze catching on Sarah's. "Cathy comes from a family rich in magical practices," Sarah explained, unaware that she was answering the question playing in his mind about how Cathy knew that information.

"Magic, demonology, paranormal beings," Cathy inserted. "You name it. I've studied it, or rather study it. There's a lot to learn and know. But what I can tell you for sure is this—even the most experienced dark practitioners don't delve into resurrecting the dead. There is a belief that raising the dead has consequences, a price that would be too horrific for anyone to bear."

In his four centuries of living, Max had crossed paths with a few people who had touched the dark arts. He'd made a fast path in the other direction. He made it his goal to avoid anything to do with it. Which made this little test in Nowhere all the more ironic.

"But if you wanted to bring someone back from the dead," Sarah asked, "it's possible?"

Reluctantly, Cathy inclined her head. "Yes." She listed off several ways this might be done, ending with, "I've also read about certain higher-level demons granting such wishes...for a price."

"Really?" Sarah said, perking up. "Max mentioned a demon, as well." She cast him an expectant look. "Didn't you, Max?"

Max took his time answering, knowing it was time to lay down his cards, but not eager to do so. He hated lying to Sarah. Hated it with a passion.

Stalling, he reported on the laptop. "Its board is fried," he said rotating around to face Sarah and her team. Edward cursed in response to the news. "Just like the one at the sheriff's office. Which isn't a coincidence. I would bet every computer in this town is fried. I don't believe in coincidence."

Max glanced at Sarah and baited her into questioning him. "Nor do the people I work for."

"Which is who?" Sarah asked, just as he had hoped.

Hesitating, Max pretended he didn't want to answer, ready to feed them the cover story. "A special-ops team."

"Military?" Edward asked.

"More covert than that. We fight the kind of wars the military would never claim existed."

Edward wasn't satisfied yet. "As in the supposed alien-research center our government had been covering up for years? That kind of thing?"

"Something like that," Max said, trying to tell as much truth as possible.

Quick to end the questions, he got back on task. "Which brings me back to the problems going on in Nowhere and my statement about there being no such thing as coincidence. We have a man we believe could be evoking a demon, in a town that has a legend about a demon. Seems to me we have two plus two here."

Sarah studied Max a minute, her gaze probing. "I can buy that. But what about the connection to Raphael?"

Max's eyes locked and held with Sarah's. Clearly, she hadn't let go of his reaction to hearing Raphael's name. He didn't want to lie about this. At this point, the truth was definitely not an option. Even if he did tell them that Raphael oversaw an immortal army of demon hunters, and that he himself happened to be one of those immortals, it wasn't as if they would believe him. He needed to do some fast thinking and talking.

Fortunately, Cathy aided his efforts with her own insertion. "Raphael is the healer of humanity, and that is why he is often called upon for healing in prayers and from those who practice angel magic," she said, proving she'd done her homework in this area, as well. "But he's also believed to be a protector of humanity and a mighty warrior when it's demanded of him. If we choose to assume the legend is true, including Raphael's involvement, then that indicates to me that the demon in question is a powerful one, worthy of angelic intervention. In other words, an upper-level demon, which would be required to resurrect the dead. Who knows what a powerful demon such as this one is capable of doing." Her brows dipped. "If Allen Walker is evoking this kind of upper-level demon, he could inadvertently set it free." Cathy looked from Max to Sarah. "I need to do more research for information on this kind of practice. Maybe one of my reference books will help. Did either of you see the name of the demon?"

"No name," Max said. "Part of the page in that book was torn away. Maybe the sheriff can help us there."

His eyes met Sarah's for several long moments. Max could see that she knew there was more to tell that he hadn't shared. Hopefully her instinct to trust her mate would make her tolerant of his silence. Damn it, he hated this need for secrecy. He tore his eyes from hers, exiting the van. "We should go," he grumbled. "I need to grab a room and pull some supplies from my bags."

And then he walked away, feeling Sarah's stare on his back, his heart pounding with the turbulence of his thoughts. He prayed he was making the right choices. What should he tell Sarah and what should he keep to himself? He wanted to tell her everything, but he also knew that too much too fast could push her away. And if that happened, protecting her could become difficult. He needed to keep her close and safe. To do that, like it or not, he had to keep these secrets. And when he did share his world, he wanted it to be forever.

And right now, he wasn't sure he had that to give.

Sarah watched Max depart as she leaned on the door of the van, her stomach twisting into a knot of conflicting emotion. Why did she want to call him back rather than let him walk away? He'd be right back. What was wrong with her?

"I've never seen you trust anyone so quickly," Cathy warned, as if reading Sarah's mind. "The man has secrets. Lots of them. I think we should take everything he gives us with a grain of salt until we can confirm his story."

"How will we do that?" Edward asked with a snort, hand on his hips. "Call the army and ask if they have a covert paranormal team that they pretend doesn't exist?"

"Don't be a smart-ass, Edward," Cathy said, cutting him an irritated glance. "We're dealing with something really evil here. For all we know, Max could be part of it. He was the only other person who didn't go psycho at the inn earlier. Just being a part of some special-ops team wouldn't make him immune to evil."

"What are you suggesting?" Sarah asked, apprehensive as she waited on Cathy's reply, worried about where this might be going.

"We know what makes you different and why you weren't affected by the rage, as the rest of us were," Cathy said, waving her hands around in an animated fashion. "But why wasn't Max? What if it's because evil is immune to evil?" She continued immediately, "If we are going to intimately invite this guy into our investigation, don't you think we need to know more about him?"

"I hate to admit it," Edward said, "but she does have a point."

Satisfaction flickered in Cathy's eyes. She loved being right and Edward rarely allowed her that privilege. Obviously empowered by the approval, she added, "If we think Allen's cabin is the source of evil, or close to that source, taking Max might be a mistake. What if he somehow makes that source stronger?"

"On the other hand," Edward interjected, sitting on the bumper and crossing his booted feet, "if Max is one of the good guys, he might know something we don't. He might be the ticket to beating this thing."

Cathy scowled at Edward while Sarah drew a deep breath. "I'll talk to Max and decide from there," Sarah said after a moment of consideration. "That's the best I can do under the circumstances." She glanced at the stormy sky as the wind kicked up speed, lifting her hair from her shoulders. The change in weather brought with it concern that it somehow signaled some new event about to unfold. "Tell the sheriff I'd like to be out of here in fifteen minutes." Sarah didn't wait for a reply; she started walking toward the inn.

She needed to talk to Max, to figure out what he was really all about. To make a decision about his involvement, though she wasn't really sure how.

Cathy was right to be cautious. Sarah's trust of Max wasn't anywhere close to her normal reaction to strangers. Still, even knowing this, she couldn't shake the nagging feeling that keeping Max by her side had life and death consequences. If only she could figure out why.

Cathy's suggestion that Max could be connected to evil came to her mind. Was this connection she felt to Max a product of evil? She didn't think so, but how could she be sure? And if she wasn't sure, could she allow him near the cabin, the place from where they felt the evil originated? Wouldn't that be pressing their luck?

Thunder rumbled in the background and hail started to fall. Sarah climbed the steps to the inn at a trot, feeling a sudden urgency to get a move on things. Time was a luxury she didn't have. People's lives could well be on the line in this town, and she had to take action to make sure everyone was safe—and do so now.

She drew in a labored breath, hating the choice she knew she had to make. But, she couldn't take risks by allowing strangers into their inner circle. That's how she had operated since her parents' death and it had worked. Max couldn't go with them to the cabin, and he wasn't going to like it one bit. But if she let him, and something happened to Edward or Cathy, she'd never forgive herself.

This was the right decision.

So why did it feel so wrong?

Chapter 7

Max sank down onto the mattress in the center of the cozy little room, with its floral curtains and lacy pillows, feeling like a fish out of water. More so than he'd ever felt. Somehow, the environment emphasized the darkness growing inside him.

The truth was he knew nothing of the softer side of life, of family and love. He'd come from a noble English family, and in those early days, he'd been known as Maxwell Kingsley, "the spare to the heir," the younger of two boys. Despite how belittling his family had been to him, how abusive and downright vicious at times, they had been all he knew, all he had. And they had been taken from him—stripped away by the Beasts and violently bled dry.

The centuries since had done nothing to stop that horrible day from replaying in his head in vivid, sickening color. Keeping others from falling prey to the Beasts had been the only peace his life had held, the only purpose.

He shoved off the bed and flipped open a long suitcase full of weapons, the velvet lining inside hugging several long blades, the tools of his trade. The method of destroying a Darkland Beast. They were tools that held no answers to defeating this new enemy, to finding a path that would deliver him to victory rather than defeat—and victory was the only answer. His hands slid over the silver of one blade; the power he wielded with it was fresh in his memories of battlefield victories.

Whatever meant to harm this town would not succeed, Max silently vowed. He would protect this town. And he would protect Sarah. His mate. He became more confident of their bond with every passing moment, her presence touching him deep in his soul. A knock sounded on the door and he knew who it was without ever opening it. Sarah. She wouldn't be here if not to ask for answers. Answers he wasn't sure he could offer her.

He walked to the door and pressed his hand to the wooden surface, closing his eyes. Damn. She was so close and so far away at the same time. He wanted to rip away the barriers, to open the door and pull her close. To tell her everything and more. "Max?" she called when he didn't respond. "It's me. Sarah."

He forced himself to keep that door shut, that barrier between them. "I'll be down in less than five minutes," he said, hoping she'd accept that and leave.

Nothing. Silence. But he could still hear her breathing. Could feel the turbulence of her emotions, feel them with odd certainty, as if they were his own. He'd heard the mated Knights speak of such things. Even with the heavy wood between them, the warmth of her presence wrapped around him, overwhelming him with its intimacy, with her nearness.

"Max…"

He turned back to the bed, shoving the suitcase lid down to hide the weapons and setting it on the floor. A second later, he yanked the door open, bringing Sarah into focus. Instantly, her green eyes melted into his, his groin tightening with the impact. He grabbed her and pulled her into the room, shutting the door behind them, his actions pure, protective instinct.

He flipped the locks firmly into place and turned to find Sarah directly behind him, barely inches away. He clutched his fists by his sides to keep from reaching for her. "What is it, Sarah? What's wrong? Did something else happen?"

Confusion flickered in her eyes as she searched his face, probing with intense scrutiny. "Nothing. Everything is fine." But it wasn't fine. If he hadn't sensed her turmoil, then her hesitation before continuing would have been enough to make that clear. "I simply wanted to tell you we're headed out to Allen's cabin. I was hoping you'd keep an eye on things back here? Maybe check in on the deputy?"

He'd expected questions, not this. He rejected her words with force. "You're not going out there alone. I'm going with you."

A flash of anger darted through her eyes. "You're not in a position to make demands. The sheriff hired me, not you. I make the rules and I say you're not going with us. That's how this is going to happen."

"No, sweetheart, it's not. I'm going and that is final."

She laughed with disbelief. "You're a piece of work, Max. Your macho, bossy attitude goes over well for about all of one minute." She hardened her voice. "You're not going, Max. That's the bottom line here. My team doesn't trust you."

He didn't miss her reference to her "team's" distrust. What about her trust? "Do *you* trust me?" he asked, knowing she did, knowing their destiny as mates would make that a given.

"I don't even know you, Max."

Those were the wrong words for one mate to utter to another, though he wouldn't have known that before she issued them. Possessiveness rushed through Max with the force of a volcanic eruption. Sarah knew him better than any other person in existence, and he wanted her to realize that, wanted her to know it as she had never known anything else in her life. The fierceness of those emotions sent Max into action. This was his woman, and everything male in him demanded she be clear on that fact.

One minute they were glaring at each other in a standoff, the next she was in his arms, her soft curves molded against his aroused body, her sweet lips pressed to his. He felt her fingers pressed to his shoulders as if she would resist, her body stiff, yet she made no movement to exit the embrace. Nor was Max about to give her the chance to come to her senses.

Wasting no time, his tongue swept past her teeth, gliding along them, and tempting her into response. She moaned, a sensual purr of a sound that drove him wild with desire. His palms flattened on her lower back as her arms slid around his neck, her chest pressing into his.

Never in his life had Max felt as complete as he did

with Sarah in his arms, with the sweet taste of her on his tongue. He belonged to Sarah, with Sarah, as he had never belonged in his entire life. Peace filled him, and when he would have reveled in the purity of it, the feeling was yanked away, the beast flaring to life with vicious intensity. It wanted her. All of her. To claim her. To make her his beyond a simple moment in time. A taste wasn't enough. A touch wasn't enough. Yet the man in him knew it had to be enough. For now, it had to be. He couldn't cave to the urges of his darker side. A war raged inside him as he battled between the right thing to do and what the beast demanded of him.

If there had been any doubt in Max's mind that Sarah was his mate, then those moments where beast and man battled did away with it. Only when answering the mating call did a Knight bear the cuspids of a Beast. And the truth became dangerously obvious as Max's gums tingled, and his teeth threatened to elongate.

In some far corner of his lust-hazed mind, Max knew he should pull away, put distance between them. But the fire coursing through his veins, all-consuming and demanding, wouldn't allow him to set her free. The primal urges of his beast were flaming hot, pushing him to take more. For a moment he did, but he was not alone in this. Sarah took, as well, kissing him with long strokes of her tongue, her hands all over him, torturing him with erotic touches. But it was her hips that did him in, her hips that arched against his erection, teasing him with possibilities, moving against him with a sensual glide up and down his long, hard length. Suddenly, they were on the bed, sharing crazy hot kisses, Sarah beneath him, on her back. Max didn't even remember how they got there. Her legs eased open for him without hesitation, inviting him intimately into her world as Max settled his hips into the V of her body, telling himself to stop before it was too late. Only the beast in him didn't want to stop, it wanted inside her, to feel the warm, wet heat of her surrounding him.

He couldn't get enough of her, couldn't get close enough. His hands were traveling, exploring. She moved beneath him, pressing closer, hips arching into him, driving him crazy as she teased his groin. The room, the danger, the need for anything but each other seemed to slide away as passion consumed and controlled.

More was all he could think of. More. His fingers slid beneath Sarah's flimsy T-shirt, the warmth of her skin inviting him upward, even as a soft moan told of pleasure. He filled his hands with her lush breasts as his mouth found her jaw, her neck, her shoulder. Her nipples pebbled beneath the silky material of her bra, and he shoved down the barrier, his fingers tweaking her nipples, his mouth hungry to do the same. But he found himself hungry with a primal burn, pressing her shirt away, exposing more of her neck, her shoulder. It would be so easy to claim her, to sink his teeth into her shoulder and mark her as his mate. She was the one. His woman. His life. Even her body fit his, perfectly. She was his. The words replayed in his mind as he deepened their kiss.

Wouldn't their mating make him pure? Wouldn't that save him from his potential fate in hell?

"Max," Sarah whispered his name, her voice full of sensual heat, full of surrender. She'd give herself to him, their connection as mates overshadowing everything but her need for him, their need for each other.

Which meant she trusted him. *Trust.* The word dropped into his head like a bomb being unloaded and brought with it a heavy dose of reality. To take Sarah, without her knowing who and what he was, would be wrong. To take her at all in his present situation—his destiny possibly eternal hell—would be unfair in every way.

Somehow, Max managed to tear his lips from hers, staring down at her desire-filled expression, his chest heaving with the effort that his restraint claimed from him. He squeezed his eyes shut, guilt sliding into his gut with a knot of pain. What if he'd lost control? What if he'd claimed her and she couldn't save him? He could have taken her straight to hell with him.

He rolled off of her onto his back, thankful he'd stopped before it was too late. "I'm sorry," he whispered. "I'm so sorry, Sarah."

She didn't move, lying there as if she were as stunned as he was by what had just happened. Seconds passed. "I don't know what's wrong with me," she said, her hand covering her face for a moment before dropping to her chest, as if trying to calm her racing heart. "I lost all sense of the here and now. I…God. People are counting on me and I didn't even care."

Without warning, she sat up and shot off the bed, her fingers running through her hair as she turned to face him. "What just happened to us?" She shook her head, as she appeared to struggle to swallow. "That wasn't normal, Max. I know you know that. It's the demon, isn't it? Doing something to distract us, so we can't stop it."

Max eased to a sitting position on the side of the mattress, shocked by her assessment. "What?" he asked, brows furrowed. "No. It's not the demon, Sarah." He quickly weighed his options and ruled out shooting straight with her. Who knew how she'd react in her present state. But he also couldn't let her dismiss what had happened between them as some sort of evil trick. He repeated his prior declaration for good measure. "It's not the demon. Things just got out of hand. We're under stress and we turned to each other. That's all."

"It's more than that," she insisted. "It was too intense not to be. It's the demon messing with us. I know it is."

There was a real franticness about her expression, in her voice. Max pushed to his feet, grabbing her hand before she could resist and pulling her close. Thankful she didn't back away.

Gently, he eased his hands into her hair, tilting her face to his, making sure she read the truth in his words. "No demon, Sarah. Just two people who want each other. I promise."

"What if it's more?" Her hands went to his wrists, her grip tight. "I've seen demons do things. I've seen—"

He kissed her. A fast, sensual kiss that he forced himself to end quickly, proving the fire between them could be ignited by another kiss at any time, but it could also be ended with the right restraint.

"Max," she whispered breathlessly, as he pulled back to look at her.

"We want each other, Sarah," he said, his voice low, husky, his groin tightening again despite his best efforts to contain himself. "There's nothing evil or unnatural about what we share." His lips smiled teasingly. "And if you keep insisting some demon made us feel this way, I am going to get insulted."

"I'm sorry." Her lashes lowered and then lifted. "It's

just that…well…someone close to me was possessed by a demon and it didn't end well."

Holy crap. Max didn't see that one coming. Thank God, he hadn't told her about the mating ritual. And no telling what she'd do if she knew his soul had once been touched by a demon. He'd scare the hell out of her.

"Talk to me," he urged. "What happened?"

Max searched her face, noting the retreat in her eyes as he waited for answers. She'd withdrawn, shut him out. The door inside her circle of trust had been firmly slammed shut, with him on the wrong side. Silently, he vowed to win his way to the right side.

Sarah drew a long, deep breath and stepped out of Max's arms, shocked she'd let that admission slip out. Shocked at how cold she felt without his touch. It would have been easy to blame the demon for what had happened with Max, but the truth was, she'd needed the escape—the moments of having big strong arms wrapped around her, without the world on her shoulders.

But those moments in his arms were gone now, and there was a demon to deal with. "People died. I won't relive that again."

He stared at her for several intense seconds, appearing frozen in place, without a breath, a blink, a movement. Then, he went into action. "Nothing is going to happen to you, your people or this town." He grabbed a duffel bag and tossed it on the bed, yanking out a holster of some sort and tightening it around his hips. "I'm not going to mince words here. You want to know what I do and why you need me, and I'm going to tell you. I hunt demons, Sarah. We call them Darkland

Beasts because they first appeared in the Mexico deserts. Nasty monsters that have fangs and bad attitudes. Their entire goal in life is to steal human souls. If I'm here, there's a good chance my people knew they would be, too."

Her blood ran cold. Spirits she understood. Fanged monsters, she did not. "When you say steal the souls, what exactly does that mean?"

"If they choose to turn a human to Beast rather than kill them, they strip the soul. There's nothing left then but pure evil. That human becomes a Darkland Beast."

He picked up the suitcase and put it on the bed, opening the lid. Sarah's eyes went wide at the sight of several long swords. The lethal-looking blades made anything she had seen him wearing before look like butter knives.

"They're saber swords," he explained, before she could ask. "They kill the bastards better than any other blade I've found. Guns won't kill them." He grabbed another holster. "Can you fire a gun?"

"Yes. My parents…" She stopped. Damn it, no more of the "personal." "Yes. Why? You said guns don't kill them."

He tossed her a shoulder holster and she caught it. "Put that on," he said, reinstating the bossy attitude he couldn't seem to shed. Still, she did as he bid. She wasn't a fool. She'd take all the protection she could get under present circumstances. He continued, as she tightened the shoulder strap. "Unload the ammo into the demon's head—and I'm talking all of it. You get enough bullets in a Darkland's head, and it will knock him down for a minute or two. Long enough for me to get to you."

He retrieved a gun from his bag and walked over to her, offering her the butt of the weapon.

A sizzle of excitement mingled with fear touched Sarah as she accepted the gun. The same feelings she'd shared with her parents when exploring new forms of the supernatural. Fresh guilt twisted in her gut. How could she derive excitement from a world that had taken their lives? Emotion welled in her chest, and she refocused on survival, sliding the gun into the holster.

Cathy and Edward needed protection, she realized. "Do you have enough to go around?"

"I've got Cathy and Edward covered, too," he promised, reading her mind.

"I've never dealt with a demon that would only die from a sword," she said, swallowing hard as he slid a long saber into a holster at his hip.

"I've never dealt with one who wouldn't," he commented, his fingers brushing her cheek, drawing her gaze to his. "I guess that's why we need each other."

Sarah felt the touch of his eyes, the intimacy of his words, with all the implications, hopes, fears. She hadn't let herself need anyone in years, nor did she want to now. But, deep down, Sarah knew it was already too late. Max had done what she swore nobody would ever do again. He'd made her need him.

Chapter 8

They're coming.

With Vars's words a whisper in his mind, Allen rushed to his truck, keys jiggling nervously in one hand, a small suitcase of supplies in the other. He didn't know who "they" were, only that they intended to stop him from getting his Kate back. No one was going to stop him. No one. His hand shook as he opened the driver's door of his candy-apple-red F-150 pickup. Kate loved red. He thought of her excitement the day they'd brought it home, and his chest tightened with the memory. Now, he had to bring her home. His temples were throbbing, his pulse pounding at double-speed—a product of his jacked-up adrenaline—yet despite the urgency to flee, Allen was careful with the case he held, taking care to slide it securely to the floorboard of the passenger's side and under the seat.

It held valuable supplies that Vars said would be
needed for the task before him. Allen had to collect three
power sources and bring them back to the cabin. With
these sources, he would have everything he needed to
free Vars. And with Vars's freedom would come Kate's.

Allen didn't know what these power sources were
any more than he knew who "they" were. But it didn't
matter. All that mattered was that he act quickly. He
started the engine, hitting the accelerator with a heavy
foot. As he pulled out from beneath his patio, he noted
the eerily dark clouds, and satisfaction filled him. If
Vars had the ability to conjure weather from his prison
cell, then once he had his freedom, Vars surely had the
power to bring back Kate. Soon the demon prince would
be free and Kate would live. And finally, Allen would
have ended the hell he'd suffered without his wife. The
world would be right again.

Still reeling from Sarah's touch, from the implications of the hell that might have become her destiny had
he claimed her, Max followed her down the inn stairs
to join the others. It had taken some effort, but he'd convinced Sarah to agree to keep his revelations about the
demon hunting to herself. Anyone who knew about the
Darklands would become a target. He'd only told Sarah
to ensure she understood the dangers they faced. That
and, ultimately, her destiny lay inside his world and
that of the Knights.

Still, there was no doubt that Sarah's crew would
have to be prepped for this lethal form of danger, and
Max needed a reason for carrying his sabers. The final
outcome of these concerns led Max and Sarah to fabri-

cate a story of sword-wielding demon worshippers, which wasn't so far from the truth.

Feeling anxious to get to Allen's cabin, to take action toward resolution, Max hoped to avoid any further delays. Relief washed over him as he noted the lobby was vacant except for Cathy, Edward and Sheriff Jenson. The fewer people present, the less chance of another detour before hitting the road.

The instant they approached the group, Cathy's eyes settled on Max, her expression turning sour. Before Max could comment, Sarah took charge. "He's coming with us," she stated, making her position on Max crystal clear.

Max smiled to himself at the victory, pleased with Sarah's support. He was, after all, only intending to protect them all, Cathy included.

It was a victory that had lasted only a few moments. Suddenly Max found himself being confronted by the sheriff. "You're not going anywhere packing those weapons," Sheriff Jenson said, scowling at Max. "You trying to scare the hell out of my town, or what?"

"I'm trying to save them, Sheriff," Max countered. "Exactly why I'm keeping the weapons."

The sheriff took a step toward Max and appeared to want a confrontation they didn't have time for. Again, Sarah grabbed the reins, placing herself between them. She faced the sheriff, directly in front of Max. "Why don't we take this outside before we draw attention? There are new developments you need to hear about before you demand that Max throw away those weapons." Sheriff Jenson hesitated, but agreed. Sarah cast Cathy and Edward a look. "You'll both want to hear this, as well."

A few minutes later, the trip to Allen's cabin was underway; the story Max and Sarah had fabricated had been accepted with grim regard, and satisfied the sheriff enough to allow Max to remain armed.

With the sheriff riding shotgun, Edward maneuvered the van along a bumpy dirt path. Cathy sat in the back of the vehicle directly across from Max and Sarah, absorbed in a chant she called a "protection spell."

Max doubted that any magic Cathy might manage to muster would touch the category of evil they were obviously up against, but he held his tongue. Who knew? He'd been surprised more than once in his long life, and Cathy certainly seemed to keep herself educated on the magical elements.

Leaning his head against the wall, allowing his eyes to shut, he feigned boredom. In reality, every nerve in his body was charged with Sarah's presence beside him. At the same time, he was on edge, worried for her safety.

Several minutes, and a huge pothole later, Max looked up to find Cathy holding a crossword puzzle book. This hardly seemed the time for games. Sarah apparently noted his expression, and responded. "Crosswords are her way of dealing with stress."

Max glanced at Sarah, and was overcome by their intense connection. The bond between them was growing, carving itself inside him. Did she feel it, too?

"It's crosswords or nonstop talking," Edward commented from the front, jerking Max back to reality. "Trust me. Crosswords are the lesser of two evils."

Max laughed at that, expecting Cathy to jab back at Edward as his fellow Knights would, the sense of friendship evident in the jests shared between the two.

Instead, Cathy tuned Edward out. "I need a five-letter word for a place between heaven and hell." She frowned. "Five letters?"

"Texas," Edward said. "That's five letters, and we're here now and definitely in hell. We need gas. Damn it, I should have filled up."

"It's not much farther up the road," Sheriff Jenson said.

"Limbo," Max said.

"Limbo," Cathy stated. "I think that's it." She frowned and wrote it down. "What is limbo?"

Max shrugged. He'd always kind of figured he was in limbo, but didn't say that. "Depends on who you ask, but the general gist is neither heaven nor hell—it's a place where the unbaptized must stay."

"I've always wondered where the spirits are who talk to me," Sarah said. "I never seem to get that from them."

"Any word from Allen's wife?" Cathy asked.

"Nothing," Sarah said.

Max still wasn't quite used to all the spirit stuff. "Is that good or bad?" he asked.

"Silence is approval," Sarah said, and rolled her eyes. "Believe me. If the spirits don't think I'm getting the message, they find a way to scream louder."

"We're here," Sheriff Jenson called back to them.

Max turned to look through the windshield. A small cabin was now visible on the horizon, and a sizzle of alarm was ringing in his body, the hair on the back of his neck standing on end. The same feeling he got when he was about to face an enemy, about to face war.

They pulled to a stop in front of the cabin. "Well, damn," Sheriff Jenson mumbled. "I don't see his truck."

Sarah reached out and grabbed Max's arm, intent on

stopping his departure; a chill raced down her spine. The ghost of Kate touched her mind, issuing a warning. "Something is wrong," she whispered, frowning as she realized Kate seemed to be fighting against some other energy source. One minute Kate was there in Sarah's head, communicating, and the next, she was gone, almost as if she'd been ripped right out of Sarah's head. Her grip on Max tightened. "Very wrong."

Max narrowed his eyes on her but didn't ask questions. Apparently, her word was enough. Then he took things into his own hands.

"No one leaves this van until I say it's clear," Max ordered, slipping his jacket off, ready to go to war.

"Oh, no, son," Sheriff Jenson said. "I'm not going to put Allen on the defensive. I'll go talk to him, and then see if he'll allow you all in. I can't go accusing him without evidence."

"Sheriff, please," Sarah said. "Listen to Max. I have a bad feeling about this." But it was too late. Sheriff Jenson shoved open the door and exited.

Max cursed and started for the side door. When he got there, he rotated around in a squatting position to look at Sarah. "Stay here until I know it's safe. You remember what I said about the gun?"

"I remember all too well," Sarah said, hoping she wouldn't have the opportunity to unload a weapon into a demon's head.

He shoved open the side door. "Hold it in your hand. It'll make me feel better. And lock the doors."

A second later he was gone, and Cathy didn't hesitate to lock up behind him. Edward did the same up front. They both knew if Sarah said something was wrong, something was wrong. Sarah eyed Cathy who hated guns. "Pull your gun."

"You know how I feel—"

"Pull the damn gun, Cathy," Sarah said, her tone uncharacteristically sharp, but she didn't care. She had Max and Kate feeding her the kind of information that created nightmares. This wasn't the time for coddling Cathy. Better to have her alive and irritated than dead.

Not waiting for Cathy's response, Sarah moved to the front of the van to claim the passenger's seat next to Edward, who had his gun resting on the steering wheel, aimed straight ahead, ready for use.

The sheriff was knocking at the cabin's front door. Max appeared to be scouting the exterior of the place. Sarah drew a breath, her chest tight. All they could do now was wait and pray all hell wasn't about to break loose.

Max met the sheriff at the front door of the cabin after a quick sweep of the perimeter. All might have seemed in order, but instincts, and Sarah's warnings, had urged him to peek inside the windows. The crazy drawing on the floor and half-burned candles confirmed Allen was into some sort of magic.

"We have to go inside, Sheriff," Max said.

"I don't have a search warrant," he countered.

"Then look the other way and I'll go inside."

Max didn't have time to talk in circles with this man. "Look," he said, hands settling on his hips. "Arrest me if you have to, but I'm going inside." He inclined his head toward a window. "You might want to take a look in that window before you make any rash decisions, though." Sheriff Jenson's lips thinned beneath his thick mustache as he huffed and then stomped toward the window, apparently none too happy about the decision put before him. Max rested his weight on one foot, watching Sheriff Jenson survey the inside of the cabin before cursing under his breath.

"Fine," he said, walking toward Max. "We'll go in."

Max didn't have to be told twice. Before the sheriff made it back to his side, Max had popped the lock and shoved the door open. He would have headed inside, but his gut twisted at the idea of allowing Sarah out of his sight for even a moment.

"I'll check it out first," the sheriff said forcefully.

Perfect. Max didn't argue. Let the sheriff ride his power trip. At the moment, it served Max's needs well. "I'll get the others."

Sheriff Jenson hesitated. "Make sure they know this has to be quick. In and out. The last thing I need is for Allen to drive up while we're inside." He turned and entered the cabin.

Max made fast tracks to the van; he stopped at the passenger's window as Sarah rolled it down. "Well?" she asked anxiously.

"No obvious signs of danger," Max said. "But I did find markings on the cabin floor."

"What kind of markings?" Cathy asked, her voice lifting with urgent interest as she poked her head between the seats.

"I'd rather you look for yourself," Max said, casting Edward a glance. "Drive under the carport and park." He wanted them sheltered as long as possible— just to be safe.

"You forget we need gas." Edward patted the dashboard. "This baby is running on fumes. I don't want to power her up again until we leave."

"Damn," Max muttered.

"All's clear inside," the sheriff called from the door, motioning everyone forward.

Max waved his understanding before turning back to the van. "When you get out of the van, don't linger. Run to the cabin and get behind closed doors."

"You said you didn't see any trouble," Cathy countered, her tone full of concern.

"That's true," Max agreed, trying to calm her before she got worked up. "I'm just playing things safe."

"Let's get this over with," Edward said, looking over his shoulder at Cathy.

"All right then," she conceded with a heavy sigh that indicated she wasn't all that sold on the idea.

Max yanked open Sarah's door as Cathy and Edward exited the driver's side.

"Something isn't right here," Sarah said. "Kate was trying to tell me something, and I felt another spirit there, something dark." He watched her swallow, her throat bobbing with the action. "And then she was just gone."

Max wasn't sure what to make of that, but it was clear that Sarah was rattled. All this spirit stuff had him grasping in vain for a game plan that had some semblance of cohesiveness.

Edward and Cathy rounded the van, and Max eyed the Sheriff who stood on alert. "You two go on inside." They didn't argue, moving toward the cabin at a fast walk. Max watched their progress, scanning to ensure they were safe before turning back to Sarah. "Stay behind the door. Once they're inside, we'll follow."

She didn't respond, her expression troubled. "I wish I had the answers," he said. "But we'll find them. We'll get through this. Have faith."

She made a frustrated sound, shoving her hair behind her ears before hugging herself. "I gave up on faith when it burned me years ago." Her gaze slid to the ground. "I'll stick with caution as my guide."

Clearly, something in her past had worked her over in a big way. Max understood pain, Lord only knew. But his reaction to Sarah's emotions delivered a shocking bit of personal introspection. In four hundred years, no matter how dark his world, no matter how hard he struggled against his inner beast, he'd hung on, and he'd never lost his faith. He'd doubted himself plenty. At least once a week, he questioned why he'd been chosen as a Knight, rather than his elder brother. He'd beaten himself up daily for not saving his family. But when he went onto the battlefield, he believed in what he fought for. And that—*that*—was what kept him fighting *off* the battlefield.

He reached out to slide his hand down her hair. To be his mate, her soul had to be pure. She had faith and hope inside her. He'd felt it in her kiss, in her touch, as it had calmed the darkness within him. She simply had to find her way back to her true self. No matter how much he wanted Sarah to be the magic key to save his soul, the truth was, she needed a bit of saving herself.

Max slid his finger under Sarah's chin as he lifted her gaze to his. "Then I'll have enough faith for both of us," he vowed, and motioned toward the cabin.

Her eyes flashed with vulnerability, and he wanted to kiss away her pain. Instead, he forced himself to focus on the imminent need for action. "Let's go find some answers," he said, backing away a step to offer Sarah some space.

His attention turned to the cabin where the sheriff stood waiting at the door, his impatience evident in his glowering look. No doubt he was worried about Allen's return.

Max reached around Sarah and shut her open door. "Once we step out of the shelter of the van's cover, start moving and don't stop until you're inside."

She nodded and they went into action. They started for the cabin, and Max felt a sudden rush of awareness track along his nerve endings, a feeling of being hunted. He held his breath, not daring to let it out until Sarah disappeared inside the doorway of the cabin.

Max paused at the entrance, his senses screaming, on the alert. Beasts. A Knight could sense a Beast from miles away, though a Beast couldn't sense a Knight. A definite edge over his enemies that Max had been thankful for more than a few times. Without question, Max knew his enemy was near. The question was—did the Beast, or Beasts, know he was present? He grabbed his phone from his belt and checked for a signal, hoping to call Jag for backup. Nothing. Still dead. He scanned again but saw nothing, no movement, no Beasts.

The wind picked up with sudden fierceness, and Max realized it had all but disappeared while he and Sarah had been standing at the van. Back now, it packed vicious gusts, seeming almost angry, pounding anything in its path.

One more look around and Max entered the cabin, shutting the door and locking it, his mind racing, adrenaline coursing through his veins. He had three humans to get out of there safely and no idea how many Beasts he faced, let alone what other evil he was up against. He needed backup, and he needed it now.

You'll get it when you're intended to have it, he reminded himself. *Faith. Hang on to your faith. It's gotten you through four hundred years. It'll get you through one more day.*

In the near distance, a spark of fire appeared in the air and took human form. Adrian, leader of the Darkland Beasts, appeared on the outskirts of the small town of Nowhere, Texas. The wind lifted his long blond hair from his leather-clad shoulders as he surveyed the small wooden cabin. He was seething with resentment that his king, Cain, had ordered him to aid Prince Vars's escape. He despised the royal chain of command, despised his inability to rank within those standings. No matter how much hell he brought to earth, Cain would always keep Adrian in his place, hold him one notch beneath in the gifts he was allowed, the powers he wielded.

He didn't give a damn about Vars's promise to help defeat The Knights of White. Adrian had no desire to see his victory credited to Vars.

Adrian crossed his arms in front of his chest. There were a few enticing angles to using Vars's legion of demon spirits to battle the Knights. If those spirits claimed innocent human bodies, the Knights wouldn't want to kill them. And it would shift the power to the dark side. But that power belonged to Adrian, not Vars. Which meant that Vars's legion of demon spirits had to become Adrian's, as well.

If Vars were to be destroyed, his legion of demon

spirits would be inherited by the first power who claimed them. What better time to battle Vars than during his first few moments of freedom when he'd be weak and unpracticed.

Adrian laughed, realizing his king had given him a gift. Cain knew Adrian would not allow Vars to steal his glory. No doubt the king intended Adrian to steal Vars's legion of demons.

Adrian snapped his fingers, and fire once again stroked through the air. Two nameless servants appeared beside him, tall and dark, with dark eyes, and faces chiseled into harsh features—Hell Hounds in human disguise. They were gifts from Cain. Pets who did as he bid without daring to think on their own.

"Secure the cabin and kill anyone who gets in your way," he ordered. His pets instantly responded, shifting into their Hound forms. The two massive animals lunged down the hill, muscled bodies shifting with otherworldly force, their long fangs bared in warning to any who dared approach.

Adrian watched the creatures depart; they were so easily at his command, just as his army of demon soldiers were. He could almost taste the power of owning Vars's legion of demon spirits. He might not possess the royal title he desired, but Adrian was well on his way to being indestructible. He stared at the little cabin, thinking how inconsequential it appeared, but how important it had become. Because inside that cabin, Vars would be set free, and when he was, Adrian would be there to destroy him.

That cabin had become the stage for war, and the stepping-stone to Adrian's next level of power.

Chapter 9

Sarah hesitated as she entered the cabin, finding herself lingering, waiting for Max. Why— she didn't know. Only that keeping him close felt important. As if her safety, and his, somehow depended on it.

Behind her, she heard him push locks into place, sealing them inside the cabin. A momentary feeling of claustrophobia, an impulse to turn to Max and tell him to unlock the door, shot through her body. She shivered and hugged herself against the pure evil that seemed to pour from the walls.

As if he sensed her need, Max stepped to her side, his hand grazing her back; a wave of calm rushed over her. She inhaled, chest expanding, wondering how Max had such an impact on her. How could a man, a stranger, somehow give her a sense of security when people she'd known for years could not?

Together, operating almost as one, Max and Sarah began surveying the room. It was a tiny cabin with a fireplace in the corner, ruffled curtains and framed pictures decorating the walls. Normal enough except that the furniture had been stacked against the walls to make room for the magical circle and triangle in the center of the room. Scented incense laced the air—most likely used for a summoning ritual.

Cathy sat on a big blanket that had been spread out on the ground. It was covered with books and magic supplies. Edward stepped to the center of the circle drawn on the floor and studied the intricate details of the star inside its frame.

"What do all the details inside the circle mean?" Sheriff Jenson asked.

Cathy looked up from the book she held. "There are specific types of circles used for different magical purposes, but the general gist is that the conjurer stands in the circle and evokes to the triangle. The demon or spirit, or whatever it might be, should theoretically be trapped inside the triangle. Unless the conjurer is foolish enough to call on a demon more powerful than they can handle." She held up the book. "This is the *Grand Grimoire.* Black magic in its rawest form. It's bad stuff. Allen didn't start small. Once he dipped his toe, he went all the way, which leads me to believe he was one of the foolish ones who called on powers well beyond his own."

"Your job is starting to make mine look easy," Max said softly, for Sarah's ears only. Somehow, from what Max had described of the Darkland Beasts, she doubted that. She would have replied to that effect, but paused with sudden awareness.

"Kate," she whispered. "Kate, she's trying to find me again, but she's still fighting something. She's—"

Pain shot through Sarah's head with a force she'd never experienced before. She squeezed her eyes shut and found herself reaching for Max to keep from falling. Images charged into her head, violent flashes that cut in and out like a television with static interference, each flash delivering a jolt of pain.

"Oh, God," she gasped with shock. She'd never had a vision come in such a burst of images, never felt trauma of this magnitude from a spiritual communication.

In some remote part of her mind, Sarah felt Max's arms around her, felt herself sink against the wall of his chest, taking comfort in his presence, his protection.

The bit of reality that Sarah tried to cling to, slid into darkness, and there were just the images flashing in her mind, and pain—so much pain. Her head felt like it would explode, but she fought through her discomfort and fixed her mind on what she was being shown. Allen in the circle. A demon in human form— a huge man with long, black hair—standing inside the triangle. A name. The demon's name. Vars. More pain. More images. A blood bond. A promise of one favor for another. Some thing else. Something important. She reached out, trying to understand, fighting through the blackness. Kate screamed, a horrid wrenching sound that tore through Sarah's mind, her ears, her head. And then, Kate was gone—but not before she gave Sarah one more important detail. Not before telling Sarah what Vars had asked of Allen and how he intended to get it. Sarah clung to that last bit of information as darkness overtook her. Complete, utter darkness.

* * *

Max sat down against the wall, Sarah cradled in his arms. She was in pain, and damn it, he couldn't do anything about it. There had been only one other time in his life when he'd felt this helpless, and that had been when the Beasts were killing his family. He couldn't stand doing nothing.

"You're sure this is a vision?" Max demanded, fixing Cathy in a desperate stare. She kneeled beside Sarah, holding her hand. Edward and the sheriff hovered behind her.

Cathy opened her mouth to speak, but the words were lost in a choked scream of pain as Edward grabbed her hair, dragging her toward the other side of the room.

Max blinked, certain he was seeing wrong. A glance at the Sheriff's shocked expression said he, too, didn't believe what he was seeing. The sheriff acted quickly, pulling his gun and trying to find a shot that wouldn't put Cathy at risk. He shouted orders at Edward, but Edward acted as if he didn't hear him.

Edward's eyes flashed red as he fixed his attention on Sarah before charging at the sheriff, half dragging Cathy with him for cover. A second later, the sheriff was flat on his back, Cathy on top of him, and Edward charging at Max and Sarah.

From there it was a blur. Acting on instinct, Max covered Sarah with his body and rotated at the hip landing a hard foot in Edward's stomach.

He barely had time to face forward and right himself before Edward came at them again, his eyes flashing red—seemingly unaffected by the blow Max had blasted him with. And it had been a hell of a blow, considering Max had supernatural strength. Which could mean only one thing—a demon. That was all it took for Max to let his beast flare, to embrace his darker side.

This *thing,* whatever it was, wanted to kill Sarah. Max had seen it in Edward's glowing red eyes. Max slammed a fist into Edward's jaw. Edward's head snapped back, and Max used the opportunity to slam him to the ground. A split second later, Max straddled Edward, pinning one of the man's hands beneath his knee, holding the other.

Battle instincts in play, Max used his free hand to unsheathe a blade, ready to destroy the demon bastard pretending to be a friend, pretending to protect when he meant to destroy.

"Max!" Sarah's scream pierced the air. "No, Max! No!"

Max heard her voice, reaching for restraint but struggling. He'd handed over control to his beast at some point, and the beast pressed Max to finish this, to take out his enemy. Max's body literally shook with the effort to hold back, the muscles in his neck and shoulders contracting painfully. He wanted to kill Edward. He wanted to kill him in a bad way.

Sarah appeared before him, kneeling above Edward's head, facing Max. Her eyes were imploring, and Lord help him, Max couldn't hide what was inside him, couldn't hide the beast. No telling what she saw in those moments, what she would think of him, how she might fear him.

"Edward's body is possessed by a demon," she explained hoarsely. "But Edward might still be in there. We have to try. *Please.*"

As if denying Sarah's words, Edward started squirming, shouting nasty things at her. Max ground his teeth, holding Edward with ease, but feeling rage bubbling within, threatening to consume him.

"You're sure?" he asked, his teeth clenched. "Sure enough to take a chance with your life, Sarah? He tried to kill you. Even now, he wants you dead."

"We have to try," she said, repeating her words and eyeing the sheriff. "We need something to tie him up with."

Max wasn't convinced Edward was still human, if he ever had been in the first place. "Sarah—" Edward spouted out nasty words, cutting off Max's sentence.

"It's the demon talking," she assured Max. The sheriff came over with some rope and Sarah continued her argument. "We'll tie him up until we can figure out what to do. Cathy comes from a family with deep and varied magical roots. If anyone can figure out how to get Edward back, she can."

He shoved the blade back into his belt holster, still uncomfortable about his actions. "Do it," he ordered the sheriff. "Tie him up, but you'll need more rope. He's unnaturally strong right now."

The sheriff grunted. "You aren't kidding."

"I'll find something," Cathy said.

"Electrical cords," Max said. "They'll be strong."

"Let's tie this bastard up good and tight," Sheriff Jenson said, offering his approval.

Sarah studied the sheriff with a probing gaze. "You okay, Sheriff?"

"No," he said in a grouchy voice, working the rope around Edward's wrist, as Max continued to hold it. "I'm living a nightmare no one is going to believe."

Cathy reappeared with several cords and Sarah surveyed her, as well. "You look pretty beat up," she said.

"I'm fine," Cathy said, touching the scratch on her face. "Nothing that a little Band-Aid and some ointment won't cure."

"He dragged her across the room by her hair," Max commented, moving away from Edward, the restraints secure. "I've seen grown men whimper over less." He gave her tiny frame and cutesy bobbed hair a once-over. "You're tougher than you look."

Cathy's expression registered surprise and appreciation. "I do believe that was a compliment."

Cathy's obvious dedication to knowledge, coupled with her warrior spirit, was beginning to earn his respect. "It is."

Cathy's lips hinted at a smile but Edward threw his head from side to side, drawing her attention, and her expression quickly sobered.

"Actually," she said, "I think I got the good end of this deal. Edward is lost in there somewhere."

"I hope you're right," Sarah whispered, hugging herself, her voice shaking a bit. Max looked at her and realized she was rattled. Not a little. A lot. This thing with Edward had hit some sort of nerve. She wasn't any more certain than he was that Edward was still human. Yet, unlike him, she'd wanted to save him.

Edward mumbled more profanity and ended with, "Bitch!" right before the sheriff gagged him.

Max noted the way Sarah took a solid backward step. Max stared down at Edward, the implications of what had gone down between the two of them starting to take hold. He didn't know what to think about Edward but if Cathy were right, if Edward was still inside that body, then Max had almost killed another human. He'd been so sure

that wasn't the case, so driven by the rage of Edward trying to take Sarah from him. The same way he'd seen red
when that human had tried to kill Des's mate. The beast
had risen and Max had handed over power.

Max squeezed his eyes shut, recognizing that this
could have been part of his test, tormented by how close
he'd come to failing. Salvador had known Max would
face humans such as Edward, possessed and out of control. Had known Max would have to fight to determine
right and wrong, to show he still knew the difference.
His human side did, indeed, have faith, but how much
of the human was left? Enough to be saved? After this,
he wasn't sure.

Sarah's hand settled on his arm. "Max?"

The touch slid along his nerve endings and delivered
calmness that he wouldn't have believed possible in
that moment of turmoil. Slowly, he turned to face her,
not sure what to say, or how to explain his actions toward Edward. He'd been ready to convict the man rather
than save him.

Touching Max delivered a calmness Sarah didn't
quite understand, but she didn't fight the feeling. She
needed calm now, needed a bit of comfort. Seeing
Edward taken over by a demon brought some demons
of the past back to Sarah. She'd seen a friend possessed,
seen him kill her family. Was Edward evil? Could a
demon control someone truly good? Her gaze went to
the turbulent expression on Max's face, and her heart
clenched. He'd been so afraid for her.

As if he read her mind, he spoke. "I was afraid he was
going to kill you."

Sarah stared at Max and the minute her gaze locked with his, she felt herself at a loss for words, felt her chest tighten with emotion—-his emotion. Just as she'd felt his utter fear for her during her vision. How could she feel what he felt? The same way she would feel a spirit sliding into her mind and body.

Somehow, she found her voice, though it was gravelly, and laced with the potency of her feelings. "If you hadn't been here," she whispered, "he might have succeeded."

"And if you hadn't stopped me, I would have killed him."

"But you didn't," she said, uncertain about what to do next. Maybe she should have warned Max about the potential for possession. She'd been so afraid to trust him, to let him know her past, her secrets. Cathy and Edward both knew about her parents, about the friend that had killed them. Her fears of exposing herself to yet another person had impacted Max, left him unprepared. What had just happened to Edward should make her less willing to trust Max, but oddly, she wanted someone to trust right now more than ever. Max shared a connection with her. She sensed his emotions and they didn't feel evil. Besides, Max was involved; he was working with them now. He deserved to be armed with data that could protect him—protect all of them.

Decision made, she leaned closer to him and lowered her voice. "There are things you need to know." She discreetly glanced at the others. "Just not here and now."

"Did you find out anything with that little vision of yours?" Cathy asked, breaking into their private conversation, as she and the sheriff piled books into a box.

Reluctantly, Sarah pulled her attention from Max, their unfinished business bothering her. "I did," Sarah said, snapping back into the imminent danger of their circumstances. "I assume that's why Edward was turned against me. The demon imprisoned beneath the town is directly below the cabin."

"Did you get a name?" Cathy quickly asked, her voice lifting with urgency.

"Why is the name so important?" the sheriff asked.

Cathy explained, "You have to have the true name of the spirit or demon to evoke it or summon any form of control over its actions."

"Right," Sarah agreed. "And it has to be the exact, proper name. Problem is, I'm not sure if I remember it correctly. Prince Vars is what keeps replaying in my head."

"A prince," Cathy said. "Interesting. Royalty in the demon world spells power. Each member of royalty in the Underworld is thought to have an army of evil spirits beneath him. If that's true, then we can assume one of Vars's spirits is inside Edward."

Sarah looked concerned. "I just hope the name is right. When Kate was trying to speak to me, there was some sort of evil entity there, shoving her away. Maybe Vars. Maybe some of his demon army. I don't really know. Bottom line—I couldn't absorb everything the way I normally would in a vision."

Cathy patted one of the leather books in front of her. "I'd venture to say one of Allen's resources here will refer to the name or something similar because he had to find it somewhere. Most likely in a reference to the town legend."

"And the library has the same book that I have in my office," the sheriff offered. "Minus the torn page."

Sarah continued relaying the details of her vision. "Vars—if that is the right name—told Allen he would be strong enough to bring Kate back from the dead once he had his freedom."

Max frowned at that. "Which he achieves how?"

"Honestly, that's where things are a little cloudy." Sarah leaned against the wall, digging deep into her mind, working through the pain still splintering her head. "This is where it gets a little weird."

"It gets weirder than this?" the sheriff asked, motioning to where Edward lay on the floor, tied up. "I doubt that."

"'Fraid it does, Sheriff," she said, her tone grim. "From what I gathered, Allen needs the source of power held by the three Shadow Masters." She frowned. "I'm not sure. There are stones of some sort, I think. The stones have some sort of power and these 'Masters' guard them. I think. Damn it, I'm really not sure. For some reason, that doesn't seem quite right."

"The three Shadow Masters," Cathy repeated, brows dipping. "That's remotely familiar. I think they are part of some sort of cult." She let out a breath. "I could find out if we actually had communication with the outside world."

"Okay," Sheriff Jenson concurred. "Maybe it does get weirder."

Cathy's voice became grim. "I doubt I need to say this, but we need to get to Allen before he gets to these Shadow Masters. He'll come back here, though, once he has them. I'm sure of it. Most likely he intends to return by the next full moon ten days from now. That would be the optimal time for a ritual. This is where Vars is contained and where he must be released. But I need to point out a tiny little problem. Stopping Allen might not be all that simple. Vars could potentially use Allen like a vessel for his own magic, if they made a blood pact. And they did. I see dried blood in the circle."

"Ten days is something at least," Sarah said. "We have some hope of heading this off." She glanced at the sheriff. "Thank goodness you called when you did."

"It's not a lot of time when you consider the implications of Vars escaping," Cathy reminded her.

Max quickly offered support. "My people will help; they'll respond quickly and secure the town." His lips thinned. "But I have to get out of this town and to a working telephone."

"Then we should move on that now," Sarah said. "I get the feeling every second counts."

"Wait now," Sheriff Jenson chimed in, hands going up stop-sign fashion. "Someone is going to stay here in Nowhere to help me, right? As much as I hate admitting I'm over my head, clearly I am. I need help."

"He's right and I'll stay," Cathy said without hesitation. "I think I can bind the demon inside Edward for at least a while, but I need a calm environment and focus to do it. Plus, he's in no condition to travel. That means not moving him beyond the local doctor's office." Her expression turned bleak. "But I don't think I'm strong enough to expel it alone. I'll need you to call for help."

"I don't feel good about leaving town with you and Edward still here," Sarah objected. "I should stay, too. You have no way to contact us if you get into trouble."

"We'll be fine," Cathy assured Sarah. "You and Max

have to go after Allen and those Shadow Masters. Max is the muscles, and you have the connection to Kate. It makes sense for me to stay here and help the sheriff. Just send help. Our people. Max's people. Whoever. I'll take what I can get."

With surprise, Sarah realized this was what she had sensed earlier, she and Max would have to team up to defeat this enemy. But after the situation with Edward, she felt torn. To trust anyone frightened her. But Max was different. She thought. She hoped. She needed it to be so. And it seemed their teaming up was the logical answer to finding Allen.

"I still don't like this," Sarah murmured, half to herself, fretting over the choice put before her, even though she knew there wasn't one. She had to leave Cathy and Edward in town and go after Allen. "But I'll go."

"Obstacle one is getting out of this cabin safely," Max said, spilling the hard-core facts. "Based on what we have seen thus far, I find it hard to believe we are going anywhere without some resistance."

With those words, Sarah thought of the demon directly beneath the cabin, felt the evil within the walls closing in on them. She had no doubt the source of that evil would destroy anything, or anyone, in its path. It had already tried to kill Sarah to keep her from relaying what Kate had shared.

They'd come there determined to find answers, and they had, indeed, found them. But would they get out of there alive?

Chapter 10

Max wasted no time dropping Edward to the floor of the van, right next to the box of books that Cathy had collected from the cabin. The feeling of being watched was still biting at his nerves. He quickly turned to check on the sheriff. He was pouring gas into the van's tank from a can they had found next to the lawn mover in the storage shed out back.

"Done," the sheriff confirmed, tossing the can to the side of the driveway, clearly no longer worried about Allen knowing they'd been there. He joined Max near the front of the van. "Let's get the hell out of here."

"Agreed," Max said, one hand resting on a weapon, in ready position as he motioned Sarah and Cathy forward. The sooner they were out of this place, the better.

The two women darted forward, clearly as eager as the men to get moving. Sarah and Cathy were almost at the van doors—Cathy at the driver's side, Sarah at the passenger's side—when Max felt the hair on the back of his neck prickle and then stand on end. He barely had time to blink before two Hell Hounds darted around the side of the cabin. One headed straight for Sarah; the other charged toward Cathy.

The sheriff pulled his gun at the same moment Max unsheathed his swords. "Shoot between the eyes," Max shouted at him, as Cathy managed to get inside the van and the sheriff slammed the door shut, firing his weapon as he did.

Sarah screamed, yanking at her door which appeared to be jammed. With a full body tug, she managed to jerk it open. But the Hound was stalking her. It had jumped to the hood of the vehicle, and then to the roof to come at her from above. Max went from a fast run to a stealth-like vault on top of the hood. The Hound turned away from Sarah to face off with Max, giving her the time to escape and slam the door shut.

Max leapt at the Hound, knowing the creature would go up in flames when he killed it, concerned about fire making contact with the gas tank. As he shoved the Hound toward the edge, the damn thing sunk its teeth into Max's leg. Pain tore through his body as he went over the edge with the Hound. Swords in hand, Max had to either drop them and risk facing the Hound without protection, or try to control how he fell. He maneuvered the blades, trying to make sure they didn't end up in his body, but with limited success. A slice ripped down his midsection, opening up a gaping wound.

Max shoved aside the pain, survival instincts controlling his actions. He maneuvered to his feet at the same moment the Hound did. Even wounded, defeating a Hound was nothing, compared to a Beast, and in a swift practiced move, Max took the creature's head. The animal burst into flames and crumbled into ash as Max turned away; he stalked toward the other Hound that had the sheriff trapped at the driver's side of the van.

Max rounded the hood to find the Sheriff Jenson on the ground and Sarah hanging out of the window firing a gun at the Hound. The Hound took several bullets to the head and stumbled before falling to its side. Max held up his hand, silently telling Sarah to hold her fire—not interested in adding a bullet wound to his other injuries.

Once he knew Sarah understood his request, he went into action, lifting his sword and rearing back. A second later, Max's blade claimed the creature's head. Fire and ash consumed the Hound almost instantly, and Max turned away, not giving himself time to consider what Sarah might think of his ability to kill so readily. Reminding himself she'd been quick to fire her own gun, that she understood this world enough not to fear him for what he'd just done.

He slid his swords back into their holsters and turned his attention to the sheriff's wounded body lying on the ground. Max squatted next to him, checking for a pulse and finding it—weak, but there. At least, he was alive.

"Is he okay?" Sarah asked, her voice urgent, worried, as she shoved open the van door and darted forward. Her eyes went wide. "Oh, God. You're hurt, too." She squatted down next to Max, her hands shaking as she steadied them on her knees, her gaze raking his leg and stomach. "You're hurt bad, Max."

"I'm fine," he said, his attention on the sheriff as he

noted numerous cuts and scrapes, but the worst was the huge slit in his wrist spouting blood. "He's losing too much blood." Max reached for the knife inside his boot, the wound on his leg all but numb, though his gut hurt like a son-of-a-bitch. He leaned back to cut off part of his shirt and decided it was too blood soaked.

Sarah gasped, her gaze locked on Max's midsection. "Your stomach is wide-open," Sarah whispered.

Max sliced off some of the sheriff's shirt to make the bandage. "It looks worse than it is," he said, referring to his injuries. Which was the truth. Max, like all Knights, didn't die easily. Beheading or bleeding to death were pretty much the only ways he'd die. He was a long way from bleeding to death, though he couldn't ignore the need for medical attention forever.

Cathy appeared, standing above them, and stared at Max. "Oh, crap," she gasped, just as Sarah had moments before. "You're bleeding as much as he is. What can I do? How can I help? Are you okay?"

Max noted Cathy's rambling. If Edward was right, it was a sign of nerves. Unfortunately, Max wasn't exactly in a position to offer comfort right now. Max tied off Sheriff Jenson's wrist with a tight knot. "I need you to drive, Cathy." He eyed Sarah as he reached under the sheriff to pick him up. "Can you open the side door for me?" She nodded and rushed to do as he asked.

Weakened from his own blood loss, Max forced himself to work through it. Lifting the sheriff took more effort than it should have, the pain in his gut ripening with the movement. But Sheriff Jenson had sacrificed himself to save Cathy, and that made him a hero in Max's book. Guilt added to the pain in his stomach. He should have gotten to him sooner, and maybe he wouldn't be in the shape he was now.

Max settled the sheriff into the back of the van, hating that he had to place him next to Edward. The minute the injured man was on the floor, Max turned and pulled Sarah inside, eager to get her into a secure place, out of the open.

He slid the door shut. "Now, Cathy," Max called to her, sitting down before he fell, and sliding to the wall to use it as a support. "Hit the accelerator and don't stop until you get us to a doctor."

Max knew he needed to tie off his wounds to stop the bleeding before he allowed himself to rest. He reached for his knife and started for the sheriff, needing a piece of his shirt to make a bandage. Sarah held out her hand. "I'll do it." She pointed to the wall. "Sit back and rest."

He started to argue and decided he was in no shape to win. "I was going—"

"—to cut off some of his shirt to make another bandage. I know. I'll do it."

He would have smiled at her determination if not for the dizziness floating around in his head. Instead, he leaned back against the wall as ordered, and let his eyes shut. He healed quickly. Even small bouts of rest would allow his blood to start clotting, the magic of immortality to start taking hold, to start healing his injuries.

He didn't want to sleep, didn't want to let down his guard, but his body demanded attention. A few minutes of rest…and then he could fight again.

Sarah surveyed Sheriff Jenson, quickly checking for a pulse, and for any wound needing attention that hadn't received it yet. Satisfied he was stable, she reported as much to Max and Cathy, certain Max wouldn't let her help him until he knew the sheriff was well taken care of.

She sliced long pieces of material from the man's shirt, ignoring Edward's snorts and grunts behind her, because they spoke with brutal reality about just how close the demon remained to them. How easily it had insinuated itself into their group. Once again, her life had been touched by a demon possession. She hadn't completely gotten her mind around that yet, and she wasn't sure she wanted to. Not now, when she had to stay sharp, ready for the next challenge.

Rotating, she scooted to Max's side and onto her knees. His head was back, eyes shut. Not wanting to startle him, she reached forward and pressed her hand to his jaw. "Max," she whispered, watching his lashes lift as if weighed down. "I'm going to tie off your wound. Okay?"

"The sheriff—"

"Is stable," she assured him, wrapping the cloth around his leg and tying it off as hard as she could. The Hound's fangs had shredded his pants, and she couldn't bear thinking about those nasty teeth in his flesh. "Were those the Darkland Beasts?" she asked.

He laughed but the sound held no humor; his eyes drifted shut. "Those were nothing but pets. Nowhere near as nasty as the Beasts."

"Oh," she said, not happy with that answer. If those were "pets," she didn't want to see the real thing. But one thing was for sure, she knew she had been right to believe Max. Her instincts were on target. Now she had to shoot straight with Max, so neither of them could be taken off guard.

She nudged his legs. "Lay them flat so I can see your stomach."

"As long as you promise not to get all worked up over it," he said.

"I'm already all worked up. I saw how bad it is." She firmed her voice. "Put your legs down."

He did as she ordered and she studied his wound, her chest tight with worry. She didn't want him to die. What if he died? What if Edward died? Everyone around her got hurt. She inhaled and told herself to calm down and take action, rather than fret. She wondered how Max managed to carry the sheriff with that kind of wide-open gaping wound in his gut.

Another inhaled breath and she went to work quickly tying strips of material together. She leaned forward and braced her hand on his chest. Max's eyes shot open, his hand going to hers, covering it. Despite the darkness of their circumstances, the intimacy between them shot to red-hot in an instant.

Sarah cleared her throat, trying to find her voice, her eyes still locked with his. "I need to wrap the bandage around your waist," she explained, leaning forward, worried about the blood he was losing, not wanting to waste time.

She had nothing to soak the blood up with, and her T-shirt was already thickly covered with a combination of the sheriff's and Max's blood. "How close are we to town?" she called to Cathy.

"Another ten minutes," Cathy replied. "I think I saw the doc's office when we first arrived. I'll head straight there and hope someone is home."

"That works," Sarah said, sliding the cloth behind

Max's back and around his waist. She tried not to think about the wave of warmth washing over her body, the sexual awareness well beyond inappropriate at this moment. The way she sensed this man on so many levels, so without reason or rationale, confused her.

Once she finished her work, Sarah found it to be poor at best. Blood was already staining the cloth. "Thank God we're almost there. You need a doctor."

Max grabbed her hand and pulled her close. "I need all right," he murmured, his fingers lacing into her hair, their mouths only an inch apart. "You forgot something."

"What would that be?" Sarah whispered.

"A kiss to make it all better," he replied, a smile hinting on his sexy mouth, pain clearly keeping him from more.

She didn't hesitate, not about to deny a wounded man—especially not one she found so damn appealing. She pressed her lips to his, feeling him inside out with that simple act of intimacy, wishing deep in her soul she could escape with him into that moment. That she would wake up in a warm bed, him by her side, all of this nothing but a bad dream.

When she finally found the will to pull away, she took a few lingering moments to drown in those hazel eyes of his. "Now, damn it," she said, "get well. That's an order."

Adrian watched from a distance as the van sped away, a smile touching his lips. Normally, the presence of a Knight would make him furious. Every time he turned around, those damn Knights got in his way. He wanted their destruction and nothing less would do. But he knew this Knight. Max. He was one of the original Knights—Raphael's first attempt at battling Adrian's

Beast of Darkness

army—most of whom had succumbed to their dark sides and now fought for the Beasts. Adrian had been collecting the former Knights, forming a special unit to lead the battle against their present-day counterparts. Max walked near the darkness, barely touching the light. That he had survived so long spoke of his strength. He would be an excellent addition to this unit. Of course, it was a pity Adrian had shown his hand with the Hounds. They would surely alert Max of the Darkland presence. But he wouldn't know for sure.

His next move must be considered carefully. Or perhaps his next move was to do nothing at all. Though Cain had ordered him to contain the town, to stop anyone from leaving, Cain would appreciate the magnitude of this opportunity. A trap could be set. Max would leave Nowhere and find a phone. He'd call his faithful brothers-in-arms and they'd race to the town's aid. Yes. Adrian rather liked where this was leading. The more the merrier as far as Adrian was concerned. Cain would feel the same. Once the Knights were here in full force, Adrian could put his Beasts and his new legion of spirits to good use in battle.

On the other hand, the last thing Adrian needed was Max, or the woman who he sensed was Max's mate, getting in Allen's way. Adrian wanted Vars free so he could steal his powers. The woman would have to die. Which was really quite a perfect idea. Max would then be sealed in darkness. Max would fall to the beast and become one of Adrian's army. Perhaps a little chat with Vars was in order. He'd allow the Vars to feel involved in his little plan to destroy the Knights, use his resources, build a little trust with the demon prince. Then, when the time was right, Adrian would destroy Vars just as he would the Knights.

Who would have thought a place called "Nowhere" could deliver such satisfaction?

In fact, this could prove a good test for his high-ranking Beasts, as well. He needed a new second, his last *Segundo* having betrayed him by trying to steal his place with Cain. The Beast who reined supreme on the battlefield against the Knights would begin his training as the new *Segundo*. Adrian smiled at the sheer brilliance of his own mind and then flashed out of the town, fire and malice lacing the air in his aftermath, his destination the Underworld. Cain would be pleased with his plan to destroy the Knights, although he'd leave his plot to destroy Vars out of things. Once he had Vars's powers, Adrian might well be strong enough to overtake Cain.

But first, Nowhere and the Knights who would come to protect it, would fall.

Chapter 11

Ready to leave town, Max followed Sarah down the inn stairs, fresh bandages in place, compliments of his stop by the doc's office. Max still felt like crap, but his natural healing abilities were aiding his efforts at hanging tough or at least faking it well. Though right about now, he wasn't feeling the results of that ability. He'd lost a lot of blood. He needed rest to allow his body to do the job of healing.

After several hours of attention by the doctor, the sheriff was stable—at least for the time being—and Edward was sedated, with Cathy by his side, working on her demon-binding spell.

Sarah paused at the front desk, assuring the innkeeper that help was coming. Max stepped onto the porch, the clouds above black and ominous, though no more rain had fallen. He let his senses reach out, searching, expecting the scent of a Beast, but finding none. The presence of Hounds had to mean they were near. Were they? Max grimaced. He didn't know anything for certain. This was a situation like none he'd ever faced before. Maybe the Hounds belonged to Vars. As soon as the thought crossed his mind, Max dismissed it. He'd sensed Darkland Beasts back at that cabin. Which meant more were near, ready to devour this town and its people.

The faster Max got Sarah out of here, the better he'd feel. In a short window of time, a possessed Edward and a Hell Hound had come after her. Clearly, she'd been marked for death.

The inn door opened behind him and Sarah's voice followed. "The doctor doesn't want you to travel," she said for the fifth time in ten minutes.

Max cast her a sideways glance as she stepped forward. "The doc has his hands full with the sheriff and Edward. He doesn't need to deal with me, too."

She turned to face him, her action showing the determination behind her words. "You've lost too much blood," she said. "I'm worried."

He turned to her then, surprised and warmed by the unfamiliar words of concern. No one worried about him except the Knights, and it wasn't the same as Sarah doing so. He smiled through the dull throb in his gut. "If I don't go, who'll protect you?"

She gave him the evil eye and then lashed out at his male ego. "Oh, please. You're in no shape to protect me. In fact, I'd have to protect you."

Max couldn't help himself, he laughed—it hurt like a bitch, but he laughed. Never before had he known a woman who had the guts this one did. She'd seen those

Hounds, and yet, he believed she'd charge back into danger to save lives. "You have more balls than a lot of men I've known in my life, Sarah Meyers."

She blinked at him, apparently not seeing the humor in any of this. In fact, her moment of taunting and teasing had disappeared completely. Her gaze dropped to his waist, where the bandages bulged beneath his shirt, lingering a moment before lifting to his face again.

With her brows knitting together, her voice quavering ever so slightly, she said, "Don't you dare go and die on me."

His gut tightened but not from pain this time—from the emotion in her voice, from her genuine fear for him. Max took her hand and pressed it to the bandages, determined to convince her that he was okay when that wasn't anywhere near true. The small improvements his body could make without rest weren't enough to overcome the extent of his wounds. He needed sleep and he needed it soon.

"I'm already healing, Sarah," he assured her. "Can't you tell I'm moving around more than before? I'm not like other people. I don't die easily."

She stared at him blankly before making a little huff of a noise. "There is a time and place for the macho—"

"No," he said, interrupting her, covering the hand she had pressed to his stomach with his own. "It's not like that. I'm different, Sarah. Different in ways I can't explain right now. I promise I'll be fine until we can get to a phone line."

Her expression held a hint of well-contained shock. "Are you saying the government did something to you? Kind of like a super soldier of some sort?" Max had never claimed to work for the government and part of him wanted to clarify that, to make sure she didn't think he'd misled her. But his instincts told him to hold back. Inviting more questions meant potential delays they couldn't afford. The time for some honest conversation had come, though.

"I'm not saying anything at this point," he said. "We need to have a heart-to-heart, honest talk, but let's get out of this town first."

"*If* we can get out of here," she said.

"Oh, we're getting out of here," Max declared. "One way or the other, we're leaving." They climbed into the van, Sarah in the driver's seat.

We're getting out of here, one way or the other. Sarah replayed Max's words in her head as she drove over the town bridge—the bridge where Kate had been killed. She glanced in Max's direction, noting his battle-ready position. He held several guns, ready to fire from the window, intent on at least slowing any pursuers. She gripped the steering wheel with a white-knuckled hold, certain they were about to be attacked at any moment. But nothing happened. Nothing. Ten minutes passed and not a peep of trouble.

Max set his guns down, but kept them easily accessible as he started dialing his cell. "No signal yet," he said.

"I can't believe we just drove out of town," Sarah said. "No trouble at all."

"Seems a little too good to be true," Max commented, punching the buttons on his phone again. "Which means it probably is."

Sarah reached for a logical explanation. "Maybe

reaching out to Allen from a distance is draining the demon's powers."

"Maybe," he said, but he didn't sound convinced.

"You don't buy that, do you?" she asked, casting him a quick look.

A frustrated sound slid from his lips as he hit the end button on his cell. "Damn it, we need a phone line." He pressed his eyes shut a minute and then admitted, "In answer to your question, no, I don't think the demon's powers have weakened. I think letting us leave served an agenda we don't understand yet."

"There's a sobering thought," she said dryly. "Thanks for that."

"Better to keep it real and stay on guard," he retorted.

Kate brushed Sarah's mind as a Motel 6 sign came into view and she did a quick turn into the entrance. "What are you doing?" Max asked, his wide-eyed gaze fixed on her, a stunned look on his face.

"The land lines are working here," Sarah explained. "Kate says they're working." She pulled into a parking spot in front of the lobby.

Max gave her a blank look and then cautioned her. "You're a lot more trusting of spirits than I am right about now." He grabbed the door handle and pushed it open, noting only one lone car in the parking lot, no signs of human life anywhere.

Sarah met him at the front of the van, not willing to let his comment go by unanswered. "These spirits aren't evil, Max. They want me to succeed because I'm helping them."

"Just be careful," he said. "We don't know what this Vars is capable of doing. That's all I'm saying."

She inhaled, realizing he was right. They didn't know what Vars could do. It was an unsettling thought. She'd always found the spirits she helped were in her comfort zone. Always assumed she could sense their true essence, just as she'd sensed the evil in that cabin. But what if she couldn't?

"Call me paranoid," Max said, changing the subject, "but I'm not about to part with my weapons, and I doubt they'll be well-received inside. I'll wait by the door where I can see you in case you run into trouble. If the phones work, let's grab a room and we can wait for backup here. If not, let's get in and out, and move onward."

Right, Sarah thought, her adrenaline suddenly spiking. Phone. Room. Alone with Max. Why did she find the latter made her heart pound at triple time in her chest?

Ten minutes later, Max followed Sarah into the hotel room, locked the door and started for the phone but stopped as Sarah seemed to stumble. He caught her with his arm, holding her upright. "Wow. Are you okay?"

Sarah nodded and inhaled. "Kate's trying to communicate, but it's...it's as if there is a battle raging in my head. Like the darkness from the cabin is beating at my mind, as well, trying to stop her."

Max helped her to the bed, noting the way she swayed a bit, the way her skin seemed devoid of color. She'd been through a lot today, and neither of them had eaten or slept in—how many hours was it? He didn't even know.

He eased her onto the edge of the mattress, and he kneeled in front of her, hands on her legs. He wished he could wipe away her pain, take it as his own, but he didn't know how. "What can I do?"

She managed a weak smile and touched his jaw. "Just get help for that town. I'm going to go to the bathroom and splash some water on my face." Her stomach growled. "Okay, so maybe food and a little rest is in order, too."

"I'll call for help and then ask the front desk about the nearest food."

"That sounds good," she said, pushing to her feet and standing there a minute. "The dizziness seems to have passed."

She'd rested all of a minute. Max wasn't convinced she'd recovered. "Just the same, leave the bathroom door open so I can hear you call out if you need me."

"You're the one that's injured," Sarah reminded him. "I have a headache. Nothing more."

He hoped she was right. "At least leave it cracked."

"I'll leave it cracked in case *you* need *me,*" she teased.

Max laughed at that and moved to sit on the bed by the nightstand, shaking his head at Sarah's comment. Damn how he loved her spunk. If they both weren't so exhausted and beat up, he'd worry about being alone with her, worry he'd lose his willpower and make use of the bed for much more appealing pleasures than sleep.

He grabbed the phone and the sweet sound of a dial tone slid into his ears a second before Sarah screamed and fell to the bathroom floor. Max dropped the phone. "Sarah!"

Max found her curled up like a child, her hands on her head. "Max," she whispered. "I... My head hurts. It hurts bad. Every time Kate—" Her words disappeared into a sob.

"It's okay, baby," he said, pulling her close. God, she was shaking. "I'll get you help. I promise. I'll get you help."

Lifting her, Max carried Sarah to the bed, and began rubbing her arms and back, trying to calm her down. He knew from experience that the adrenaline and fear a person experienced from pain would intensify their physical reactions.

He leaned against the headboard and pulled her close to his uninjured side and under his arm, reaching for the phone cord with the free hand and tugging. When it was in reach, he dialed Jag's cell, relieved to hear his leader's voice after only two rings.

Jag didn't bother with hello. "We were about to come looking for you," Jag said. "You aren't answering your phone, and Des had one of those new visions of his. He said the Beasts—"

"I need Marisol and I need her now," Max said, cutting off Jag.

"We'll be right there." The line went dead. Max set the phone back in place, telling himself everything would be okay now. Jag's gifts included an ability to locate anyone he made verbal contact with. Jag and Marisol were the only two in their group who could travel by orbing—they could travel through space at light speed. Once Jag had found Marisol, they'd be here in a flash. And Jag had said they were about to come looking for him, which meant he wasn't on his own. In the far corner of his mind, he'd worried that because of his test, there would be limits to what Jag would be allowed to do to help. But deep down, he knew that if innocents were in danger, there were no limits. Whatever test Max had to pass would not put others in danger. Only himself.

Sarah breathed in and out with labored effort, alternating silence with soft murmurs of pain. Max lay there holding her, minutes passing as if they were hours, fear for her life tearing him up inside. How long had it been since he'd cared for someone as he did Sarah? He remembered his family, remembered the emptiness their deaths had left inside him—he lived with that each day of his life. But the caring, the worry, the daily emotions that came with love—these things he didn't remember at all. Only that what he felt now, with Sarah in pain, in his arms, touched him deeply. Love bound together two mates, destiny linked their souls. Love. It hurt. It excited. It scared the hell out of him.

Jag and Marisol appeared in that moment at the foot of the bed. Max wasn't sure what calmed him more, the dominating warriorlike confidence of their leader or the soft promise of hope that clung to their healer. "You two are a sight for sore eyes," Max said. "She's in pain, and I don't know how to help."

"You don't look so good yourself, man," Jag said instantly, as Marisol moved forward, easing onto the bed, tucking her long white skirt under her legs, and shoving her mass of raven hair behind her ears.

"What the hell happened?" Jag demanded. "Why couldn't we get through to you?"

Marisol reached out to touch Sarah, but Max gently shackled her wrist. As much as he wanted her to heal Sarah, it wouldn't be fair to let her begin without the facts. "You should know what you're dealing with first."

Max knew Marisol could fight off beastly influences if she touched a human soon enough after a bite, but these were not Darkland Beasts they were dealing with. These demons were demon spirits. He went on to explain more about the demon spirits, including a condensed version of what had taken place back in Nowhere, his focus shifting between Marisol and Jag.

Drawing to a conclusion, Max shared the sheriff's and Edward's dicey medical conditions before fixing his attention back on Marisol. "Can you help her?"

Marisol's eyes comforted, her presence alone somehow warm and full of healing. She reached out and touched Sarah. "She's not sick. She's exhausted." Her gaze went from Max to Jag. "She's also very special. Her gifts are strong, her mind, too. These evil spirits are draining her, though."

"What does that mean?" Max asked. "If they keep attacking her, will this keep happening?"

"When was the last time either of you slept?" Marisol asked, but didn't give him time to respond.

Sarah murmured something.

"She doesn't seem as if she can rest," he said.

"I'll put her into a deep healing sleep," Marisol said. "After I heal you," she said, her gaze sweeping his stomach.

He quickly rejected that idea. "No. Healing weakens you. The sheriff and Edward are not well and who knows how many others have been injured since we left."

"It takes a lot to drain me, and who will protect her if you die?" Marisol said. "Bleeding to death serves no purpose. She's your mate. It's your duty to protect her."

"Mate?" Jag asked, his brows lifting. "Sarah is your mate?"

"I believe so," Max said, glancing at Marisol. "How did you know?"

"Not with magic or my healing touch," she said. "It's

in your eyes. That same look of utter devotion Jag and Des have for their mates." She gave him a reprimanding look. "Now, let me heal you, so I can get on with taking care of your woman."

Jag chuckled and eyed Max. "The lady has spoken. I think you better listen."

"You're sure you can heal the others if you heal me?"

Marisol rolled her eyes, pushed off the bed and stomped around to Max's side. "Stop asking questions and let me do my job."

"I'll gather a team to go into Nowhere," Jag said, inclining his head at Max and grinning at Marisol's reprimand. "I'll meet you out front so we don't disturb Marisol and Sarah when I return." He didn't wait for an answer before flashing out of the room.

Thirty minutes later, completely healed, though still exhausted, Max stood outside. Fortunately, they seemed to be the only visitors at the hotel, allowing them to engage in open conversation. Des, Rock, Rinehart and Jag surrounded Max. These were the Knights who made him feel as if he belonged, who he hoped would allow him to become a permanent part of their team. To really be a part of their circle of trust. He knew they had doubts about his involvement, but since he'd saved Des's mate, they looked at him differently, with more acceptance. But he also knew that Des, especially, knew how close to the darkness Max walked. Des had been there the day Max had taken that human's life.

With a quick recap of everything that had gone down back in Nowhere, Texas, Max brought the Knights up-to-date on the troubles they faced. When Max finished, Des was the first to interject his opinions.

"Chingado," Des muttered using a familiar Spanish curse word—at least familiar to anyone who spent any amount of time around Des. "I knew something was wrong, man. These damn visions are freaking impossible to understand." He laughed incredulously. "I kept seeing you with a shovel refilling a deep-ass hole in the ground. I guess that was you trying to keep this demon in his underground prison. I don't know how I was supposed to know what that meant and send help."

"They'll get easier to decipher with time," Jag offered, one booted foot resting on a concrete step leading to the second floor of the hotel. The sparse accommodations offered only outdoor entry to the rooms.

"Says Salvador," Des said dryly. He'd never been fond of Salvador's coded messages and vague statements.

Jag narrowed his gaze on Des. "Says me. Every day with Karen, my abilities become stronger."

"You're here now," Max inserted. "That's what counts. And that town needs you." He frowned. "There's something bothering me, though. Why was I allowed to leave? Surely Vars knew I'd bring back help."

"Sounds like a trap," Rinehart reflected, shoving his cowboy hat back from his blue eyes that were sharp with suspicion.

"Oh, yeah," Rock chimed in. "Definitely a trap. But hey—" he shrugged "—we're used to that."

Rinehart snorted, irritated at Rock as usual. "Are you nuts, kid? Going into that town is playing right into their hands. We can't just charge in without any idea what we're dealing with."

Max didn't like it, but Rinehart made sense. He eyed Jag. "The town doctor could only do so much for the sheriff. He'll die without immediate help." He hesitated. "If it's not too late already. And this Cathy who works with Sarah. She actually has several people she wanted me to contact who could help. She's got a lot to offer. She understands the magical aspects of all of this."

"Let's recap what we all know," Des said, resting a hand on his hip. "We've got three Shadow Masters, and three Shadow Stones. Somehow, together they can give Vars the power to be free. We don't known anything about these stones or these Masters. Really, we don't know squat."

"We know we have to get to them before Allen does," Rock interjected.

"Or keep Allen from getting back to the cabin with them in tow," Max added.

"Wait," Jag said. "Allen has to go back to the cabin to free Vars?"

"Right," Max agreed. "Which makes securing the cabin critical. If we can't stop Allen from getting the power he needs to free Vars, we need to stop him from getting back to Vars."

"Which is likely what they're counting on," Rinehart inserted. "Get us there and trap us."

Rock nodded his agreement before offering a suggestion. "Why not put a group of Knights on the outskirts of town, ready to aid our efforts in case of attack, but out of harm's reach?"

Rinehart, a military man in his human life, quickly axed that. "That's expected. The Beasts could simply come up behind them and push them forward."

Jag considered a minute. "Okay. Here is what we'll do. I'll talk to Salvador. Des will go back to the ranch and make contact with Cathy's people and come up with a list of targets Allen might be after. From there he will communicate with Max and Sarah to go after Allen. Rock, Rinehart, you two head into Nowhere and investigate. Take Marisol so she can heal the sheriff and attempt to help Edward."

As if on queue, Marisol opened the door and motioned Max and Jag forward. The two of them joined her in the room. "She's resting now." Marisol looked at Max. "She should sleep awhile now. Let her. She needs it. You do, too. I know you don't want to but you need to. Let us take over long enough for you to recuperate."

"You're sure she's okay?" Max asked, staring at Sarah's pale face, dark circles coloring the skin beneath her eyes.

"She just needs rest," Marisol said.

"We can take her to the ranch where she'll be safe," Jag offered.

"No," Max said quickly. "I haven't explained everything about our world to her." He paused, torn about saying more than he had to. Jag might not agree with his handling of Sarah. Reluctantly, he added, "I don't know if I am going to."

Jag narrowed his eyes on Max and then cast Marisol a look. She quickly picked up on what he wanted. "I'll leave you two to talk, so I can attend to the others who need me."

"Marisol," Max said, as she walked to the door. She turned back to him and he added, "Thank you and be careful."

A sad look flashed in her eyes. "I'd tell you to do the same, but I know you won't listen." She glanced at Sarah as if she wanted to say more, but didn't, turning away and exiting without another word.

"I've never asked a favor before," Max said the minute the door shut, "but I need one now. I need to know if I don't pass this test, if I don't survive, that Sarah will be looked after."

Jag tilted his head, his gaze probing Max's face. "You've decided your fate already." It wasn't a question.

"I almost killed Edward today," Max said. "I *wanted* to kill him."

"But you didn't."

"Didn't you hear what I said? I wanted to. I could damn near taste his blood. He tried to kill Sarah and I lost it." His lips thinned. "Just like before. Just like with the other human. The beast took control."

"If the beast had control, you would have killed Edward."

"I stopped because of Sarah." He hesitated. "Because I didn't want her to see what I really am. Not because I wanted to spare the human." And he realized, it was also because he'd felt her fear, her guilt. She would have blamed herself for Edward's death, for not saving him, for not protecting him from the demon.

"A Beast wouldn't have stopped for any reason. You know that as well as I do."

"And if you're wrong?" Max asked. "She has enough demons in her world without dealing with mine. I have to find a way to come through this or leave her without her ever knowing who and what I truly am."

Jag glanced at Sarah and then back at Max. "She has no more peace than you at present. I feel…loss in her. She's lost much in her life. She's afraid to lose more." His gaze went back to Max. "She needs you as much as you need her. Give her a chance to help."

"If I claim her and then fail this test, will her destiny be the same as mine is—in hell?"

"Yes," Jag said. "Once your souls are linked through mating, she will share your future. Which leaves you with only one option." He paused for obvious effect. "Don't fail this test. She is your incentive to succeed."

Jag inclined his head as he often did before departing a room. "I will contact you with an update soon." And then he was gone, leaving Max no chance to respond. No chance to ask questions.

Max scrubbed his jaw and walked to the bed, staring down at Sarah. He wanted to live for her, wanted to succeed. But what if he didn't? What if he let her down as he had his family? What if he failed?

He couldn't risk that. He couldn't. No matter what—he would see Sarah and this town through this danger. But he'd do it without claiming her or telling her who and what he was.

She murmured a soft something in her sleep. God, he loved her, he realized. He'd always heard a mate's love was instant, and he knew, in that moment, that it was true. He wouldn't cause her pain or put her in jeopardy for his own comfort, his own hope.

But Jag was right. Sarah was incentive enough to keep him fighting. New resolve formed and he vowed to defeat his beast and pass this test.

Vars heard Adrian's summons and it infuriated him. He'd called on Cain for hours with no response and now he was being called by the idiotic fool he wanted to destroy. Vars materialized in the cabin at Adrian's summons, but given the circumstances, found these confines more frustrating than his prison below. Fury consumed Vars as he brought the blond-haired, leather-clad, arrogant bastard into his sights.

"I asked one thing of you," he ground out, with anger lacing the words. "One. You were to ensure no one left this town. Cain will hear of this, and he will know you for the idiot you are!"

Adrian laughed, a mocking sound that bit at Vars's nerve endings. "I am not the one who is imprisoned beneath the ground, begging for my freedom like some pitiful dog begs for a bone. Consider yourself lucky I've lowered myself to dealing with the likes of you. Cain knows what I have done and it serves a purpose. One broader than your small mind can apparently wrap around. The man is no man, he is one of Raphael's Knights of White. The woman is his mate. The Knight will lead his army here to their own destruction."

Vars would have choked the life out of Adrian if he wasn't stuck in his pathetic shrine of powerless confine-ment, his abilities drained by the magic he was pump-ing into Allen right now. He bit back his anger and ground out a nasty reply. "The woman has connections to the other side, you fool. She will try to stop Allen before I get my energy sources."

Adrian waved off the words. "The woman will be dead in a few hours. Now—" he crossed his arms in front of his body "—I understand you need these energy sources by the next full moon. You have only ten days. Do I need to fetch your Shadow Stones for you so we are sure it gets done right?"

Adrian couldn't do the job if he wanted to, and Vars took pleasure in that knowledge. "For centuries now, each eldest son of the Shadow Masters' families have placed their souls in a magical Shadow Stone. In exchange, I endowed them with great health and wealth. The Masters will not release their souls from the stones to anyone but me, their *royal* master. They will find me through my bond with Allen, and he, and he alone, will receive their souls. Quite simply, you are not worthy of the stones. So, do your job. Protect this town. Protect Allen. Or is that too much for you?"

A sudden rush of menace filled the air, Adrian's eyes flashing yellow and red. "Do not test my limits, Vars, or you will remain beneath the ground." A second later Vars found himself thrown back into the pit of his prison, fire consuming him, pain—however momentary— scorching his every muscle. When the flames subsided, Vars pushed to his feet, vowing to make Adrian pay for his actions.

Adrian flashed to his home deep below the Mexican mountains where he lived in luxury and housed his sex slaves and army of Beasts. Rage burned inside him, rage directed at Vars. He was beneath no one, beneath nothing.

He snapped his fingers and a brunette beauty appeared. The sheer pink gown she wore showed the bright red of her puckered nipples. She was bound to him by the marks on her shoulder, her soul stuck between dimensions, allowing him to control her every need. He kissed her, savoring the sweetness of her taste, sex an outlet for the thunder raging inside. But one human would not sate this rage. He snapped his fingers and another slave appeared—this one blond, voluptuous, full breasted. She wore the same pink gown. Pink was a favorite of Adrian's. It made him think of the innocence he'd stolen from them. He tasted the second female's lips, his cock throbbing with need. Then he waved his hand and flashed them into the king-sized bed behind him, discarding their gowns with his magic.

He had a business matter to attend to before he could devour his prey. With another wave of his hand three Beasts appeared in their demon forms, half their faces distorted, their yellowish red eyes alert with the call of their master.

They were part of the Unit of his prior second-in-charge. U1, U2 and U3 were the only names they deserved—for now. "Each of you have the chance to earn the spot of my next *Segundo.* How you perform your next assignments will decide your futures. One of you will achieve greatness by my side. The other two—" Adrian paused for effect, an evil smile playing on his lips "—will be beheaded."

Fear crackled in the air at the words and Adrian drank it in, reveling in the power he had over the Beasts. Adrenaline and lust spiked within him, as he continued to speak. "U1 will ensure the Shadow Stones are recovered. Take a team and follow the human called Allen Walker. Kill any Knight or human who dares to interfere." He flashed U1 out of the room.

Adrian focused on U2. "You have a special assignment. You will kill the human called Sarah Meyers. I've come to understand she is the mate of your former brother. You are not to kill him. I want him on our special-forces team." Adrian could feel U2's edginess, his desire to see his brother dead. "Destroying her will ensure he crosses over to the dark side. Have your way with the woman, torture her, torture him for all I care. I really don't care. Just make sure she's dead and he watches her die. I want her blood spilled by the next dawn." He touched U2's chest, heat flaming from his palm to the Beast's skin, painfully reminding him who had control. "Fail me and die." He didn't give U2 time to respond, flashing the Beast from the room.

One final Beast remained, U3. "You will handpick the Beasts that are the strongest. Use them to defeat the Knights who gather in Nowhere, Texas." The final Beast was flashed from the room, and Adrian thought of Vars. "I will destroy the demon prince myself and enjoy doing so."

Now that he had his Beasts after blood, he turned back to the naked beauties in his bed, ready to explore the pleasures they represented. Ready to sate at least one of the desires burning within him. Satisfied to know his other needs would soon be fulfilled, as well.

Chapter 12

With Rock at her heels, Marisol walked toward the door of the exam room where Cathy and Edward were resting. He was scared to death to leave her alone, afraid the Beasts would attack. The young Knight acted like her keeper, as if she couldn't simply shimmer out of the room and away from danger. Secretly, she loved his protectiveness, just as she knew she loved him. But it was forbidden that she ever act on those feelings. Her love for Rock worked against her duty, her vows as a healer. She was not of this world, she simply served it.

She turned to him, silently telling him she needed privacy to talk with Cathy. He stepped to the side of the entrance. "I'll be right here if you need me."

Her heart clenched with his words and she resisted the urge to reach out and touch him. "Thank you," she said, softly, not daring to look into his eyes for fear he would see how much his concern touched her.

She stepped around Rock and opened the door, pausing as she took in the sight before her. The man she assumed to be Edward was strapped to a table and sedated, yet still he tossed about, driven by the demon possessing him.

Beside the table, sleeping in a chair, was the woman called Cathy. Poor thing was exhausted and Marisol could feel her turbulent emotions. Cathy didn't know help had arrived, didn't even know Marisol had healed the sheriff who was now talking with Jag and Rinehart.

Marisol walked toward Cathy, surprised at the charge of energy that flowed from the female. She was gifted with magic beyond what she practiced, born into powers she had yet to realize. Jag would find this interesting. For he had learned what Marisol's centuries in another realm had taught her well—nothing happened without a reason. Cathy had been delivered to them to play a role in this battle against evil, a battle that would most likely transcend the one fought in this town.

Kneeling in front of Cathy, Marisol touched her leg. "Cathy," she whispered.

The woman blinked and lifted her head, staring at Marisol. "My God, you have beautiful green eyes."

Marisol smiled at the compliment, which wasn't uncommon. "Green is the color of healing," Cathy said. "You're the healer Max spoke of," Cathy said, her hands going to the sides of the chair. "The sheriff—"

"Is as good as new," Marisol said. "He's chatting with the others in my group."

Cathy went a little pale. "That's impossible."

"You're welcome to go see for yourself," Marisol

offered, pushing to her feet. She spotted a mirror on the wall and inclined her head. "Or you can stand in front of that mirror while I heal that cut on your face."

A moment passed as Cathy cocked her head to the side and studied Marisol. "All right." She stood and walked to the mirror. "Let's see what you've got."

Marisol smiled and approached the other woman, touching her face. The wound was small, and took little effort to wipe away. A second later, she pulled her hand from Cathy's face and smiled. "Good as new."

Cathy stared in the mirror and moved closer to the surface, inspecting her face. She whirled and faced Marisol. "You know what's the most amazing part of this?" She didn't give Marisol time to answer. "It's not what you did but what I felt when you did it." She touched her chest. "I felt warm and…touched by, well, something special."

"You know what's the most amazing thing to me?" Marisol asked.

"What?" Cathy asked, her eyes wide with interest.

"That you know what you felt was special. That you are close enough to the source of my power to feel it. That makes you special, Cathy."

She snorted at that. "I'm not special." Edward made a low growling noise and her expression turned serious. "Can you help him? I've tried everything I know to do."

Marisol walked over to Edward and touched his hand. Evil rocketed through her body, and she gasped, stepping back and breaking contact.

"That didn't look good," Jag said, leaning on the doorjamb.

"It wasn't," Marisol said. "Whatever is inside him is

far more evil than a Beast. I need to consult my *Book of Knowledge*."

"*Book of Knowledge?*" Cathy asked.

Marisol eyed Cathy. "It's my reference…it's special. It may hold the answer to saving Edward." She looked toward the doorway. "This is Jag, the leader of The Knights of White."

Cathy did what all women do in Jag's rather intimidating masculine presence. She stared. Besides being gorgeous, with shoulder-length black hair and a body that would set any woman on fire, Jag carried an air of power and sexuality. He also adored the mate who waited for him at home more than life itself.

"You're Max's boss then?" Cathy asked. "He called you here to help?"

"We are here to help, and yes, Max called us." Jag's lips twisted in a hint of a smile. "As for being his boss, I don't know that anyone can claim to being Max's boss. I am, however, honored to have him on our team."

"Glad to meet you," Cathy said. "I have a feeling I owe Max an apology for doubting him." She frowned. "Or two or three." She glanced between Jag and Marisol. "Did Sarah talk to my people? Are they coming here, too?"

"It's too dangerous for your people to come here, Cathy," Jag said. "We can go to them."

"They won't talk to you," she insisted. "I wasn't completely sure they'd talk to Sarah but at least my mother has met her and liked her. The world of magic is a private one. There are secrets that simply aren't shared—not without consequences from those in the circle."

Jag considered her words. "We can take you to your people."

"I can't leave Edward," Cathy said, her arms crossing in front of her body. She shook her head. "That's simply not an option."

"Cathy has some gifts I can harness to heal Edward," Marisol said, "and perhaps others who might be afflicted as he is. Perhaps her gifts may even help us fight some of the evil we are faced with. I really need her to stay, so we can figure out what we are capable of together."

"What are her abilities?" Jag asked.

"I know a little magic," Cathy answered, casting Marisol a curious gaze.

Marisol, in turn, gave Jag a look that was meant to tell him she had more to say on the subject later—when they were alone. His eyes narrowed and then he gave her a barely discernible nod. "Where does that leave us then?" he asked. "My men are researching, but so far we have nothing on these Shadow Masters."

"And my guess is you won't find anything," Cathy inserted with confidence. "We are talking about the blackest of magic here. No one talks about this kind of evil openly for fear they will be punished by those using it. They certainly don't write it down nor do they discuss it over the phone. Nor do they talk to strangers. My family knows the magical world. They have connections. That's why we need to get them involved. But you can't do that without me."

Marisol gave Jag a pointed look. "Can I talk with you?" He inclined his head and Marisol glanced at Cathy. "Give us one minute."

Jag and Marisol stepped into the hall to join Rock. "Let's go outside so we can speak freely," Jag said.

A few seconds later they stepped onto the porch, the

sky black despite the fact that the dawn hour had come and gone. Rock and Jag framed Marisol, their big bodies almost like a shield to the outer world.

The two men turned to her, Jag speaking first. "What's Cathy's story?"

"She's unique, gifted with inbred magic she doesn't even know she has. I really think we have a better chance at saving Edward together than if I go it alone. I can use her magical energy to strengthen mine. And if we can figure out how, maybe we can turn that combined energy on Vars in some way."

Jag ran his fingers over his goatee. "Well, then," he said. "That's an interesting twist of events. Any idea what the source of her power is?"

"I'm seeing a familiar pattern to the women who enter our world," Marisol said. "I'm guessing a little research will find her tied to that list of angelic bloodlines we recently discovered. In other words, I think she is part of our world and someone's future mate."

Jag's eyes lit with that explanation. "A Knight's salvation."

"Or perhaps a future Knight," Marisol suggested.

Jag took a sudden step forward, his eyes traveling the horizon. "Beasts," he murmured. "Do you feel them, Rock?"

Rock stepped to his side. "I do," he said quietly. "Our men should arrive soon."

"Not soon enough, I fear," Jag said, turning back to them. "There is a distinct flavor of power in the air. Adrian, I think."

"Adrian?" Rock said. "As in, the leader of the Darklands? I didn't think he came into the trenches."

"He doesn't," Jag said. "Which is exactly why I'm worried. Both of you be on guard and warn the others to do the same." He looked at Marisol. "Perhaps Cathy came to us for a reason. Her powers may be needed. Do what you can to help her awaken them." He didn't wait for a reply. "I need to speak with Salvador and then I'll take Sarah to meet with Cathy's mother. I'll update you soon." He inclined his head and vanished without another word.

Marisol drew in a breath and focused on Rock. "I need to get my *Book of Knowledge,*" Marisol said, eyeing Rock. "Can you stay with Cathy while I'm gone? I can't shake the feeling she will be important in the future. I don't want to risk someone else figuring that out and coming after her."

"I'll protect her with my life," Rock said, willing as always to meet Marisol's needs.

She rolled her eyes at his over-the-top gallant words. "You're laying it on thick today, Rock."

He grinned. "Just making sure you know I'm here for you."

Her expression turned serious. "I know you are, Rock," she said, and shimmered into air, disappearing before he could respond.

Allen pulled up to the gate of the fancy Houston mansion and hit the buzzer, knowing he'd be expected. He checked the name on the marble plate beneath the buzzer and confirmed he had, indeed, found the one he sought—Caden Neil, a dark sorcerer who'd be bringing together the Shadow Masters in the Stone Ceremony.

Vars had arranged his visit, though he didn't know

how and didn't really care. The rich bastard who owned this place had apparently come by his money with help from the dark side. Figured. Allen used to wonder how some people had an overabundance of luck and money. Now he knew. They used magic. The Shadow Masters certainly had. But they'd also sold their souls for all they possessed. A bargain that would now destroy them. But that didn't matter to Allen; his only concern was getting Kate back. These Shadow Masters were evil. In truth, he was doing the world a favor. He'd be ridding it of the black sorcerers, and bringing back into it a lovely, wonderful woman. A good woman.

He touched the vial hanging from his neck, the one he'd created with the magic Vars had given him. A vial that would soon hold the souls of the Shadow Masters. And those souls would wield the power to free Vars. Allen simply needed this Caden to extract the souls from the stones. He wondered what Caden got in return for all of this, and how Caden had been connected to Vars. It was clear everything in this world operated on trade. Give me this and I give you that. Not that Allen cared. He just wanted this done.

A camera swung around to fix on him, and he stared into it. Seconds passed and the big steel gate slid open. Allen smiled and put the truck into Drive. Soon the Shadow Masters would be no more—soon Kate would come home to him.

Chapter 13

Sarah tossed and turned in the bed, screaming out in her mind as the cold bitterness of the familiar nightmare claimed her. Once again locked inside those moments so many years before when someone close to her—someone she trusted like a brother—had pulled the trigger of a gun two times, two deadly bullets hitting their targets and stealing her parents' lives.

Sarah lived that moment again, collapsing over her parents' bodies, touching them, searching for life that wasn't there to be found. "No," she whispered, shaking, her gaze lifting to the one who held the gun—to Kevin, a man who'd worked closely with her family for years. Had he always been this...this evil thing? Had she missed the signs? "Why?" she sobbed, her voice and hands shaking. "Why?"

But what she saw when she looked at Kevin wasn't

Kevin at all. Red eyes, evil and full of malice, stared back at her. "Who are you?" she demanded, but she knew already. She knew this was the demon they'd been hunting, the one the police thought was a serial killer. How long had Kevin been controlled by that demon? How long?

She let her lashes flutter, eyes shut. She would die next. But seconds passed and nothing happened. "Do it!" she screamed, wanting to die. She'd lost everything; she'd failed her family.

When she fixed her gaze on Kevin, for a moment she saw the man she'd known—or she thought she did. She couldn't be sure. And then, before she could stop it, before she even knew what was happening, the gun turned on Kevin.

"No!" Sarah shrieked, pushing to her feet, not sure if Kevin was really Kevin anymore—if he could be saved—just that she had to try. But it was too late.

The shot rang in the air, a loud thunder that made her jerk, and Kevin crumpled to the ground. Slowly, Sarah fell to her knees, tears pouring from her eyes. Why was she alive? Why? Would this demon come for her later? Was he taunting her? Why was she alive? She looked at her mother's pale face, and rocked back and forth. Why couldn't it be her and not her mother? Her gaze went to her father, and she screamed from the injustice of it all. Screamed until it hurt, until it felt as if her throat bled. Until everything went black.

The nightmare shifted to a hospital room, the smell of medicine lacing her nostrils. She blinked awake and memories flooded her, the pain of loss filling her. God, how it hurt. She'd failed everyone she loved. She'd let the demon take them. Let the demon get inside their

world and destroy it from the inside out. Why hadn't she
sensed it? Why? Had Kevin ever been their friend? Or
had he always been possessed, a part of that demon?
Tears spilled from her eyes, tears so full of self-hatred,
they burned her cheeks. She wanted to destroy that
demon one moment; the next, she wanted to die. She
shivered, cold, alone, empty—so very empty.

Abruptly the cold began to fade, shift, move. Warmth
surrounded Sarah and she moved closer to it, needing
it, desperate for it. A soft masculine voice slid into her
mind, her name a baritone murmur. She blinked and her
lashes lifted. Sarah was awake for real this time, outside
her nightmare, and strong arms held her, absorbing the
emptiness, making her feel whole again.

"Max?" she whispered, as she stared into his rich
hazel eyes. Reality began to register and she vaguely remembered passing out.

"Yes," he said softly, his voice full of gentle comfort
that so contrasted with the strength in his masculine
features, in the powerful body holding her. He rested
against the headboard, legs stretched out in front of him,
shirt off, his bare chest cradling her body. "I'm here."

She shivered, and he rubbed her arm, tugging the
blanket over her. "Are you cold?"

"No." Not anymore. Not with him here, holding her,
somehow making the nightmare fade when nothing else
would. "I had a nightmare." She leaned up on an elbow,
taking in the surroundings, trying to remember how she
got in bed. She was dressed but her shoes were off. The
room was dimly lit, only a small corner lamp on; a
glance at the window confirmed night had fallen.

She swallowed hard. "You took care of me." Then another thought followed before she could digest that one. "How long was I out? Did we call for help? The sheriff and Edward—are they okay?" Her mind was racing now. Max was hurt! What if he'd looked out for her and waited too long for care? "Oh, God! You need a doctor."

She tried to yank back the blanket and sit up to inspect his injuries, but Max pulled her back down; her chest was pressed to his side, one of his legs grabbing hers and pulling it beneath him, holding her in place. Shock mixed with pure fire surged through her body.

"Max!" she objected, confused by his actions. "What are you doing?" His mouth was close to hers, the air crackling with tension—charged with sexual energy, with attraction—but there was more there, too. She tried to identify the feeling. Apprehension perhaps?

"Everything is in order," he said. "You slept for six hours. My people have gone to Nowhere to offer aid, and they're researching the Shadow Masters. They will protect your team. I promise."

She would have felt relief, but for the look of tension on Max's face. A fizzle of fear raced through her and started to spin out of control. Her hands dug into his arm. "What's wrong? Just tell me. What's wrong?"

"Nothing that wasn't wrong when you went to sleep," Max said.

"I don't believe you," she whispered vehemently. "Tell me."

He shut his eyes and his torment washed over her. Suddenly, Sarah felt his sorrow, his pain. The connection she shared with him was so intense, so alive, it was almost as if he moved inside her. She'd never felt anything like this with another person. Nothing remotely close.

Her hand went to his jaw. "Max?" she softly prodded. "Talk to me."

"I need to show you something, but I need to know you won't freak out on me. I'm not like other people, Sarah. I don't want you to be afraid of me." Fear fluttered in her chest and she stiffened ever so slightly. After that nightmare, the unknown set her on edge. Max didn't, though, she reminded herself. Max calmed and comforted her. He needed acceptance now, too, she realized. Just as she often wanted acceptance, but rarely found it from those around her. And, my God, the man had saved her life several times already. He deserved her support.

She wanted to be there for him as he had been for her when she'd collapsed. "I understand being different. I live it each day of my life."

His throat bobbed. "Not like me, Sarah." He hesitated and then yanked the sheets back and exposed his bare abdominals.

Sarah blinked and blinked again. She couldn't be seeing what she thought she was seeing. His wound had disappeared, healed completely. He reached out and took her hand, pressing it to his stomach, the touch intimate, and packed with a punch. Heat darted up her arm and then coiled low in her stomach.

Her fingers itched to move and explore while her mind warned of her need for answers. "How can this be?"

"When you collapsed you were in a great deal of pain. I was desperate to take away your pain. I summoned Marisol. She is special, Sarah. She heals by touch. She eased your pain and helped you rest. Then, she took care of me. Hopefully, she's aided the sheriff and Edward by now, as well."

"I don't even remember her being here," Sarah said, frightened that so much was going on out of her control. Errors happened when she didn't keep things well under thumb. People died. But then, if what Max said was true, maybe people had been saved—her people. The sheriff. "When will we know if she helped them?"

"Soon I hope," he said, but offered nothing more, his attention turning back to the prior conversation. "My world is different from yours, Sarah." Something in his voice drew her gaze to his. "I'm not like other humans." His hand flattened on hers with more force. "But I need you to know I am one of the good guys. I'll fight to my death to protect you. I won't leave you to deal with this challenge alone." More conviction slid into his voice. "I won't."

For the first time in years, Sarah trusted someone at their word. She looked into Max's tormented eyes, and she let herself be lost. Lost to him, to the moment, to the whirlwind of emotions taking hold of her. She wanted him as she had never wanted a man, beyond reason, beyond explanation. The world was crumbling only a few miles away, but for just the briefest of times, she wanted to escape, to pretend nothing existed but the two of them.

"I believe you," she whispered, her body turning toward his, her hand sliding from beneath his, to the sprinkle of dark hair on his chest.

Max felt the brush of Sarah's lips on his and it was all he could do to remain still, to hold back. But he had to hold back. Had to. If he dared to explore where this could lead, he risked breaking the promise he'd just made. Because attached to him, mated to him, she would not be protected. She would share his destiny, his potential hell.

"Sarah—"

She pressed a finger to his lips. "Don't talk. I need you, Max. Make love to me."

Her mouth pressed to his, her tongue sliding past his lips, inviting him into a seductive game, dangerous and enticing, impossible to resist. Neither man nor Beast had enough willpower.

Suddenly, Max was kissing her, passion exploding within him, the completeness of his desire for this woman, his mate, consuming him at all levels—heart, soul, body. His fingers laced through her hair, her taste as addictive as her touch. And she was definitely touching him, showing no hesitation to explore his body. Her hands were everywhere, fingers tracing his muscles with tantalizing results, her leg over his, as his had been over hers earlier. As if she was the one who feared *he* would escape. But the only escape he wanted was inside her, his body intimately bound to hers. She was the sweetest thing life had ever given him, and for this one night, he was going to be strong enough to enjoy her without losing control.

"Max," Sarah whispered, easing her body on top of his, straddling his hips, the V of her body teasing his groin, thickening his cock. His hands gripped her hips, pressing her more firmly against him, pelvis lifting upward.

She moaned and pulled her blood-stained shirt—stained with his blood from when she'd taken care of him—over her head. The thought warmed him for an instant before fading away, as Sarah tossed her bra to the floor and leaned forward, pressing her chest to his chest, skin intimately touching skin.

Her lips lingered above his, her nipples pebbled against him. "I meant what I said earlier," she said, her voice barely audible.

"Which was what?" he asked, having a hard time remembering anything beyond the present, his hands skimming the softness of her bare back, to ease up her sides.

"I don't make a habit of getting naked with strangers."

He brushed the sides of her breasts and she moaned. "We might have only just met, Sarah," he murmured, his lips caressing hers for a quick moment, fingers sliding around the lush fullness of her breasts to tease her nipples. "But we aren't strangers." His teeth tugged on her bottom lip ever so gently. "Haven't you figured that out by now?"

She didn't immediately respond. Their breathing mingled, the air crackling with sensual tension. Slowly, Sarah eased back a bit, staring down at him, her eyes heavy with passion, with questions. "I've never felt this before."

He didn't ask what she meant by *this* because he understood. "That makes two of us," Max replied, his voice leaden with desire, with tenderness he hadn't known he possessed. But as quickly as that tenderness had consumed him, so did other, darker emotions.

Primal instincts flared inside Max, pushing him to take Sarah, driving him to claim. The need to control the pace, to control Sarah's actions rang in his mind as important. He couldn't risk her taking him beyond the place where man contained beast. If Sarah pressed him over the edge, he might not make it back. There was no option—he had to dominate. Had to control.

Max responded to the growing demands of his beast,

rolling Sarah onto her back, spreading her legs as he had back at the inn, and settling between them. The beast clawed at him, making its presence known, but Max suppressed it, dominated, pressed it back into the deep depths of his soul. He'd fought his darker side for centuries, and he would fight it now. Control belonged to the man, not the beast.

His mouth closed down on Sarah's softer one, as he forced himself to be gentle, to reach inside to calm himself. But that kiss quickly went from tender to fiery hot. Their tongues tangled in a seductive dance that turned into a full body sway. The kiss he'd meant to help him slow down, to put restraint in place, simply wasn't enough to satisfy either of them.

"I want you, Max," Sarah announced against his lips, fingers entwined in his hair, urgency lacing her words. "All of you." She reached between their bodies and slid her fingers over his erection before working his zipper with no success. "Take them off."

He hesitated, wanting this, but aware he was about to cross into the land of no return. This was where his willpower would be stretched, his limits strained.

"Now, Max," she ordered, her voice lifting.

Her demands drew laughter from him when he'd never have believed that possible. Not when he felt this depth of passion, not with the beast so close to the surface. No woman had ever done that to him, but Sarah could. Sarah was special. He nipped her lips. "You're very bossy."

She didn't laugh, but her eyes sparkled with mischief. "You haven't seen anything yet," she countered. "Now, get rid of the pants."

His cock pulsed with those words. Sarah had this knack for being both sweet and sexy, meek and powerful, all in one moment. It got him hotter than hot.

Max brushed his lips over hers. "Your wish is my command," he replied, pushing off the bed to stand and undoing the button on his pants. He would have demanded she undress, but she was already doing it; the sight of her jeans sliding down her legs, panties in tow, stilled his actions. She was beautiful, her silky white skin a direct contrast to the ripe red of her aroused nipples, her breasts high and full, stomach flat, hips rounded with womanly curves.

"What's taking so long?" she asked, easing toward him on her knees until she stopped directly in front of him. "And please tell me you have a condom packed in one of those pockets."

"Old battle injury," he said, his eyes tracking the hard peeks of her nipples, the lift of her full breasts. "I shoot blanks."

"Really?" she asked, surprise in her voice.

"Disappointed?" he asked, watching for her reaction his chest tightening as he realized he could never give her a normal life. No kids, no white picket fence.

Her response came quickly. "Not at all," she said, smiling, her gaze sliding up and down his body. "It's perfect. You're perfect."

Max sensed no remorse in her, no loss at the implications of his words. "*You're* perfect," he told her, meaning it. Her body was perfect, but even more so, she was perfect. Perfect for him.

Her hand went to his zipper again but this time with success. Together they shoved his pants and boxers down his legs. Max made quick work of kicking away his clothing, thankful his boots were long gone.

Before he knew her intent, Sarah's soft touch closed around his erection, stealing his breath with the bold action. And with that touch any hope he had of keeping their joining on his terms slid to oblivion, and he didn't give a damn. Sarah leaned into him and tilted her mouth up in an invitation, and he devoured her with greedy pleasure.

He ravished her with his kiss, tasting her deeply, his tongue growing more demanding with each stroke of her hand along his hard length. When he thought he could take no more, Max reached for restraint by claiming control. He filled his hands with her breasts, thumbing her nipples, before pressing her back onto the mattress. Leaning over her, he lapped at her nipples, teasing them with his tongue and teeth, licking and tasting. She moaned, arching her back, murmuring his name with raspy sensuality. So sexy, so alluring. The sound pressed him further to the edge, made him see fire and heat and possessiveness.

For a fleeting moment, he considered lifting her legs over his shoulders and sliding inside her, keeping their bodies distant, his mouth away from the temptation of marking her. But another second flashed by and he couldn't bear moving away from her, couldn't bear separating skin from skin. One instant he was lapping at her nipples, the next he was sliding his cock along the silky wet core of her body, seeking entrance. He sunk into the warm, wet heat that pulled him into the depths of blind passion—passion born of the joining of two mates. Their mutual sighs filled the room as he hit her core, a tantalizing sound of merging pleasures.

His forehead settled against hers, and he drew a shaky breath, emotion rushing over him, a feeling of belonging with Sarah. Their lips lingered close, their bodies intimately joined, unmoving. His chest was tight, his body on fire. He leaned back to look in her eyes, seeking the confirmation that she felt what he did and finding it. Their gazes held and locked, the contact intensifying the connection, the love shared naturally by mates radiating between them. He ran a gentle finger down her cheek and whispered her name. She took his hand in hers and brought it to her lips. Their stares fired into desire, and what was softness and sensuality turned red-hot, combustible.

Suddenly, they were kissing, bodies moving, rocking, swaying. He wanted to go slow, wanted to explore, linger, enjoy what might be the only time he'd ever make love to Sarah. But he couldn't slow down; he couldn't hold back. She was driving him crazy with need. Her body arched into him, her legs wrapping around his thighs to get closer, higher, pull him deeper.

Max thrust into her, harder, faster, and with the build of passion, with the build of release, the beast grew stronger. He felt it, but he couldn't seem to stop moving, couldn't seem to hold back. Sarah. He simply had to have more, had to get deeper. Had to touch her breasts, her hips, her face, her hair. All of her. Any of her. He simply had to have her. Long minutes passed, their lovemaking intense, passionate.

"Max," she gasped between moans, arching into him and stiffening.

He knew she was about to climax and he wanted her pleasure, wanted it as he'd never wanted another woman's pleasure. He kissed her jaw, her lips, her nose. "Come for me, baby," he urged.

"I'm, oh, I'm—" She lost the words as her body erupted in spasms that grabbed at his cock with erotic pressure, tantalizing and explosive. In that moment of pure, white-hot pleasure, Max's teeth elongated, his willpower dissolving. Damn it. Knights only had fangs during mating. He knew this but he'd been sure he could stop it from happening, been sure that centuries of suppressing the beast wouldn't fail him now.

He buried his face in the bed by her neck, fighting the urge to sink his teeth into her shoulder. No! The beast didn't listen. The beast wanted Sarah. Demanded her. He just needed one taste of her. One. Taste.

No! He screamed the word in his head over and over. No!

Max fought the primal urge to claim, fought it with other desires, with the burn of his body's need for release. He plunged deeper into her core, thrusting harder—thrusting faster. But it wasn't enough. The beast kept him on the edge, unable to find completion, wanting him to take more than pleasure. If he didn't find release soon, he'd lose the battle with the beast; he would lose control. He was close to the edge, close to explosion. He just needed a little deeper. Needed to move a little faster.

Desperate, Max raised up on his hands and plunged hard and deep. Once. Twice. And there it was, there was relief, control, satisfaction. He spilled himself inside the depths of her core, her heat consuming him, shaking with the intensity of orgasm. But in that moment, he also forgot those fangs, forgot the monster that passion had brought to life.

Suddenly Sarah's sigh of satisfaction became a scream. Max had shown her the beast within himself, and there was no way to hide the truth.

Chapter 14

"Get off me!" Sarah screamed, her heart about to explode out of her chest. Max had fangs. Fangs! She'd let her guard down and been fooled. She never let down her guard. Not since the day a friend had turned demon and killed her family.

Max held her, his big body still on top of hers; good God, he was still inside her. "Wait. Sarah. Please."

"No!" She kicked and squirmed, but found movement near impossible. Grinding her teeth, she stared up at him. "Let me up."

"Not until you hear me out," he said. "I told you I'm different. I tried to explain before...before we made love."

"Had sex! Just sex!" she shouted, refusing the feelings she had for him. She kicked some more. He grunted and rolled off of her.

Sarah grabbed the sheet and yanked it around her

body, turning to square off with him. "Who are you, Max? What are you?"

"I mean you no harm, Sarah," he said, standing there naked and glorious, his big body powerfully male. "I know you feel that. I know you trust me."

"How can I?" she asked. "How?" But the truth was, even now, she wanted to. Desperately, Sarah prayed Max would give her a reason to make those fangs not matter. But how could he? What would make this better? Nothing. Nothing at all, and damn, it hurt. His betrayal, her past, her life—it all hurt. So she did all she ever knew how to do when that pain bit into her. She pushed back. "My parents were killed by a friend we trusted who was possessed by a demon. You want me to trust a man who tells me he fights demons and then shows signs of being one himself? Tell me how I can do that? Tell me! I'd be a fool to trust you. I was a fool once in my life, and that cost me everything. How can I trust you? Tell me that. How?"

Max digested that news as he would a solid punch to the gut. She'd lost her family to a demon just as he had. He understood that pain, understood the loneliness. To have a close friend be the killer, well, he certainly understood why that would breed distrust. That had to be hell to live with. He wanted to be there for her, to ease her pain. But almost certainly, this demon connection assured that Sarah could never accept him as her mate. Even if he passed this test, his time was short-lived. He couldn't fight the darkness without a mate much longer, and he wouldn't go to the other side. He'd die first. He'd let a Beast take his head and end this before he'd go to the other side.

A decision became clear. Leaving this world with lies between them or even with unspoken words simply wasn't an option. They would only feed the fear and distrust she obviously harbored toward others after the death of her parents.

He stared at her, wanting to speak, but tormented by what he found in her face. Her eyes were wary, accusing. Her back pressed against the wall as if she couldn't get far enough away, the sheet clutched in front of her body. She covered herself as if he were an enemy rather than her mate, her lover. Damn it! Frustration and anger formed within him. Why did it have to be this way?

Snagging his boxers, he pulled them on, trying to make her more comfortable. "This is exactly what I didn't want. I didn't want you to be afraid of me, Sarah. I told you, I'm different, but I'm not dangerous." Okay, that might not be the truth so he added, "Not to you. I'd sooner die than hurt you." That was the truth. The complete truth. He let out a heavy breath. "I was trying to tell you about me, about my people." He held his hand up in frustration. "Things just got out of control."

Her hand shook where it held the sheet in place. "How can I know that, Max? How?"

"Think back to what we've been through. How many times could I have hurt you if I meant you harm? How many times did I save you and your friends?"

"Don't you see?" she asked. "It's not about what you did. It's about secrets. The friend who killed my family—to this day I have no idea if he was ever a friend. Was he always possessed? He seemed normal up to the minute he pulled a gun and shot my family." Her lips pressed together, and she continued as if she couldn't rein in her thoughts, "How do I know you're not with Vars? How do I know you aren't supposed to earn my trust and turn it on me? The demon my family hunted was a serial killer. He possessed human bodies, changing forms with each murder. The police never had a chance of catching him. For all I know, my friend was always working for this demon, telling him every step we took. I've been through too much to see what I just saw and ignore the risks. I've had someone close to me steal everything I knew and loved, and I won't be foolish like that again."

Max's gut clenched at the pain in her voice, in her face. "What happened to the demon?"

"I destroyed that bastard," she said. "And, Max, as much as I've wanted to trust you, if I find out you want to hurt people I care about, hurt anyone for that matter, I'll find a way to stop you."

As much as her need to threaten him tore him up inside, he admired her courage.

He hated the story he had to tell. Inhaling deeply, he made an effort to distance himself from his words. "I lost my parents to the Darkland Beasts. Watched them die right in front of me. They didn't bother converting my parents. They just killed them, drained them dry. My brother was another story. They took his soul, and he became one of them. I watched the transformation. One minute he was my brother—the next, something so evil I didn't even recognize him. I would have turned out like that, too, evil and beyond salvation. But a man came then. He killed the Beasts that didn't run, and gave me back my soul. That was how I became what I am now. How I became a Knight of White. We aren't military, Sarah. We aren't even human. We exist to fight evil."

His chest filled with emotion, and it took him a minute to continue. "That was four hundred years ago. I've spent those long years fighting the Beasts…and finding that battle the reason to keep going." But now, with no hope of light, no hope of Sarah to save his soul, there was no reason to continue. "My journey has been long and it's about to end. Once I see you through this, it's over for me."

Tormented by the prospect of Sarah's rejection, of never having her in his life, his impervious shell threatened to crack. He cut his gaze from Sarah and grabbed his pants and shirt. "I'm going to take a shower. You can leave, but I don't advise it. There have been several attempts on your life. Obviously, the Darklands are partnering with Vars. They'll hunt you down, Sarah. I'll keep you safe if you let me. I told you back at the cabin, I'd have enough faith for both of us. Now I'm afraid you're going to have to find some of your own. But if you do, Sarah, if you reach deep and you find that faith, I won't fail you."

He headed into the bathroom, leaving her alone, knowing she might walk out the door. It was one of the hardest things Max had ever done in his life. He wanted to tie her down and force her to let him protect her, but that wasn't the answer. Not yet at least. He didn't know what he'd do if she walked out that door.

A demon. She had been in the arms of a demon. Sarah laughed, a choked, nervous sound even to her own ears. That was impossible. Max wasn't a demon.

But she'd seen the fangs, she reminded herself. He might feel human and even look human, but so had Kevin, the friend who'd killed her parents. Fangs! Damn it, Max had fangs. Her hand pressed to her stomach, nerves fluttering. She'd never been so confused in her life.

Have faith, Max had said. Her parents had said that often. Every time they'd headed into an investigation, every time things seemed grim. Sarah wasn't sure she knew what faith was anymore. Where had faith gotten her in life? Alone, that was where—looking over her shoulder and afraid of the shadows. Pretending she was afraid of nothing, when she was afraid of everything. Every investigation terrified her. Having others close to her was a twofold terror. Who would get hurt? Who would turn evil? If someone became possessed, were they evil to start with? Had Kevin been evil? Was Edward? No. She refused to believe that Edward was evil. So where did that leave her?

She inhaled, thinking of what Max had been through in his past. If he was telling the truth, he'd lost his parents as she had lost hers. Or was he simply an enemy playing with her, dragging her into a seductive game to distract her from finding Allen?

She felt as if she was going to be sick. She didn't want Max to be an enemy. He was the first person, in what felt like forever, that she actually wanted to let into her life. With Max, she had the oddest sense of belonging. It didn't matter that they'd just met. Thinking back to the moment he'd walked into the inn, she realized the feeling had been instant.

The very fact that he'd given her the chance to leave spoke volumes. Fangs or no fangs, Max felt safe. He felt right.

Her hand went to her chest, her throat dry, her heart drumming at a fast beat. What had he meant when he'd said his journey was about to end? Why did the idea of his departure bother her so much?

Faith. She rolled the word over in her mind and reached deeper inside than she had in a very long time. Max had protected her and her friends. He'd been hurt doing it, too. He deserved the benefit of the doubt—no, a little faith. He deserved a little faith.

Her eyes slid shut, and for the first time in years, she prayed. She prayed for the strength to act, for the wisdom to know what to do. Seconds passed and she let that prayer take root in her mind, let it slide through her body and soothe. She opened her heart and her soul; she prayed that it was the right thing to do.

And when she was done, she acted. She didn't give herself time to think, not even time to dress. If she did either of those things, she might talk herself out of what she was about to do. Instead, she wrapped the sheet snugly around her and marched to the bathroom.

She needed answers and she intended to get them.

The water was running. Perfect. Somehow, his being in the shower made him the prisoner and offered her control. And control was exactly what she was after right now. She reached for the doorknob and turned, letting out a sigh as it opened. Steam poured out of the room and clung to her skin. She swatted it away and moved forward, sitting down on the toilet.

"Max," she said, struggling a bit for her voice.

The curtain moved instantly, his head appearing around the side. "Sarah?" He disappeared again and the water turned off.

An instant concern formed. She'd meant for him to stay in the shower. Of course, he wouldn't. Maybe she should have done a little thinking before acting after all. A naked Max would mean distraction in a big way. She grabbed a towel and shoved it behind the barrier. He snatched it, and a second later the curtain moved back to expose him, dripping wet, in a too-small towel. Wet hair clung to his high cheekbones, to his muscular chest. A droplet of water ran down his stellar abdominals, and her gaze followed it as it disappeared inside his sunken belly button.

"Sarah?" He repeated her name as a question, and the one word held vulnerability she didn't think a man so strong could show.

The emotion in his voice drew her attention, and she searched his face, probing for the true man beneath the warrior shell. What she found in his eyes took her breath away. Torment and pain laced those hazel eyes. Eyes speckled with yellow. Eyes she loved, she realized.

Lonely hurt eyes that still held warmth where another's might be cold. Hope flooded her body then— hope that touched deep in her soul. Hope that her trust in Max hadn't been wrong.

A surprising realization took hold. "I'm not afraid of you. I should be, but I'm not."

He reached for her and she held up a staying hand, afraid now, but not of him. Of herself. Of forgetting what she'd seen in that bedroom, and forgetting her caution, her questions.

Frustration flashed across his face and a hint of fresh pain. It was almost enough to send her into his arms, but she forced herself to remain in her seat. "I would have walked—no run—out the door and never looked back if I didn't find a little of that faith you asked for." Her voice softened, holding a bit of defeat over the obvious. "But, Max. You have to know this fang thing is messing with my head. If you aren't a demon and you aren't human, what are you?"

He closed his eyes, his lips tight. She could feel his hesitation to the point of almost tasting it. He didn't want to explain. He didn't want to tell her. That meant whatever he had to say wasn't good. She hugged herself, seconds passing as she waited, before his lashes lifted, water clinging to them.

"Immortal, Sarah. I belong to Raphael's army of demon hunters."

She could barely breathe when she heard those words. "Raphael."

He nodded. "Yes. That's why I knew that legend had to be relevant to what was going on in that town."

His urgency to know which archangel was involved in the legend made sense now. Still, this seemed a fairy tale, not reality. But then, fangs and Hell Hounds seemed a nightmare. Fangs. Max had fangs.

"Why would an archangel give his army fangs?"

"There is only one time when a Knight possesses fangs."

No way. "Are you telling me every time you have sex—"

"Not sex," he said, his voice lower, his eyes hotter. "Mating."

She sucked in a breath at the sound of that word. Unbidden, a hint of excitement fluttered in her chest that she couldn't begin to understand. "What does that mean?"

"There is only one mate for our kind, and we know that person when we find them. The desire to bind them to us for all of time is primal, instinctive—a matter of survival. The male marks the female's shoulder with his teeth, and with that bite comes the melding of souls. The two are linked together for all eternity."

Her body reacted to his words of its own accord, completely out of her control. Heat pooled low in her limbs and her nipples tingled. The images she played in her head were erotic, seductive, far more appealing than they should be. Most of all, they felt right. They felt like what was supposed to happen between her and Max.

This was crazy. Insane. Mating? Bound for all of eternity. Or was it? She knew there were things beyond this realm of existence. She dealt with spirits all the time. And there was no doubt she felt a connection to Max. Lord help her, she felt as if she knew him beyond time. As if they'd been lovers in another life, or something. She knew him. She was Max's mate? Maybe it was true. Maybe that explained the need to trust him. The idea of having someone close to her, someone to fill the emptiness, both excited and frightened her. But someone to love was someone to lose, as well.

"So if you bite me…" she said, hugging herself, her teeth worrying her bottom lip. Had she ever been this confused in her life? "What exactly happens?"

His response came fast and hard. "Nothing, because I won't damn you to my future, Sarah. I won't. I only told you this because you saw the fangs, and as long as I'm around you I can't promise I won't feel the urge to take you again." Without warning, he stepped out of the tub and stared down at her. "Which means I can't touch you again."

An emotional door slammed shut in Max, and she felt it like a punch, but she saw the look in his eyes a second before he walked away. He wanted her, even needed her. She jumped to her feet, following him, not about to be dismissed that easily. She didn't know if she wanted to be Max's mate; it was all too overwhelming. But one thing was for sure—she wanted all the facts. She rounded the corner to find him already buttoning his jeans and started to confront him. He didn't give her time.

His hand ran over his wet hair, pressing it away from his face. "Don't ask anything else, because I don't even know how to answer you."

"You have to answer me," she argued. "I deserve answers and you know it. Damn it, Max. Tell me what is going on!"

"Fine," he said. "You want to know?" He didn't give her time to answer. "When I was saved, my soul retained a dark stain. I've battled that stain for longer than most. These Knights I fight with are not the original Knights. Almost all of those who were first created eventually fell to the darkness inside them."

"What does that mean?"

"It means they turned into the very thing they battled—they became Darkland Beasts. Since then, a new breed of Knights has been formed, and they now have a chance to erase the stain on their souls. If they find their one chosen mate in time, the mating will imprison the demon side of the Knight and save him forever. But I have fought this battle four centuries now. More and more, I can't control my dark side." His chest expanded as he looked away from her as if ashamed. "I couldn't control myself when we were together. I don't know what I am capable of." He looked at her again, his eyes stormy with emotion. "One of the biggest fears a Knight has when he finds his mate is biting her and killing her. I'm hundreds of years older than any of these Knights I fight with. There is far less human in me than there was in them when they claimed their mates."

She sucked in a breath. "You're telling me I could save your life if we mate, but you could kill me in the process?"

"Don't worry, Sarah. I won't be biting you. Mating is not an option. It's simply too late for me, anyway. I broke a sacred rule and now I'm being tested. If I fail this test, I go to hell. If you are linked to me, you will, too. Which is exactly why I can't touch you again. And I'll want to, Sarah, just as you will want to touch me. Passion between mates is as natural as breathing."

If she believed all of this, and the fangs seemed to make it pretty believable, then the passion between mates made sense. It explained why she couldn't keep her mind on her job. Sarah swallowed hard, trying to take all of this in. As for going to hell, she didn't know if Max meant literally or not, but she knew she didn't want to find out. And where the biting her shoulder thing had seemed rather erotic a moment before, possible death-by-fangs certainly zapped the passion out of the idea.

"Tell me about the test and the rule you broke."

Max didn't respond. His body tensing, his expression registered alertness. A second passed and he turned away from her, his attention fixed on the door as if he knew something she didn't. "Get dressed," he said without looking at her, a second before a knock sounded.

Max walked to the window and looked outside.

Sarah's heart pounded as she ran to do as he said, fear making her heart race. "Who is it?"

"It's Jag," he said, tapping the window and holding up a finger. "Our leader."

Sarah had her clothes in her hand. "That's good then, right?"

He laughed at that, though it sounded a bit forced. "Yes. He's one of the good guys."

"I'll go into the bathroom and change so you can let him in." A thought occurred. "Wait. Was he in town? Will he know about Edward and Cathy? About the sheriff?"

"Probably, yes."

She rushed at him then, almost tripping over the sheet. Max grabbed her and kept her from going down. "Ask him for an update. Please." Her hands clung to his arms. "I'll wait right here."

He looked as if he might argue and then he nodded. "Give me a second."

"Thank you, Max," she said, her stomach in knots. "I just really need to know they're okay."

His knuckle gently brushed her cheek. "I understand."

The act was tender, sweet. It touched Sarah inside, beyond simple skin-to-skin contact. She watched as he turned and exited, rocking on her heels and hugging herself as she waited. Thankful when he returned after only a minute.

"Cathy and Marisol are working together on Edward's situation, and the sheriff is healed."

Relief washed over her at the news. Cathy and Edward were still alive. "Sheriff Jenson is healed?" she asked, surprised. "Completely?"

"Marisol is good."

She blinked. "Yes. I can't quite get my mind wrapped around such a talent. I don't know if I will believe it until I see it." Her gaze went to his stomach where the injury had disappeared. "Okay, I believe it, but I'll still feel better when I see the sheriff up and about myself."

"So far no one has anything on the Shadow Masters. I worked the Net myself while you were sleeping and found nothing. Cathy sent word to remind you to call her mother. But she said not to bring up the Shadow Masters on the phone. It's too dangerous. We need to go see her."

"I hope she can help," Sarah said, worry etching her features. "I'll call as soon as I get dressed."

"Your shirt has blood all over it," Max told her and inclined his head at the closet. "I brought your bag in while you were sleeping."

She hadn't been taken care of in, well, forever. It was a small gesture, but it meant something to her. "Thank you," she said, her eyes locking with his. She started to turn and hesitated. "There can't be double standards in this relationship."

A frowned touched his eyes. "What?"

"If I'm going to have faith, you can't go losing yours. It doesn't work that way." She didn't wait for a response, pushing to her toes and brushing her lips quickly over his. Then she headed to the closet to grab her bag before disappearing into the bathroom.

She shut the door and stared into the mirror. Her hair was a mess, and aside from the smudged mascara under her right eye, her face bore no makeup. She was a mess on the outside and confused on the inside. But she also felt a sense of belonging she hadn't felt for a long time. A sense of needing and being needed.

They'd figure out this test he faced, just as they'd figure out how to save Allen, and the town of Nowhere. They had to. Failure wasn't an option.

Suddenly, she realized Kate had been silent since she woke, despite previously desperate attempts to communicate with Sarah. Her mind stretched to that communication. Kate had told her something—something important. A place maybe. A location. Somewhere Allen was going. Sarah dropped her sheet and stepped into the shower. By the time the hot water poured over her, she was lost in her thoughts, desperate to find the clue lurking in the depths of her mind. She had to remember…before it was too late.

Chapter 15

Once Sarah entered the bathroom, Max spent the next few minutes pacing the room. Jag had disappeared, no doubt orbing to some distant place, his return certain at any moment. Frustration welled in Max's gut over his situation. Damn this test. Why give him some secret test that could doom him to hell and deliver him to his mate at the same time? Why? And the thought of dooming his mate to hell, as well, was unbearable. He began pacing again, scrubbing the now overgrown stubble on his jaw.

A knock sounded on the door and Max reached for it, his frustrations funneled into the action as he yanked it open, biting back angry words of confrontation. A good thing because Jag was no longer alone. Karen, his mate, stood beside him.

"We thought you might be hungry," Karen said, smiling as if she didn't notice the scowl on Max's face, her blue eyes twinkling. Blond and beautiful, she was strikingly light in appearance and personality—a direct contrast to the dark edge that clung to Jag's presence— yet somehow the perfect match for him. She held up the bag to make sure he saw the name on the side, and added, "I know how you love Big Macs."

Max cast Jag a disgruntled look. He didn't make a habit of confronting Jag—he respected him too damn much—but right now this test and Jag's Big Mac party were pushing the wrong buttons. Very personal buttons. "I know what you're doing and it's not okay." Max ground out the words between his teeth. "I don't want to pull Sarah into my world when I don't even know if I'm going to be here for her."

"You will be," Jag said, "because I refuse to let you fail this test."

"That makes two of us," Karen said, shooing him with her dainty little hand. "Now, step aside. I'm hungry and I want to eat." She grinned. "And meet Sarah."

Max slid his teeth together and obediently did as he was instructed, easing back into the room, allowing Jag and Karen to enter. But then his restraint snapped; the agitation that had pushed him to pace only moments before bubbled over into actions. Max shut the door in a near slam and whirled around to find Karen on the bed pulling food from the bag, and Jag leaning on the dresser.

"How am I going to pass this damn test when I don't even know what it is?"

"By believing you can."

The softly spoken answer came not from Jag, but from Sarah, who had entered the room as he spoke. She paused just outside the bathroom wearing slim-cut black jeans and a red T-shirt. Freshly showered, her hair damp, her face fresh, she looked lovely—like an angel. His angel. Max felt his frustration melt away as he looked at her. Felt the calmness take hold. She did that to him. She brought him a peace he hadn't felt in centuries.

He watched her closely, expecting her to focus on Jag in awe as most people did when they first met him. Jag had a way of drawing both male and female attention. It was an aura of power he oozed, a bit of magic even. But Sarah wasn't looking at Jag. She was staring at Max, as lost in him as he was in her. God, this connection he shared with her made him whole. He felt it as surely as he knew this was what had been missing all his life. He wanted to believe he could pass this test. He did. Wanted to believe there was enough human left in him to deserve to stand beside his fellow Knights, as well. To deserve Sarah and mate without harming her. But he'd killed a human; his beast had dictated that action. Four hundred years of fighting the beast had taken its toll and beaten down the man.

Out of his peripheral vision, Max saw Jag cross one booted foot over the other, and he knew Jag's action was meant to gain his attention. "Smart woman," his leader murmured softly.

Sarah glanced at Jag. "Actually," she corrected him, "my mother was the smart one." Her attention went back to Max. "She said that doubt breeds weakness and bad choices."

Without warning, Sarah's stomach rumbled rather loudly, shifting the mood in the room. Sarah's cheeks flushed red as her hand pressed to her middle. She laughed, the sound laced with embarrassment. "Sorry about that. I guess the smell of food is getting to me."

Karen started laughing, too. "I heard that. Sounds urgent." She patted the bed. "I'm Karen, Sarah. Jag's mate and wife."

Jag offered a tiny bow. "Nice to meet you, Sarah."

"Nice to meet you," Sarah said, studying him a moment with interest.

"Come sit with me," Karen ordered playfully, bringing Sarah's attention back to her. "I won't have you starving on my clock."

A smile touched Sarah's lips. "I love McDonald's," she confessed, claiming the spot next to Karen and reaching in a bag for a fry. "Hmm. I don't know if they are really good or I'm just really hungry."

"I brought choices," Karen offered. "Nuggets, double cheeseburgers or Big Macs."

"Big Mac," Sarah said, accepting a burger and inhaling the smell. "Love these things."

Karen smiled and eyed Max, a Big Mac in his hand. "You know you want it." She turned to Sarah. "He loves them, too."

"I'll grab some drinks," Jag said. "I know what everyone else likes. Any preferences, Sarah?"

"Coke," Sarah, "but I'll settle for Pepsi."

Jag looked at Max. "Why don't you help me?"

Max glanced at Jag and silently told him again, he knew what his leader was up to. Jag wanted to give the women some alone time. At this point, Max didn't see the point in arguing. Jag had expertly orchestrated Operation Bring Sarah Into The Inner Circle, and it was working like magic. Sarah and Karen were getting along as if they were longtime friends.

Max took a minute to fully dress, and for any Knight, that included arming himself with blades. Once outside, he expected Jag to corner him about Sarah. He quickly learned that assessment was wrong.

Jag pulled out his phone. "I need to check in with Des one last time before he's in Nowhere and I can't reach him. Right before I left, I sensed Adrian's presence."

Two things instantly crossed Max's mind. (1) He was damn impressed that Jag could sense Adrian's presence. Jag couldn't have done that before now. Their leader was growing stronger each day, and that meant the Knights were, as well. (2) He'd been around four centuries, and he knew the rules that guided those not of this world.

Max gave Jag a puzzled expression. "He's not allowed to interfere with activity in this realm any more than Salvador is," Max pointed out. "So what's he up to?"

"His usual no good, but at least I have Salvador alerted. If Adrian crosses any lines, Salvador will be watching. Salvador can't intervene unless certain lines are crossed. He has to work through us."

"Did he offer any insight into Vars's history?" Max asked, ready for any bit of information he could sink his teeth into.

"He uses humans for personal entertainment, subjugates them to stroke his ego," Jag offered. "He's concerned about us being lured to Nowhere by Adrian."

Max filled in the blanks. "I guess we all are. It's pretty obvious Adrian had chosen it as his battlefield."

"Exactly," Jag said. "Which means we need to turn the tables on the enemy and turn their trap into our trap."

Max grinned. "I like the way you think, Great White leader."

Jag punched the buttons on the phone, and Max moved toward the soda machine, allowing Jag the privacy to talk to his second-in-charge. He gave himself a moment to think about what had to be done. A great battle faced them all. He had to make some tough choices and ensure that Sarah was safe if he didn't make it to the other side of this war. And he damn sure wouldn't take her to hell with him if that was where he ended up. Nor would he let her live here on earth blaming herself for not saving him. He wasn't a fool. He could see she lived her life with the guilt of her parents' death.

No. Max had to get this under control and focus on the battle ahead. He'd push Sarah firmly away, but not so far that he couldn't protect her. There wasn't another option. He had to do this. But damn, he wasn't going to like it. This was going to be a little taste of living hell.

Sarah watched the door shut as the men exited the room and immediately turned to Karen. "What can you tell me about this test Max has to face?"

"Regretfully," Karen said, "not much. The test comes from above Jag, and neither of us were told the details." She held up a finger. "But I can tell you Max will be asked to do nothing he is not capable of achieving. His success, not his failure, is the goal. And frankly, I believe that you, as his mate, came to him now as a guide, to support him and help him conquer this test. If that's not proof he's intended to succeed, I don't know what is."

"So you believe I'm Max's mate, too?"

Karen gave her a curious look. "Don't you?"

Sarah hesitated only an instant, deciding there wasn't time for anything but directness, her heart telling her all she had to know. "I do," she admitted. "It's a little overwhelming to believe something like this is real, but I know it is. I felt the connection the minute I met him." She considered the situation a minute, and then asked, "If you can't tell me what this test is—can you tell me why Max is being tested? He said he broke a rule, but didn't seem inclined to explain the details."

A conflicted look flashed across Karen's features. "I'm afraid I'd be out of line to comment. I think this needs to be something Max tells you."

"But you know."

Karen nodded. "Yes. I know what he did. I just shouldn't say."

Sarah's shoulders slumped in defeat. "I suspected you would say that." Still, she wasn't willing to give up without some form of information. "Can you confirm he goes to hell if he fails the test?"

"That's true," Karen replied softly, the words touched with regret.

Sarah felt that confirmation like someone ripping her heart out. "I just barely met the man and the idea of losing him feels like torture."

"Time is irrelevant," Karen explained. "Your soul is connected to his. Max is your other half. In this lifetime or another, you would never have felt complete satisfaction without him. Don't run from the connection. He needs you too much. Accept your bond and you'll save him."

Karen tugged her shirt to the side to expose her shoulder. "This is the mating mark you will receive after he bites you." She quickly added, "If you make the choice to mate."

Sarah blinked, shocked at the star which not only looked like a tattoo but seemed familiar in a very personal way. "That star—it's related to King Solomon, right?"

Karen let her shirt slide back into place as surprise registered on her face. "It is. We call it Solomon's Star, though in his time it was named after his father, David."

"The Star of David," Sarah said.

"Right," Karen confirmed. "Unfortunately, Solomon's service ended with betrayal and he turned to dark powers. We call it *The Star of Solomon* as a reminder that Jag must protect humanity without corruption."

Sarah could barely believe what she was hearing. "I…this is crazy." Karen gave her an inquisitive look and Sarah continued, "My parents were killed by a demon. When I finally destroyed it, I used Solomon's magical writings to do it." Her chest tightened. "Just not soon enough to save my family." She shook her head. "This is so strange. The connection to Solomon seems too big to be a coincidence."

Karen's expression held certainty. "Everything happens for a reason, though you may not know that reason until much later. You were guided to Solomon's writings for a reason. I have no doubt you deserved justice and you received it. I've found the higher powers can't always stop the evil forces, but they can guide us to do it. I don't pretend to understand all of this but I know this. Your destiny is with us. We are your family now, Sarah. In time I hope you feel that, too." She touched Sarah's arm. "One day I'll share with you how the Knights became my family."

Family. She forgot what that felt like. All these years of doubting, of losing that faith Max had spoken of, and there seemed to be a higher force guiding her all along. Her mother had always said there was. Deep inside, Sarah knew that all along.

Male voices rumbled outside, signaling the men could be returning. Quickly, Sarah blurted out a rather embarrassing question weighing on her mind. "One more thing. Max said he was worried about the mating process. He said he could kill me. That there isn't enough human left in him to bite me and not turn into a Beast."

Karen rolled her eyes. "They all think that and it's simply not the case. And, yes, I know Max is an old, old man." She crinkled her nose. "He acts like it sometimes, too. He hovers over everyone in protective mode all the time. Especially the younger Knights." Her expression turned thoughtful and she continued before Sarah could ask more about Max's "old man" tendencies. "I've given some consideration to why mating requires they bite their intended mate, considering biting a human and taking blood could turn them into a Beast for good."

Sarah absorbed the last bit of information with some apprehension. Once the Knight bit a human, he converted to demon. She suppressed a shiver. "And what did you come up with?"

"I think it's because they must believe they are worthy of their duty to continue this journey they are on. If they can't believe in themselves, why should anyone else? He's been through a lot and so have you. But you have each other now. It will work out. He can't hurt you. He'd die to save your life."

She believed that. All of it. Max had already saved

her too many times to count. "This all makes sense," Sarah said, thinking of just how much Max didn't believe in his worthiness, relieved he wasn't possessed. That he couldn't turn on her. She smiled. "Thank you. I feel better already." She blushed a bit and then asked one last thing, "Those teeth of Max's are pretty long. Does it hurt? Were you worried at all when he bit you?"

"Not at all," Karen said, and grinned. "It's actually quite sexy. It's a sensual bonding of body and soul you only get to live once. Enjoy it."

Sarah smiled. "I guess that explains why I got all warm all over when he described the process."

"Oh, yeah," Karen agreed. "That's why, all right. The natural attraction between mates is quite yummy, isn't it?"

The door opened, and Karen and Sarah quickly ended their private conversation, sharing a female look of understanding, two kindred spirits. They'd become fast friends, and Sarah couldn't be more pleased about that fact. Suddenly, in the middle of a firestorm of danger, Sarah felt a bit of hope. The kind she hadn't felt in a very long time. Max wasn't a demon. He was connected to an archangel, in fact. And he needed her. If there had been anything she'd gotten out of this talk with Karen, it was that.

Max's ears filled with the women's laughter as he pushed open the door to the room. His eyes caught on Sarah's, his heart squeezing because he'd just made a hard decision. One that forced him to pull away from her.

He cut his gaze away, afraid she would read the distress in his eyes. Intentionally Max settled on the floor, against the wall, putting distance between them. Jag passed out drinks and then joined him.

The two men sat there, eating in silence, listening to the women bond as Karen shared details about Jaguar Ranch. Changing subjects, Karen shifted the conversation to Sarah's personal life. "How long have you been able to talk to spirits?"

"Actually, they talk to me," Sarah said. "I can't really talk back, though I try. I was twelve when it started. The same age as my mother and her mother before her. I have an older brother, but he's normal and, believe me, he likes it that way."

"Interesting that only the females carry the gift," Karen said. "Des's mate, Jessica, can sense evil. A person you and I might think seems perfectly nice will put her nerves on edge. She's remarkably accurate, too."

"Really?" Sarah said. "She'd be great to have around on an investigation."

"You won't get her without Des right by her side," Karen commented and eyed Jag. "Like Jag, he's quite protective."

Max watched Sarah closely as Karen talked, understanding how Des felt. He wanted to protect Sarah. Exactly the reason he had to push her away. Part of him said claiming her would contain his dark side, and that passing the test would then be ensured. But the other part of him, the part that logic ruled, knew he couldn't take a risk with Sarah's future.

"You've heard nothing from Kate since Marisol helped you sleep?" Jag asked, his long legs stretched in front of him as he reached for a bag and pulled out a second burger.

Sarah shook her head. "Nothing yet."

"What does that mean?" Karen questioned, her expression concerned. "Is something wrong with her? Did the demon spirits get to her?"

"I don't think it's anything like that," Sarah assured her. "Spirits only communicate when they have something important to say. My guess is the information she had before was time-sensitive. It's too late for it to matter now."

"That doesn't sound good," Karen mused. "It must have been important. Why else would demon spirits try to stop the communication?"

"You think Allen has the stones already?" Jag asked.

"I don't know," Sarah said, leaning forward to set her drink on the nightstand. "But Cathy mentioned that the ritual Vars would need to perform should be held on a full moon. That gives us only a little more than a week to track down Allen. Between Cathy's mother and Kate, I'm praying we get some leads." Her lips thinned slightly. "Kate was trying to tell me something about a location last night. I remember that much, but nothing more. And even if I remember the location, I don't remember the relevance it has."

"If it were still important, Kate would tell you again though, right?" Max asked.

"That's usually how it works," she confirmed. "The spirits are quite forceful and determined when they want me to understand a particular detail. Then again, I have this nagging feeling whatever she told me last night was important, and she can't, or won't, contact me again right now. She might be afraid these demon spirits will hurt me again."

"The full moon will be here before we know it," Jag pointed out. "We have nothing to go on and only a short time to find answers." He discarded half a burger into a bag, and pushed to his feet. "We should get going."

"I hope Cathy is right about the full moon," Karen said. "It seems that Vars has left us more time to counter his threat than I would have expected."

"It's not a long time when we have no clues," Max reminded her. "And Vars didn't intend for anyone to catch on to his plan."

"I'll call Cathy's mom," Sarah offered. "We can talk to her about the timelines to confirm Cathy's thoughts. I'll try to get her to talk on the phone, though. I think it's about a three-hour drive to Dallas from here."

Karen reached out and touched Sarah's hand. "Jag has a few special talents himself. When you make that call tell her you'll be right over. As in *right* over. No travel time. No drive."

Sarah blinked. "What? How?"

A smile touched Karen's lips. "Jag has this nifty little ability to transport through space in a blink of an eye. Unfortunately, he can transport only two at once. I'll get back to the ranch and help research the Shadow Masters while Jag takes you two to see Cathy's mother. I believe Des and a team of Knights should already be in Nowhere by now, so you can feel confident your friends will be well looked after. Des is one of our best Knights."

Sarah's eyes were wide as she glanced at Max. "Can *you* do that?"

"Ah, no," he said. "If I could, I'd have gotten us the hell out of Nowhere a long time before I did."

"You know," she commented, "it's kind of nice not to be the only one who's different. Around you all, I feel almost normal." Max's eyes held hers, and beside him, he could feel Jag's approval. Jag had done this on purpose, trying to motivate Max to conquer this test by letting him see what life could be like when the test was behind him. But what Jag didn't understand was that Max had to look out for Sarah—in best case and worst case scenarios. He had to be sure he was on the other side of this test before he pulled her close and kept her there.

Karen and Jag departed, leaving a file behind with all the research Karen and Jessica had done so far on Vars and various other topics that they thought might be helpful. Max rested against the door, keeping his distance from Sarah as she spoke on the phone with Cathy's mother, Sheryl.

"Okay," Sarah said after ending the call. "We're set. She expects us and she's willing to help. Of course, she's worried about Cathy. If we don't convince Sheryl that her daughter is safe, she'll take off after her." Her gaze probed his features. "You look tired. You didn't sleep at all, did you?"

He shrugged. "I wanted to be alert in case I needed to call Marisol back for you."

"Thank you, Max," she said softly. "I hate that you did that, though. I can see you're tired. You need rest."

She stood and he prayed she'd keep her distance. Especially since her concern touched him, weakening his resolve to push her away. No one worried about him. No one. Not even in his human life. It had always been his brother, the heir to his father's title, that his parents had worried for.

"I'll rest when this is over," he said, his voice low, a bit gruff from emotion. She took another step—she was too close. He held up a staying hand. "Stop. Sarah." He inhaled her soft feminine scent. It wasn't perfume that teased his senses, it was the sweetness of Sarah, his mate, his woman. "I told you I can't be near you."

"And I told you I'm not afraid of you."

She took another step and he acted out of desperation to keep his resolve, acted before he talked himself out of it. He gently shackled her arms with enough force to startle her, maneuvering her so that he placed her back against the wall.

Max pinned Sarah's hands over her head, his thighs framing hers, trapping her legs, his hips pressed snugly against hers. Instantly, his groin tightened, desire licking at his limbs, at his cock—his willpower fading away. But he had to be strong, to let her see his dark side, and not allow himself to cave to temptation.

His mouth lingered above her ear, his primal side alive, hungry for her. "Fear me or you're a fool," he rasped softly.

"You can't hurt me," she countered, her voice quivering ever so slightly. "You said so. Karen said so, too."

He leaned back and looked her in the eyes. "I lied. Think about it, Sarah. What if there isn't enough human left in me to properly mate? What if I bite you and the beast takes too much blood and kills you?"

Seconds ticked by. She narrowed her gaze on him, her eyes full of confusion, her scrutiny intense. Her voice low, taut. "This isn't working, Max. I told you I can sense your emotions, just like I do the spirits that communicate with me. You're lying and you hate yourself for it. Why? Why are you doing this?"

"You might know the human, little Sarah," he purred, nipping her lobe with his teeth, "but you don't know the beast."

Her chin lifted in defiance, but her voice quavered. "You're not a Beast."

"Are you sure?" he asked, leaning back to let her see the challenge in his expression. "I don't know what Karen told you but look into my eyes, Sarah. See the yellow? Did you know many of the Beasts have yellow in their red eyes? I'm so close to my dark side, even my physical appearance is changing."

She shook her head, rejecting his words. "Lots of people—*human* people—have yellow in their eyes, Max."

"But those humans aren't four hundred years old with a soul as black as hell. You want to know why I'm being tested?" He felt a muscle jump in his jaw, his admission hard to muster. "I killed a human, Sarah." He gave her no time to respond. "I killed a man and I don't even remember doing it. The beast had total, complete control. I. Don't. Remember."

He dropped her arms, forcing himself to take a step back from her, hating the tears he saw welling in her eyes. "So now you know. I'm no different than the demon that took your parents and your friend. I killed, too."

She hugged herself, her body shaking, though she gave him a steady look, her eyes pinning his in a probing stare. "Why did you kill this person?"

"Who and why doesn't matter."

Her voice raised in demand. "Why, Max?"

A knock sounded on the door. "Jag's back. We need to go."

Awareness rushed over Max—Beasts. They never attacked in a public place without killing all witnesses. The hotel was in the middle of open country, which left them exposed to a Darkland attack.

"Who, Max?" Sarah persisted, unaware of Max's shift of attention to the imminent threat. She turned to the door as she said, "I'll ask Jag."

Sarah flipped the lock and Max grabbed her, tossing her behind him, and not as gently as he would have liked. He simply wanted her alive and well, out of harm's way.

He flung open the door, blades already drawn, finding Jag in heavy combat with the Beasts. Max didn't hesitate. This is what he did—what he was born to do. He attacked.

Chapter 16

Sarah found herself stumbling and falling to the hotel floor, stunned to have been shoved away by Max. Even more stunned to see him pull his blades and charge out the door. Something told her she was about to meet a Beast up close and personal, and after those Hounds, she didn't want to do it unarmed.

Pushing to her feet, she scrambled toward the closet where she'd seen Max's bag. He'd have weapons, she was sure of it. She had taken only a few steps when a snarl drew her attention. She turned, her eyes going wide at the creature standing in the doorway—with half its face distorted, and one eye bigger than the other. She noted the yellowish red eyes, and her stomach clenched as she recalled Max's yellow-flecked eyes. She barely had time to take in the vinyl-looking suit the Beast wore, the long fangs, and wild mass of hair, before the Beast stumbled forward, Max on its back.

"Lock yourself in the bathroom," Max yelled, as he landed on the ground, on top of the Beast.

Sarah darted to the closet, instead, to search for a gun. Adrenaline pumped through her body with such force she could feel her stomach in her chest. She couldn't imagine how Max could take the Beast's head in this tiny room. He'd never have the room to swing wide enough. A gun would at least slow the Beast down long enough to drag it out of here. She hoped.

With desperation in her actions, she grabbed the bag in the closet and dug, relief washing over her as she found a loaded Glock. Her relief faded as she turned to find Max's back to her. She couldn't fire at the Beast without hitting Max. Sarah held the gun in ready position, searching for an opportunity; there just wasn't one.

"Jag!" she screamed, and repeated his name several times, praying for help. A good move because suddenly Jag was there. He came up behind the Beast and wrapped his arms around him. A second later he orbed out of the room, taking the Beast with him.

Max whirled around, eyes wild with concern as he focused on Sarah. "Tell me you're okay."

"I am!" She pointed. "Go help Jag!"

Max was on the move before she ever finished her sentence. She ran after him, clutching the gun—a tiny comfort she embraced wholeheartedly. But, thankfully, she didn't need it. When she joined them, Max and Jag had already destroyed the enemies, the last one going up in flames as she watched, before turning to ash. Her eyes went wide as she realized their fancy vinyl-looking suits turned to ash, too. She didn't ask how. She knew how. Magic.

Jag scanned the surrounding area as he and Max quickly sheathed their weapons. "I don't see any witnesses, but I'm going to check closer to be certain. We may need Marisol to wipe some memories."

Max inhaled and scrubbed his jaw. His voice was low, tense. "I know it's crazy, but I had the distinct feeling William was here."

Jag considered Max for a moment. Sarah didn't know who William was, but she could tell he was important to Max.

"Never ignore your senses," Jag responded, offering no further insight to clear up William's identity for Sarah.

Jag continued, "They came for your woman."

The sound of Jag calling her Max's woman sent a dart of heat through her limbs, despite her confused emotions about Max right now. She'd seen the Beasts, seen their eyes. She'd endured Max's assurance that he, too, was a Beast. It was hard not to feel a bit of apprehension, even fear.

She inhaled and forced herself to focus on the reason for the attack, not the personal side of this situation. She could see why the Beasts would want her dead. "They don't want Kate to talk to me," she whispered, the gun easing to her side.

Jag's eyes narrowed on Sarah, his stare potent, packing a punch. "Know this, Sarah," he said softly. "You are far more than a link to information. Max has resisted the call of his beast when others have not. His soul is a prize to our enemy. Destroying you would take away his hope of ever escaping the darkness—it would destroy him." His gaze shifted back to Max. "Which is why you had to save Jessica that day, Max. Had you let her die, Des would be gone now. We both know he lived too close to his beast." A second passed, then another, tension crackling in the air. "Don't forget what you did for your fellow Knight, your brother-in-arms. I won't, nor will Des. And I assure you, Salvador won't, either."

Jag walked away then, leaving Sarah and Max to face each other. Their eyes locked. Sarah felt the contact from head to toe and deeper—in her soul. He didn't speak, and she knew he was waiting for some sort of reaction from her. She couldn't find words no matter how hard she tried. There was so much to take in and try to understand. She didn't want to say the wrong thing.

Moments ticked by, and Max made a frustrated sound. "Pack up," he said. "I want the van loaded so we're mobile if needed." She felt the bitterness lacing his words and stepped backward with the impact. He'd wanted something from her, though she wasn't sure what. Something she hadn't given. He was confusing her. One minute, he made love to her, the next he pushed her away. Now, he seemed to want her to come to him.

Breaking eye contact, she turned away to do as he said, heading to the room to be alone with her internal struggles. She had to think. It was as simple as that. Images of those Beasts taunted her. The idea of one of them controlling Max made her almost sick. She could see that he was close to the edge; she'd even sensed it while he was fighting. There had been a primal ferocity to him while he fought, whereas Jag had seemed to be more warrior than Beast. Deep in her heart, Sarah knew that if she didn't complete this mating soon, it would be too late for Max. He wouldn't last much longer.

God, how she wanted to talk to Karen again, to understand more about mating. She needed more time to get to know Max, too, to understand him and his world. Sarah looked skyward. *Give me a little time. Please. And then let me make the right choices.* Sarah let her hands fall to her lap and ran her palms down her jeans. If she caused anyone else to get hurt, she'd be the one who deserved to be in the ground. She'd certainly be living in her own personal form of hell.

With Jag in between her and Max, his hand on each of their arms, the three of them appeared at their destination—Cathy's mother's home, on the front porch.

As Jag had promised Sarah, their travel experience was uneventful, and she found herself staring at the door of Sheryl's home. Despite the ease of the experience, her nerves were still rattled from the events back at the hotel. And despite Max being a big part of what caused those nerves, her first reaction was to look at Max, to share this new experience with him. She received a guarded look in return, an expression that was shielded, but no doubt cold. She'd pushed him away; now he pushed her away. They seemed to be having a tug-of-war, and she didn't like it. Unbidden, a feeling of loss washed over her—fear that she'd lost him when she'd not even found him fully yet. This didn't work for her. She had to clear the air and soon.

Doing her best to shake off the way his coldness bothered her, Sarah quickly eyed her surroundings, concerned that the neighbors might have seen them "pop" into view. But no worries—she found the porch enclosed and hidden from easy viewing.

"Has anyone ever caught you doing this?" she asked Jag. "You know—one minute you aren't here and the next you are?"

Amusement danced in Jag's eyes. "No, and I don't plan to be caught. I choose my landing spots with care."

"I'd ask how you do that, but I'm sure the answer would be as unbelievable as the gift." She stepped to the door, making a mental note to ask him the question another time when they weren't in peril.

Sarah started to knock when the door flew open to reveal an older version of Cathy with much longer dark hair, but the same big brown eyes and adorable features. Sheryl Wilburt wore a long, cream-colored, fitted dress that flattered her slim figure, showing off her curves without being too snug.

"Sarah!" Sheryl said, pulling her into a hug. Sarah had met Sheryl once before and often took her calls at the office, so they had a comfort level together. "Tell me what's going on. I've been worried sick." She leaned back to look at Sarah, her voice cracking a bit. "Tell me Cathy is okay. I need to hear it again. And Edward? Is he any better?"

"Cathy is fine," Sarah said, hoping it was still true. "And there is no change in Edward. Both are well guarded." She hesitated, as she indicated the two men framing her with their big bodies. "Just as you can see I am."

"Absolutely, ma'am," Max said, surprising Sarah. She got the feeling he really understood Sheryl's fear for her daughter as he added, "We have some of our best men with Cathy and Edward. They'll be taken care of."

Sheryl shifted her attention to Max, feminine appreciation flashing in her eyes, and Sarah introduced him. They shook hands and murmured a greeting. "Max has been working closely with our team on this particular case." Sarah motioned to Jag next. "And this is Jag. He heads the team that Max works for."

Sheryl's gaze narrowed just a bit on Jag, before she accepted his hand. "What kind of team would that be?"

"Similar to mine," Sarah responded, smiling, quick to ease Sheryl's mind of any concerns and take the pressure off the men to respond. "Only with a lot more brawn."

A tiny laugh bubbled from Sheryl's throat. "I can see that." She lowered her voice for Sarah's ears only and added, "Interesting company you're keeping these days." Then to all of them she said, "Come in." Motioning them forward as she stepped back into the house, she gave them room to enter.

Sarah went first, with Max and Jag behind her. Once in the hallway, they followed Sheryl into a living room decorated in warm blues with a brick fireplace in the center. Sarah sat on the couch next to Sheryl and Max sat on the matching love seat to her direct left. Jag walked to the mantel and looked up at the picture of a mighty-looking archangel hanging as the centerpiece.

He glanced over his shoulder at Sheryl. "You like Michael, I see."

"Michael is a brave warrior," Sheryl explained. "I feel safe with him around."

"I'm a bit partial to Raphael myself," Jag said, leaning an elbow on the ledge beneath the picture. "Raphael is a healer of earth and humanity."

Sarah and Max exchanged a look and she almost thought she saw a hint of a smile on his lips, his dark mood seeming to lighten a bit. "But Raphael isn't a warrior by nature," Sheryl countered.

"That's true," Jag agreed, looking impressed with her knowledge. "He raises his sword reluctantly, but no less efficiently."

Sheryl tilted her head. "You know your archangels."

"As do you," Jag replied. "You practice angel magic." It wasn't a question.

"My family is rich in inbred magic, though how we practice those gifts may vary. Angel magic just happens to be what speaks to me." She directed a grave look at Sarah and directed the conversation to her obvious worries. "Talk to me, Sarah. What was so dangerous that it couldn't be discussed on the phone?"

Sarah took a moment to explain the situation with Vars and Allen. The minute Sarah said Shadow Masters, Sheryl paled.

"There are stories," she said. "None of them good. Some from sources that make me believe it's true. Three men who sold their souls for wealth and power, even immortality. Their souls are said to be locked inside the magical stones. These Masters are said to be dark powers in the magic world, all able to kill you with a mere spoken word."

"I'm remembering something," Sarah said, shutting her eyes, trying to focus on what Kate had tried to communicate in the cabin. "The stones hold the souls. The demon wants the souls released from the stones so he can use them somehow to free himself." She looked at Sheryl. "Does that sound right?"

Sheryl nodded. "I've heard stories that seem to support that conclusion. It's also said that the Masters use the stones to perform black magic, and that the power collected by those stones is immense. If their souls are released, the demon would have that power to use for his own purposes."

"Such as freeing himself," Jag stated. "Any idea how Allen would be involved? How he would get the Masters to release their souls?"

"None," Sheryl said. "And honestly, I can't be certain of any of this. I am simply making educated guesses. I would conclude that the Masters will die when their souls are freed, though. Allen must be the carrier who delivers them to this demon." Sadness flashed across her face. "Poor Allen. It sounds like all he really wants is his wife back. The pain of losing a loved one can be a dangerous thing."

Sarah barely kept her eyes from Max's but she knew Sheryl's words had to touch him as much as they did her. They'd both felt that pain. Both had felt the desperation of grief, too.

"Do you have any idea who these Masters are?" Sarah asked, hoping for some semblance of a lead.

Sheryl shook her head, her lips tight. "You can't go asking questions about these men. If they're real—and I believe they are—they'll kill you before you get any-where near them."

Sarah grabbed Sheryl's hand. "If we don't find them, a lot more people will die than just us. There has to be someone we can go to who can help? Someone who can be trusted?"

Sheryl swallowed hard, her apprehension palpable. Seconds passed, and somehow they all knew to leave her be, not to press. Finally, she pushed to her feet and left the room. Sarah glanced at the men, their expressions seeming to indicate they were feeling the same uncertainty she was. Her gaze lingered on Max. His hair had a windblown look, a bit too long, a bit too wild. A bit too sexy and distracting. And as his eyes met hers, she saw through the cold shell he had enclosed himself in, saw a moment of tenderness.

Sheryl returned in a scurry of movement, and handed Sarah a piece of paper. "This is opening a door I shut tight, but if you go to this man and tell him I sent you, he will help you. I'm sure he will call me to confirm and that's…expected." She hesitated. "He is dangerous, Sarah, but he wants to please me." Her gaze went to Max who now stood behind Sarah. "Still, he's volatile. His mood can turn dark quickly. Get in and get out." She shut her eyes. "There was a time when the dark side of magic touched me more than I like to admit. I'd appreciate it if you didn't share that with Cathy. I've taught her to learn about the dark side of magic as a way of defending herself against it, and that's the right reason. She has no idea I learned about it for the wrong reasons. After her father left us, I needed someone who actually accepted our world. Someone who embraced magic. I swear, I didn't know—"

Sarah squeezed her hand. "Don't do this to yourself," she said. "You have nothing to be ashamed of. Honestly, I think you should tell Cathy because she loves you and she'll be there for you. But I won't break your trust." Concerned for Sheryl's safety, Sarah asked, "What will happen once you open this door?"

"You just stop this demon from rising," she said, stiffening her spine, her resolve firming as Sarah watched. "I can handle myself. Don't underestimate Caden, though. He knew my family had a strong foot in magic. He wanted the power he thought us joining could bring him. The man is gifted with dark magic no human should possess. It's downright frightening. But if these Shadow Masters exist, he'll know how to find them."

Sarah had the feeling Sheryl was opening herself to painful repercussions by letting them use her name with Caden. "Thank you."

"Thank me by getting my daughter out of that town safely." She eyed the men at that point. "I'm talking to all of you now."

The men were quick to promise their protection as Sheryl walked them all to the door. After hugging Sheryl goodbye, Sarah stood on the porch with Jag and Max by her side. She looked at the piece of paper that held the name *Caden Neil* and a Houston address.

"Houston," Sarah said holding up the paper for them to see.

"This could get us no place fast," Max said. "I know you're worried about the men, Jag. Houston's only a few hours from the inn. Sarah and I can drive it."

"Once I'm inside Nowhere, we can't guarantee communication," Jag cautioned. "You'll be on your own."

"Just make sure Allen doesn't get back to that cabin if he makes it back to town," Max said. "What we're doing may or may not lead anywhere."

Jag gave a slow nod of approval and looked at Sarah, offering her his arm so he could orb them back to the van. "Ready to go?"

She remembered the conversation she'd had with Karen about Max believing in himself. And she thought of the care he'd shown for Sheryl, for her team, for everyone but himself. Suddenly, it felt very important he know she saw the human in him, not the beast.

Sarah reached for Max's hand, her gaze finding his. Without words, she hoped he saw the message in her eyes—that she was with him, ready to fight. He couldn't push her away.

When she saw the ice of his stare melting, she knew she'd at least touched some part of his emotions. She turned to Jag and took his arm. "Now I am."

Jag's eyes warmed and she took strength in his obvious approval. She turned back to Max, the man who'd taken her life by storm. Her hand tightened on his, as his did on hers, their palms melting together as their bodies had only hours before.

And in that moment, as Jag orbed them back to the van, they were united, no barriers, no worries—just the two of them, no matter what the future held.

As they stood beside the van, Max knew he should let go of Sarah's hand and push her away. After all, his plan was to scare her off, not draw her close. But as he wished Jag a farewell, he couldn't seem to find the will.

"I'll check in with Karen every twelve hours and you do the same," Jag instructed Max. "If I don't hear from you, I'll try to find you based on the last update you left. At least that leaves us with some form of communication."

"And if you don't check in?"

"Karen will contact Salvador and give you instructions," Jag replied. "Unless you're told otherwise, stay your path if it feels productive." He grabbed Max's shoulder. "Be safe, my friend." With a nod, he indicated Sarah. "And take good care of our newest recruit here." He stepped back from them and disappeared.

Max turned to face Sarah, not sure what to say. She let go of his hand and stepped back from him, grabbing the keys from her pocket. "I'm driving so you can sleep."

For a moment he considered insisting that he drive, but decided she'd call him macho and she'd be right. He was exhausted, plain and simple. "A little shut-eye would do me good." She smiled her approval and climbed in the van. Once Max was inside, he leaned his seat back. "If anything seems wrong, if you get even a slight vibe of trouble—"

Sarah inserted the key and turned on the engine. "I'll scream, you'll jerk away and draw your blades, and we'll do battle. Got it." She cast him a warning look. "Lie down and go to sleep."

He did as she said, secretly smiling at her bossy attitude, enjoying it more than he should. Enjoying it because she was once again genuinely concerned about him.

And with that secret smile, he drifted off to sleep, hoping to wake with a clear mind and a solution to all their problems. A way to save lives, including his own. A way to make him and Sarah more than a fantasy.

Chapter 17

They'd been on the road about two hours when the sun set. A traffic jam had caused them to lose an hour sitting on the highway. Max had been in and out of sleep the entire time, occasionally sitting up to check on things and then sliding back into a nightmare. She knew they were nightmares because of the way she felt his emotions. It really was quite hard to get used to her sensitivity to him. Being sensitive to spirits had become a way of life, and it only came during their brief visits. But with Max, she got his emotional feed pretty much all the time. And boy, was it intense. He still had plenty of human in him. She didn't doubt that now. He also had a lot of pain that needed healing.

Another rush of feelings came over her, and this

time it was so turbulent, so full of anguish and hurt, that she tensed, fingers turning white as she gripped the steering wheel.

"William," Max murmured, his head tossing from side to side. "No!"

Her chest tightened, stomach queasy. He was dreaming of the day his family was murdered. She knew because this is what she felt when she dreamt of hers dying. He quieted, but he made a jerky movement with his hand. "William!" Then he shouted louder as he sat up and grabbed the dash, "William!"

They'd entered a tiny town and were about to pass a small ice-cream and burger joint on the right. Sarah whipped into the driveway and stopped the car.

She quickly reached for him. "Max," Sarah whispered, careful not to startle him, not sure how he would react. "You're having a nightmare. Just a nightmare." Her hand stroked his arm, offering comfort.

He blinked and turned to look at her, his eyes narrowing, focusing. "What happened?" Surveying the surroundings, he shook his head as if to clear the cobwebs and ran a rough hand through his hair. "I didn't even know we'd stopped. I should have been more alert."

"You had a nightmare," she said softly, her hand moving up and down his arm. "One of many in the past two hours. You were screaming a name—William."

Darkness flashed across his handsome features, and he dropped back on the seat. "My brother."

"I assumed as much," she said. "You answered a question for me today."

He glanced her way. "What would that be?"

"The nightmares never end. I had hoped with enough time they would."

"No," he agreed, turning away again. "They never end."

"Want to talk about it?"

Max laughed at her question, the sound bitter even to his own ears. "No. Reliving that day every time I sleep is enough."

Beside him, Sarah reclined her seat, and he glanced over to see her lean back and shut her eyes. She didn't press him for more information, didn't press him period. She simply lay there with him, for him, and he knew it. No one had ever been there for him. Not even in his human life.

He stared up at the roof of the van, replaying the nightmare, and somehow he just started talking. Still, he didn't look at her. He kept his focus on the plain black ceiling.

"I grew up in England, a part of the English nobility. My brother was the oldest, the one who'd inherit my father's title. I never cared about titles and social functions as they did." He made a frustrated sound. "That's something I've never missed."

"You don't have an English accent," she observed.

"I've had centuries to shed that accent," he reminded her, eyeing the ceiling again. In a corner of his mind, he knew this conversation compromised his plans to push her away. He should be cold, quiet, working to keep her at a distance where he couldn't hurt her. Instead, he kept talking.

Her voice was soft, gently prodding. "I think you mentioned your brother became a Beast?"

"We both did, but William wasn't saved. Salvador…"

He cast her a sideways look and explained, "That's the one who created the Knights—he's a direct descendant to Raphael." He continued, "Salvador said it wasn't William's destiny to join me. Nothing more. No matter how many times I ask, that's what I get. Everyone loved William. It makes no sense. None."

Sarah reached for his hand. "Max." He turned to look at her, sucking in a breath at the tenderness in her gaze as she sympathized, "I understand how you feel. Why didn't the demon kill me? Why my family? My friend? Not knowing tears me up inside." Darkness enclosed the van as nighttime fell around them, shadowing her expression. But he heard the anguish in her voice. "Deep down I want to believe my survival had a purpose, but it's been hard. You're part of the Knights, and they give you a purpose."

More than anything, he wanted to pull her close and kiss her, to believe he would beat this test, to believe he could be with his Sarah and control his inner beast.

"Sarah," he murmured, his body turning toward hers, his willpower fading. The air crackled with their shared attraction, the moments that passed potent as they leaned toward each other. They froze as Max's cell phone rang.

Max eyed the screen caller ID. "It's Karen." He hit the answer button and listened a minute. "Cathy?" His gaze went to Sarah. "Before you ask, she's fine. Nothing has changed."

Sarah visibly relaxed. Max held up a finger and listened. A few seconds later he hung up. He motioned to the restaurant. "Let's grab some food before we get back on the road, and I'll fill you in."

"All right then," she said, and reached for her door.

They walked side by side toward the restaurant, and he wished like hell they could be that way for a lifetime.

A few minutes later they sat together in a tiny booth eating burgers and fries again. Sarah listened as Max explained the details of Karen's call, which had been badly timed. She'd wanted him to kiss her—one more second and he would have.

"Marisol can sense magical abilities. Not the kind a human creates but inborn talents. The minute she met Cathy, she knew she was special. Most of the women who come into our circle come from certain bloodlines. Angelic bloodlines. Karen is researching to see if either or both of you are on the list we hold. Des's mate is on the list."

Sarah's eyes went wide. "Angelic bloodlines?" She shook her head. "Unbelievable." She would have asked more questions, but there were simply too many and too little time. "Does Cathy know any of this?"

Max dipped a fry in ketchup. "Marisol has talked to her." He leaned back in his seat. "Marisol hopes she can funnel Cathy's abilities into her own and dispel the demon that is possessing Edward. So far no go, but they're working on it."

"Do we know what Cathy's abilities are?"

"Not yet." He drew a sip off his straw and swallowed. "The good news is that Karen felt Cathy and Marisol were making progress on how to help Edward."

This made Sarah think of Vars. "Anything going on inside the town?"

"Jag visited Karen right after he reviewed the town's situation. It's quiet there—eerily so. He's convinced the Sheriff to keep the town on lockdown, so the residents won't be walking targets for the Beasts. He confirmed the Beasts have taken positions on the outskirts, intending to trap us inside the perimeter of the populated area. But we're ready. We have Knights in position behind their Beasts. We'll know when they move, and we'll hit them from behind."

"So we're talking an all-out war zone forming," Sarah said, a chill racing up her spine at the thought of how many might die.

"We'll try to keep the battle away from populated areas," he said, and eyed their food. "Right now, we better finish up and get on the road. I'd like to talk to this Caden person tonight. The sooner we get answers, the better."

Sarah nodded her head and reached for her burger. She couldn't agree more. It seemed that everyone she cared for had somehow become linked to the destiny of a town called Nowhere.

Adrian appeared in the back of the underground temple, a shrine to the royalty of the Underworld. Unbeknownst to those inside the temple, his Beasts surrounded the upstairs club, ensuring the property was secure from unwanted visitors.

Low chants filled the air, evil enough to be downright sensual as far as Adrian was concerned. Caden Neil, a sorcerer dark enough to be murmured about in the Underworld, stood in the front of the room, speaking to hundreds of humans who wore long black robes, their hoods covering their faces. To the humans who followed him, he was "The Dark One" capable of inhuman acts no man should be allowed to perform.

It didn't surprise Adrian that Vars had chosen Caden

to aid Allen's efforts to free him. Century after century, Caden's ancestors had made pacts with the Underworld.

Caden called out to the room of eager listeners. "The Shadow Masters are delivering to us the ultimate power of a great Underworld leader," he announced. "This leader will soon be with us.

"He will bring wrath on those foolish enough to turn away from him. Bring wealth and pleasure to those who whisper his name with praise and devotion. Vars is the name of this great demon prince."

The chants changed to the name. "Vars, Vars, Vars…"

Adrian ground his teeth. He wanted those chants to be for him, not for Vars. These people would know the truth of who had the power, he vowed, and they would know soon. He would take Vars's legion of demon spirits and make these people, every last one of them, know his name. Right after he made The Knights of White wish they hadn't raised a blade to fight his Beasts. Adrian would destroy the Knights just as he would destroy Vars.

As for Caden Neil, he served the wrong master and for that there was only one solution—when this was over, Caden would die.

He watched as the three Shadow Masters stepped forward, taking center stage, the ritual beginning. For six days, they would be treated as gods, worshipped, prepared, pleasured—the sexual magic feeding the stones' powers, feeding the stones' magic. By the end of day six, the stones would glow with energy, ready to transfer the souls of their masters into the vial around Allen's neck. The Shadow Masters let their robes drop to the floor, all displaying the naked muscular bodies of thirty-year-old men, when none of them were a day younger than fifty. They'd bargained with their souls for a life of luxury, a life where youth never ended nor did the money and sex. They thought their life in hell would be the same, but they knew not what they were dealing with. They would live in a prison, sex slaves for the Underworld royalty, used to service their wants and desires. Three robed women stepped forward, untying their garments and letting them fall to the floor, displaying their sensual curves. Adrian leaned against the wall; his anger faded as he prepared to watch the orgy. Perhaps he'd even join in.

He might not be a king in the Underworld, not even a prince, but here on earth, he could have anything, or anyone he wanted. He pointed at two hooded figures, knowing instinctively they were beautiful women. They turned to him, his magic controlling their minds. Their robes fell to the ground, lush curves, full breasts, displayed for his enjoyment. He pointed at a third female, drawing her forward. He would need more than two women this night, perhaps more than three. Because, yes, he could have anyone, anything, he wanted here on earth, but it simply wasn't enough anymore.

He drew the women close and then flashed them out of the room, refusing to take his pleasure in a place where Vars was being worshipped.

Allen stood in the corner of the room, watching as the robes fell to the ground, watching as bodies pressed to bodies. He didn't want to be aroused, didn't want to be involved. But he was here, and he *was* aroused—and he hated himself for it. Hated how disloyal to Kate that made him. He'd not touched another woman since her death. Yet, despite his guilt, his eyes fixed on a particular woman as she rubbed her voluptuous curves against her partner's body like a cat in heat.

Caden appeared before him then, blocking his view, still wearing his robe, his short dark hair covered by a hood. His black eyes piercing as they fixed Allen in a stare. He and Allen were the only ones among hundreds who remained clothed.

"The stones won't work without feeding their power," Caden proclaimed. "If you want your precious Kate back, forget your guilt and find pleasure." He stepped to the side, giving Allen a view of the woman again, just in time to see the man fondling her breast, her long red hair spread over creamy-white shoulders. "If you want her, she is yours."

Caden narrowed his gaze on Allen's features. "And you do want her. I can damn near taste your lust. This isn't a game. This is about power. The power to give life to those stones. If you want Kate, then fuck the woman and do it well."

Caden snapped his fingers and the woman looked at him. She was too far away to have heard the snap. Allen knew Caden had somehow bidden her attention with magic. The gorgeous beauty stared at Caden for several seconds, and then smiled, pushing out of the arms of her lover and walking toward Allen.

Allen damn near choked on his tongue trying to object, but no words would come. He glanced at Caden and saw the evil smile on his thin lips. He'd done something to Allen to silence him. And it was too late to object, anyway. The woman leaned into him and took his hands, filling his palms with her breasts. "Tell me what you want," she purred, her lips brushing his jaw.

"Kate," he whispered in his mind, but as the woman started to rub against him, he found himself kissing the redheaded seductress, fighting an internal battle to push her away, to cling to Kate. But as seconds passed, so did his memories. All he could think about was here and now. Kate began to fade, and he fought the cries of his body for satisfaction. And when his robe came off and he could fight no more, he promised himself this was for Kate. This was to empower the stones. To bring back Kate. She'd understand. She always understood him. She was Kate.

Chapter 18

Caden was no place to be found. A visit to his house had found no one present, aside from the two armed guards outside the grounds, which sent a pretty clear message—Caden had something to hide.

Now, near midnight, Max pushed open the door to the high-rise hotel room and tried not to think about the single bed the overbooked hotel had offered.

Seemingly unaffected by the intimate setting, Sarah went straight to the bed and sat down, her scent lifting in her wake, taunting him with its sweetness. Max inhaled that soft smell despite his best efforts not to, his body warming, firing his desire to reach for her. They'd only just entered the room, and he was already fighting temptation. It was going to be one hell of a long night.

Max hesitated by the closet, staring at Sarah as she reached for the menu lying on the bedside table. Thinking of what it would be like to be in that bed with her, naked, making love. His groin tightened and his gums tingled. Damn. His mating instincts were wildly out of control if a simple fantasy could make his cuspids start to emerge. He squeezed his eyes shut as though that would block the images playing in his head. But there was no blocking them. No hiding.

He would not touch her, would not make love to her—absolutely would not claim her as his mate. Max murmured these words in his head as he tracked across the hotel room. Sliding into the chair behind a tiny corner desk, he cut his gaze from Sarah. *Focus on work,* he told himself. *Focus on work.*

Trying to distract himself, he cataloged the room as he booted up his computer: blue drapes; blue floral comforter; tan rugs; and a nightstand by the bed. Tight confined quarters. Intimate lighting perfect for making love. He ground his teeth and looked back at his computer. Work. He needed to get lost in work.

Needed to get lost in anything but Sarah.

"They have a twenty-four-hour menu that amounts to pizza," she commented. "Is that okay?" He nodded stiffly and she asked hopefully, "Pepperoni?"

He managed a smile despite the rage of desire pumping through his body. "My favorite."

"Excellent," she said, her eyes lighting up as she reached for the phone.

Max inhaled and turned away from her, trying to make the act of powering up his computer absorbing enough to block out his desire for Sarah. A feat that proved impossible as he listened to her talk on the phone, her soft voice sensual and far too arousing.

When she finished placing the order, he could feel her attention, feel her eyes on him. But he didn't look up, didn't dare invite further contact until he'd reined in his lust. Only when the knock sounded on the door, to indicate their order had arrived, did he dare turn in Sarah's direction and push to his feet. He made fast work of paying for the order and returned to set the pizza on the bed.

And then he sat down at the desk and drew a deep breath, forcing logic into his mind. Finding Caden and stopping Vars were his objectives. These things were imperative if he wanted a future with Sarah, a part of his test—he felt it in his core. He had to pull himself together. Clarity came with those conclusions, and slowly the tension in his body eased enough for him to eat.

The next hour was filled with remarkably comfortable silence; their fingers tapping the keyboards were the only sounds between them. On some level, Sarah seemed to sense, and even understand, his need to keep to himself. A good hour after they'd finished off the last of the pizza, Sarah straightened a bit and began tapping the keyboard more rapidly, explaining her sudden spike of energy as she typed. "I've been scanning these occult sites and several of them referenced 'The Dark One,'" she commented, hitting a few more keys and then looking up at him. "After some digging, I found another reference—this one to 'Caden—The Dark One.'"

Max rotated in his chair to face her, his attention piqued. "Sheryl made it clear this guy is involved in the dark arts. That doesn't seem surprising."

"Not until you hear the rest," Sarah said. "There's a reference related to Caden and some underground worship ceremony that is invitation only. I don't have a location or any details, but—" she raised a finger, her voice lifting as she added, "here's the kicker. It's this week. I think Caden is more than a source of information. I think he's the one helping Allen."

"It makes sense," Max agreed. "And no matter how much Sheryl swore Caden would talk to us, the fear I saw in that woman's face spoke a warning beyond her words." Which brought him back to the need to find Caden. "He's not going to be at work tomorrow. He'd be smarter than that. He'll be in hiding until this is over."

Sarah nodded her agreement and started working on her computer again. "We have to find a location for the ceremony." Her voice lowered to a murmur as she seemed to think out loud. "Maybe an occult chat room."

"I had a little success myself," Max offered, drawing her hopeful gaze. "Caden owns a variety of businesses around the state, but most of them are here in Houston. They seem like obvious locations to check out for this ceremony. There's a restaurant, an antique store, a large number of bars, and the list goes on. I'll shoot the names to your e-mail so you can cross-reference them with the occult Web sites." Sarah gave him her address and he punched a few keys.

They worked on the list a good hour and ranked each of Caden's businesses based on probable ceremony sites. They were ready with a plan of attack for the next day. "I think we're set," Max announced at last, the final outline of Caden's business locations mapped out.

"Finally," Sarah said. Her gaze slowly lifted from the computer as she blinked a couple of times. Her eyes were heavy, weariness in her expression.

"We should sleep a few hours while we can," he said, worried about her ability to ward off another mental attack if she were exhausted.

"Yes," she agreed. "Sleep would be really good."

But neither moved. They sat there, silent, the implications of the one bed hanging in the air.

Max's body began a fast burn to arousal and he pushed to his feet, quick to distance himself from Sarah and temptation. He walked to the closet and pulled the extra pillow and blanket from the top shelf, aware that Sarah's attention was on him. He didn't look at her as he found a spot beside the wall and lay down, clothes and boots still in place, the blanket on top of him. Next, Max grabbed his cell phone from his belt and set the alarm for seven. That was only a few hours of sleep, but it had to be enough.

In his peripheral vision, he saw Sarah clear the bed and turn to face him. "Please don't do this, Max. You need some real rest. Share the bed with me."

He shut his eyes. "Turn off the light, Sarah, and go to sleep."

"Max—"

His lashes snapped open. "This isn't a debate. I'm sleeping here. Turn off the light."

Several seconds passed before she pounded the pillow and murmured, "This is crazy." The light went out.

No, it's torture, he thought to himself as the silence fell again, this time laced with discomfort, with sexual tension.

"Max?"

"Yes."

"I'm not afraid of you."

"You should be."

"I did a lot of thinking while we traveled." A few seconds of silence. "You said Darkland Beasts have no soul, right?"

"Yes."

"But you have a soul."

"A dark one."

"I lived those nightmares with you. I feel your feelings like I do the spirits. And no one would feel the guilt you do if they were evil. Evil people don't care about anything but themselves. I imagine soulless, evil Beasts care even less. You care. You aren't evil."

Max wanted her acceptance and her approval more than anything in that moment, and she was giving it to him. But he couldn't take what she offered and it was killing him. There was a reason he'd tried to scare her away, and he couldn't lose sight of that fact. He was protecting her.

He had to make her understand. "You've seen my eyes, Sarah. You've seen how much they resemble the eyes of a Beast. I'm on the edge. I could hurt you. I could hurt someone you love. I won't let you go through that again." Frustration rolled inside, his words laden with emotion. "Why are you trying to make me human when I'm not?"

"Because you are, Max. Immortal, yes, but still human beyond that. Just like Edward is. As was the friend I lost to that demon possession. We have to fight, Max. *You* have to fight."

Why couldn't she just be scared? He'd given her every reason to be afraid of him.

As if she read his mind, she added, "I realized something else today. When that demon took the people I loved, it destroyed a part of me, too. I forgot the higher purpose that is served when I use my gifts to help people. I've lived in fear and I refuse to do it anymore. I know what I feel when I'm with you. I know how comfortable I felt with Karen and Jag. Everything in my life has come back to right now, with you. Did you know the demon that killed my family had a connection to Solomon?"

"What?" Max asked in surprise.

"Yes." She went on to explain how they'd hunted the demon, and how Solomon's writings had helped her destroy it. "So you see, finding you has to be part of my destiny. That means you are supposed to pass this test and fight by my side. I feel it. I choose to believe it. I won't let fear of history repeating itself make me hide. Not anymore."

Admiration filled Max. "I knew you'd find that purpose again, Sarah. And I know if I'm not here, you'll make a difference in this war."

Her voice reached through the darkness. "You have to be here. It was meant to be. Why else would we find each other if you weren't?"

He wanted to be here. He did. "Maybe I am supposed to see you through this battle in Nowhere and lead you to the Knights for protection and guidance. Or maybe I was just supposed to help you find your place in this world again, Sarah."

"Do you believe that?" she asked. "Because I don't."

The truth was he didn't know what to believe, but he knew he couldn't risk her future for his. Maybe Sarah would do something great in this lifetime, and he had to make sure she survived to do it. There were so many possibilities he could think of, but he saw no point in sharing them with Sarah.

The fact was he had to get them both through this present battle before he could look for a future with her.

And he wasn't sure he had enough willpower to resist Sarah if she kept trying to pull him closer—enough to fight his inner Beast and her. Now came the big question. How did he keep her at a distance, away from him, so he couldn't adversely affect her destiny, without destroying her newfound purpose?

He knew of only one thing that might work—the one thing that might show her they'd met too late. And that was the cold, hard truth he hated with all of his being. The truth about what he'd done, why he was being tested. "Sarah." He hesitated, forcing out the words he'd spoken before, but now with the truth behind them. "I killed a man. I *killed* him." His thoughts flashed back to that day. "He was trying to give the list of angelic bloodlines to the Beasts, so they could hunt them. Jessica, Des's intended mate, tried to stop him. I saw him draw a knife—he was going to stab her. I charged after him, but I was too late. The blade had pierced Jessica's side. And then I just lost it. I don't know what happened. I blacked out. The next thing I knew, I was leaning over his dead body, a bloody blade in my hand."

Seconds ticked by and Sarah said nothing. Nothing. Pain ripped through his chest. He'd succeeded in doing what he needed to do. He'd scared her, pushed her away. He turned onto his back and stared into the dark room, moonlight illuminating the ceiling above. He willed himself to be pleased with his results, to sleep and be ready to fight this war again tomorrow. That's what he did. He fought. Alone.

He heard Sarah moving around, perhaps settling

beneath the blankets. He didn't look. He couldn't look. He inhaled. A mistake. Her scent was everywhere. All around him. Tempting him.

But then the most amazing thing happened. Sarah was there, lying down on the floor with him. "What are you doing?" he asked, objecting, and then turned to face her, on his side as she was, his back to the wall— putting distance between them.

"Relax," she said. "I'm on top of the blanket, and we have our clothes on."

She reached over the distance and her fingers brushed his jaw. Max's breath lodged in his chest at the gentle touch. He'd felt few of those in his lifetime. He'd had women, had plenty of sex. Tenderness he didn't even remember. He needed this, he realized. He wasn't strong enough to push her away right now. He hated himself for that, but he wasn't. "Sarah," he whispered. "I don't want to hurt you."

"You won't," she assured him. "I don't know what happened that day, Max, but I know you were trying to save Jessica's life. Obviously Jessica is alive, and you rescued that list of bloodlines. The way I see it, you saved a lot of lives that day."

"I killed him."

"You must have had no other option."

"There is always another option."

"If only that were true," Sarah said. "But it's not, Max. We both know that. If it were, neither of us would have let our families die." With those profound and painful words, she snuggled up as close to him as the blankets would allow, her hand going to his hip. "Go to sleep, Max."

He didn't sleep, though. Not for a long time. He was

afraid of hurting her, of losing control in his sleep. But his eyes were heavy, as were his thoughts. And soon he drifted into sleep....

Sarah woke to the throbbing in her head—Kate was trying to communicate with her, and once again, the demon spirits were trying to stop her. A shooting pain pierced Sarah's temple and Max scooped her into his arms, cradling her against his body. In some remote corner of her mind she heard him talking to her, heard his worry.

"Kate," she whispered, clinging to him. "Kate is—" The barely-there words were cut off as Sarah was hit with flashes of images with moments of blackness as the demon spirits worked to defeat the vision Kate was delivering.

Sarah felt Max near her, felt his strength. She reached through the pain, searched the images. Three men wearing robes—no—they dropped the robes. They were the Shadow Masters and they were naked. So were hundreds of others. Another black spot. Lots of blackness. Then Sarah saw Allen in a corner, watching the people as they pleasured each other. Waiting on something. The Shadow Masters. Yes. He was there for the Shadow Masters. Suddenly loud music came from somewhere. Dance music. Overhead. A club maybe. The music got louder as if Kate wanted her to know it was important. Flash to a man—he wore a robe and spoke to Allen. He was evil—pure evil. Kate fed her a name—Caden. And then everything went blank.

Sarah collapsed against Max, not realizing until that moment that every muscle in her body had been tense and now burned like fire. She swallowed against the dryness in her throat and slid her fingers along her scalp.

"Caden," she said, sitting up despite the dizziness that came along with the action. "He's using some sort of sex ritual to activate the stones."

Max followed her to a sitting position and he ignored her words. His palms framed her face. "Forget Caden for the moment. You scared the hell out of me. Are you okay?"

"Fine," she said, her hands going to his wrist. "Nothing a bottle of aspirin and caffeine won't cure." She made an attempt to smile that didn't quite work out. "We don't do mornings very well, do we? Yesterday I saw your fangs. Today this."

His expression softened and he brushed hair from her brow. "We do mornings fine. These are extraordinary circumstances."

"At least you didn't lecture me about sleeping with you and tell me we shouldn't be doing mornings together at all."

"We're supposed to do a lot more than mornings together," he said, his words laced with regret. "But like I said—extraordinary circumstances."

The alarm on his cell went off and Max ignored it. He pressed his forehead to hers. "I don't know how to protect you, Sarah. I've spent centuries fighting demons, yet, I can't destroy the ones attacking you during these visions."

Her heart clenched at the words and she leaned back to look at him. "We will destroy them with Vars, but you're right. You can't use a sword and slay the evil that touches the spirit world. But, Max," she said, her voice laced with a plea, her fingers tracing his lips, "you *can* stop trying to push me away."

His hands slid from her face and he eased his back

against the wall. "That's the one thing I can't do. Not now. Not until this is over and we know the outcome."

"Of the test," she said, exhaling against the throbbing of her head.

"Are you—"

Her lashes lifted. "I'm fine," she assured him. "Jag talked about you saving Jessica back at the other hotel. About how he'd never forget that. Think about it, Max. I have. He was telling you something. Telling *me* something."

His brows furrowed. "Like what?"

"I don't know but my guess is that everything isn't as you assume it is. You have to remember."

Frustration laced his response. "You think I haven't tried?"

"Try harder," she countered, knowing he wouldn't like her words, but knowing, too, that he needed to hear them. "If this test is based on that incident, then your life depends on it. Maybe mine, too. You fight for everyone but yourself. Fine. Fight for me."

"I am fighting for you," he said. "That's why I can't touch you again. Not now."

This time she was the one who was frustrated. "Fight, Max. Fight for yourself. Do it for me if you won't do it for you."

Sarah pushed to her feet, ignoring the slight dizziness overtaking her and walking to the phone. She ordered aspirin and coffee and then covered the phone to ask if he liked waffles. He did. That didn't surprise her. They seemed to share a lot of likes. Too bad he seemed determined to make sure he spent eternity in hell and wouldn't be sharing any of them with her. He was stubborn and making her mad. She wanted to shake sense into his big, burly ass. He could see only one way of dealing with his test—alone.

By the time she hung up the phone, she'd reined in her heated mood. Max did alone so well because it's all he knew. That wasn't the case for her. She'd been alone, yes, but for far less time than Max. And she had been close to her family. She could feel the distance Max had with his family. He'd been hungry for the love he'd never received. She'd just have to show him he didn't have to do this alone. Somehow. Some way. She'd figure it out.

He'd taken a seat behind the desk and she turned to him. "About Caden and this ritual," she said, shifting back into the current challenge of finding Allen. "Sexual energy can be quite powerful. I've read about rituals that last for days." She thought a moment, her lashes lowering, her mind reaching for the details of her vision. "Six days. This one is six days. Two for each stone and then they are empowered. Somehow that allows the souls to be extracted from the stones. I think…yes. We have some time. If we can find a location where all of this is happening, then maybe we can stop it. So what do you think?" She remembered something. "Music. There was loud music. A club. A club is above the ritual ground. Yes. It's underground."

"I'd say it's a good thing we didn't find him last night. Now that we know he's involved, I'd say questioning him would only put him on guard."

"My guess is he isn't even in his office. Not with this ritual going on." She grabbed the phone. "Let's find out." Sure enough, a quick call later, and she'd confirmed he was out for the rest of the week. "Now we have to figure out which club."

"Maybe if you see the locations, you'll remember something?" Max asked.

"I hope so," she said. "Because the full moon is fast approaching."

Chapter 19

Seventy-two grueling hours of searching for answers had passed for Sarah and Max.

It was just past ten o'clock, with the full moon closing in on them in a matter of a few days, when Max and Sarah walked up a red-carpeted sidewalk leading to the Red Room, one of the many clubs Caden owned.

Visiting several clubs a night had been a stretch, considering they were spread out from one end of the city to the next. And working the employees and patrons for information took an effort to fit in which couldn't be made by darting in and out. Nor could searches of private areas be done without some tricky side steps.

The time with Sarah had been both heaven and hell for Max. Heaven because he'd listened to stories about her life, and shared some of his own even—he'd learned about Sarah and he liked what he'd found. It had also been hell—keeping his hands off her was damn near killing him. Sarah wouldn't sleep without him. She wouldn't let him run from her, or push her away. Lord only knew, he'd tried.

They neared the entrance to the club, and Max kept Sarah close, her arm linked under his, her body pressed to his side. The closer they got to the entrance, the more his skin warmed, the more aware he became of Sarah's soft curves against his body. The feeling of sexual need formed rapidly, and Max knew he was in trouble.

Lust carved its way into his limbs, hungry for his complete submission. He was in trouble. Even his weakest moments of temptation with Sarah hadn't come close to this. The beast was alive, threatening to consume him. If he'd thought he had reclaimed control, he now knew that control to be a facade. He didn't want this to happen around Sarah. His worst fear was a blackout, like the one he'd had when he killed that human. He had no idea what he was capable of in that state, and he didn't want to find out.

Before he could even begin to consider warning Sarah, the hostess smiled and motioned them forward. He greeted her, beating down his beast. This was important. They had to find Caden.

The entry into the club was pricey for nonmembers—obviously meant to discourage anyone who wasn't a high roller.

They'd made a trip to the mall earlier today for clothes to fit the part. Max wore Ralph Lauren slacks and a sleek blue button-down with a matching tie. He didn't much like dressing up. It reminded him of the social affairs back in England. The fluff meant for nothing but upward movement. He did, however, enjoy seeing Sarah in her knee-length, figure-hugging black dress. Simple yet elegant, it matched her personality to perfection.

Max was about to hand his gold card to the hostess when a red phone buzzed, claiming the hostess's attention. She picked up the receiver, listened a moment, and cut a look at Max and Sarah that was meant to be discreet, but wasn't.

"I'll handle it," she said into the receiver, and replaced it on the base.

The woman ran Max's card and then handed it back to him, avoiding eye contact. Bingo. She was nervous. That call had been about them. Someone had caught on to their hunt for Caden.

"Your visit to The Red Room will start in the lounge on the second floor. It's a private room that overlooks the club as you enjoy beverages. It will allow you to see the various flavors we have to offer here." She motioned to another woman to cover her post. "Follow me."

Max glanced at Sarah to confirm she'd picked up on the potential trouble they were in and confirmed she had. He pulled her closer as they exited the entry hall and entered the club, her safety the most important thing. If he got any vibe of real danger, they were leaving.

The instant they entered the heart of the crowd, Max could feel the sexual charge. Music pounded through speakers with a sensual rhythm; dim lighting cast a red glow on the room. The low thrum of arousal he'd felt outside escalated. The dance floor held couples pressed together in highly suggestive undulations. Heat vibrated through his body in an unnatural way.

Sarah's hand tightened on his arm, and he felt the movement in every nerve ending he owned. What the hell was happening to him? His heart was pounding in his chest, his groin tightening. His desire for Sarah was to the point of complete, utter distraction. This wasn't just mating instinct. It was something more. If this continued, he might well be the danger to Sarah, rather than this place.

The hostess started up a winding stairwell, and Sarah hesitated at the bottom, pushing to her toes to whisper in Max's ear. "This is it. Don't you feel the sexual energy?"

He didn't look at her, not wanting her to know just how much the atmosphere was affecting him. The need to mate was obviously intensifying his sensitivity. "I feel it," Max murmured, taking her hand as he started up the stairs.

The hostess stood at the top of the landing and waved them through an open door. Max went in first, leading Sarah, prepared to inspect their destination before Sarah entered harm's way. Inside he found a room with a long, red love seat and a marble, art deco-looking black table that held two oversized red martini glasses filled to the rim. Candles flickered around the room, and in the corners on tall pedestals. The candlelight almost seeming to dance to the music being funneled through ceiling-mounted speakers.

The walls directly in front of the seating area held television screens, each displaying various locations within the club, including private areas not visible upon entry. Several of the visuals were quite erotic. Max turned toward the hostess to ask a question, finding her still in the doorway. Before he could issue his question, she departed. "Enjoy," she said, and shut them in the room.

Max immediately turned to Sarah, intending to warn her to be silent, that they were being watched. But the minute he looked at her, the minute he saw those big green eyes and full red lips, he was on fire. He pulled her close, molding her hips to his, his hand splayed on her lower back.

In some far corner of his mind, he recognized his actions—what he felt wasn't right. "Sarah," he murmured, his voice low, full of sexual intent. One hand slid into her hair, angling her mouth to his, lips a breath away from hers. "We're being watched."

"I know," she whispered, a soft little sound of pleasure sliding from her lips. "The ritual is close… The magic. It's close. Acting like a drug." But still, her arms wrapped around his neck, her actions defying the warning of her words. "We should g—"

Max kissed her, swallowing the last of her words. He hadn't kissed her in days. He told himself he just wanted a taste of her, one little taste. And, God, it was good. He savored the moment of that first intimate contact—tongue against tongue. She tasted so pure, so sweet.

He deepened the kiss and suddenly it turned passionate, hot, wild. Max couldn't get enough of her, hungry for more, desperate for all of her. In those moments, life was perfect and nothing else mattered. He wanted her, his mate, and damn it, he would take her. The beast began to flare, his teeth elongating, and he didn't care. He was done waiting. He'd take her here and now.

"It's time, Sarah," he murmured near her ear. "Time to become mine."

His teeth scraped her neck, and she cried out. "Yes. Now."

But a moment later she stiffened, her cry of pleasure turning to something different. Her fingers dug into his shoulders, and Max shook his head, trying to clear the fog in his mind. What the hell had he almost done?

Her knees started to give way, and he wrapped his arm around her waist, holding her up. "Sarah!"

"Kate says…" She squeezed her eyes shut. "She says we are…in danger. Get out." Her lashes lifted. "Your brother is here."

The shock of her words shot through him a second before the door was flung open. Max stepped in front of Sarah, protecting her with his body. "Tell Kate a little more warning would be nice!"

Just as Kate said, William walked into the room, looking every bit Max's brother in human form. Max inhaled, jolted by the sight of the Beast who'd once been family.

He'd hoped to never face this day—the day when he might well have to kill the Beast who was once his brother. "William."

"Hello, Maxwell," William said, an evil laugh following the greeting. "All that mating heat is a bitch, isn't it? None of your other senses work worth a crap when you have that pretty little thing all over you. A shame you didn't know I was coming. Maybe you should reconsider your priorities. Play for the right side of this war."

Understanding filled Max. Somehow, they knew Sarah was his mate. They'd funneled the ritual magic through this room somehow, drugging him as Sarah had suggested, dulling his ability to know his enemy was near. His hand inched toward his belt, and he silently cursed as he remembered his only weapons were hidden, beyond reach.

"Looking for something, brother?" William asked. "Tsk. Tsk. Hunting 'The Dark One' unarmed. That really wasn't bright. How did you think you'd protect your woman?" He laughed again and snapped his fingers at the two Beasts behind him. They grabbed Max's arms, shackling him from behind. William reached to his pant leg, pulling it upward to display an ankle holster. He pulled out a small, sharp blade—a blade useless against a Knight, but not against a human such as Sarah.

In his peripheral vision, Max could see that Sarah had backed against the wall, but he didn't dare make eye contact with her. He didn't dare look away from his enemy. He could take the two Beasts holding him, but he wasn't sure he could do it fast enough to get to Sarah before William did. He had to be cautious, to strategize his move.

"Join us and she goes free," William offered, holding the weapon so that the candles flickered against the shiny silver blade.

"You're without your armor," Max pointed out, knowing a Beast without his protective gear could feel a great deal of pain. They couldn't bleed but they could be tortured. "Let her go and I'll kill you fast. I promise you'll feel no pain."

William smiled, seemingly pleased with that answer. "I figured you'd make this a challenge." His eyes raked over Sarah's body. "But something tells me, with Sarah around, I might enjoy convincing you." He winked. "She's a nice choice, brother."

The words cut through Max's heart for too many reasons to pin down in that moment. Right now, all that mattered was freeing Sarah. "You aren't my brother, and I swear to God, if you touch her, I will take your head."

"It's not nice to make promises you can't keep." He slid two fingers down the blade and turned to Sarah. "Maybe we'll join the others downstairs and play a while." He grimaced. "No. I want you all to myself." He glanced over his shoulder at Max. "But you can watch." With the threatening words he inched forward, closer to Sarah.

She slid along the wall, retreating until she bumped into a tall pillar that held a flaming, three-wick candle.

"William, he's your brother," Sarah said. "Help us and maybe we can save you. Maybe Salvador will have mercy on you."

His reply was instant, his words steely with hatred. "It is my mercy you should pray for."

Max ground his teeth at William's words. God, how he wanted William to exist beyond the shell of the man he once was—he had always held on to that hope despite Salvador's insistence that he let William go.

William's eyes lit with contempt as they settled on Max. "I offer you a chance for conversion because I am ordered to do so. If you are smart, you will do what you always failed to do in our human lives—follow my leadership."

He moved then, fast and without warning. His blade touched Sarah's neck, his attention still riveted to Max. "I'd hate to kill her before I show her who the better brother is, but don't doubt for a second I will." He paused. "So here are the hard-core facts, Maxwell. You must choose. Your soul, or your mate's life. Which will it be?"

Max wasn't a fool. He'd gladly sacrifice himself for Sarah, but to do so now would be for nothing. The Beasts would see her dead anyway. He could stand here and pretend he didn't know that or he could take action.

He was tired of playing captive to the two Beasts holding his arms. As for the knife at Sarah's throat, that had to go. Now.

With heavy thoughts, Max surrendered to the inevitable. For the first time since he killed that human to save Des's mate, he had to allow his inner beast to fully take control.

His resolve thickened, his eyes lingering on the knife at his mate's neck; he let the raw emotions, the fury, take hold. Max embraced the heavy pulse of adrenaline pumping through his veins, welcomed the power of his beast as it rose to the surface—clawing its way upward, from the depths of his soul. Soon, man and beast existed as one.

The time to do battle had arrived.

Sarah watched in horror as the room erupted in chaos, the knife at her throat a constant threat. Since she wasn't dead yet, she had to assume there was a reason to keep her alive—perhaps simply to torture her and make Max watch. Either way, she had a chance to survive, which meant she had to fight.

She watched as Max wrenched one arm free from one of the Beasts and smashed his fists into the same Beast's jaw. The blow packed so much force that the Beast stumbled backward. Immediately, the second captor hit Max; the sound of knuckles cracking against bone filled the air. Sarah cringed, thankful that Max recovered quickly and returned the blow. She couldn't believe Max had gone on the attack. He was outnumbered, in tight quarters. Her heart pounded so hard, she thought her chest would explode. She had to help. Think, damn it!

Max somehow freed himself from his two attackers and charged at his brother. William turned to face Max, shoving Sarah behind him, the blade finally lifted from her skin. Sarah stumbled into the candle pillar to her right, and it wobbled. Instinctively Sarah reached out to steady the candle. But then an idea hit her. Fire. Alarm. The people downstairs panicking. That might just work.

She shoved the candle to the ground, praying the carpet would go up in flames. It did. Well, one flame. A small one, but it would grow. That little success didn't offer much comfort, though, because Max was in trouble. All three of the Beasts were pounding on him.

Sarah clung to the hope her plan offered and went into action, taking advantage of the attention being off her for now. She grabbed candles from anywhere she could find them, tossing them to the ground. Fire was beginning to form a circle around the battle, smoke rising, lifting, hopefully touching the alarm sensors. When one of the Beasts tumbled back into her, Sarah barely sidestepped the flames as she found herself crushed against the wall. Somehow, she held on to the candle in her hand, seeing it as a weapon.

Taking opportunity where it presented itself, she pressed the flame into the back side of the Beast's long hair. The strands ignited with quick speed and the creature screamed as flames traveled up his head, jumping around in the center. He was now a live weapon ready to set anything in its path on fire.

William and the other Beast backed away from the fire and finally the alarm sounded. Water erupted from the ceiling almost instantly, screams filling the air as the customers felt its downpour. Apparently, this signaled a temporary retreat to William; he darted out the door, disappearing into the club. But she'd seen how determined he was to destroy Max and how devious he was about achieving it. He was most likely regrouping, planning another strike upon their attempt to depart. His uninjured Beast followed in his wake. The one that was on fire dropped to his knees as if he were submitting to the fire licking at his body, the water barely dulling the flames. In shock, she watched as the creature seemed to be melting into the fire, proving beheading wasn't the only method of destroying these monsters.

Suddenly Sarah was in Max's arms and being carried out of the room. He dodged the growing fire as if it required no effort, charging out the door and down the stairs toward the bottom floor. Sarah searched the crowd for William, the sound of sirens touching her ears. People were pushing and shoving their way to the front door. They had to find Allen now—before he was gone, before their hope of stopping his plans faded.

She tried to say as much, but the shrill alarm drowned out her voice.

Max weaved through the crowd, and before Sarah could object, they were outside the club. Still, he didn't stop moving. "Max! Stop! We have to find Allen."

Max didn't stop. No matter how many times she screamed, ordered, pleaded, he stayed his path. They were blocks away from the club when she found herself on the sidewalk watching as Max flagged the cab that had apparently been the reason for his sudden stop. The cab responded, pulling to the curb.

Max yanked open the door and Sarah stared at

him. "We have to go back," she argued, not understanding his plan.

"I *am* going back," he said, and handed her his cell,
barely looking at her in the process. "Jag and Karen are
both on speed dial. Jag will protect you. Have him orb
you to his location and have him do it now. Then tell him
I need backup. The immediate kind."

He opened the front door and gave the driver the
hotel address and tossed money onto the seat. He
slammed the door. "Go to the room and stay there, so I
know you're safe."

"Max—"

His gaze caught hers midair, and her throat went dry
at what she saw. Yellow eyes...predator eyes. His voice
was low, thick. "Just do as I say, Sarah."

Answering wasn't an option, not that she could find
words in that moment.

And then he was running, leaving her behind. She'd
never seen Max seem quite so on edge, so dangerous.
She watched his departure, his muscular body, long and
sleek, traveling at inhuman speed.

Her mind raced with thoughts, fear pressing into her
consciousness. She rejected it as a useless emotion.
She'd seen how powerful those three Beasts had been.
There were probably many more back at that club. Max
couldn't face them alone.

The cabdriver honked, and she slammed the door
shut and waved him forward without her. A second later,
she hit the speed dial for Jag, praying he would answer.
He didn't. Next she tried Karen, pacing as the phone
rang in her ear.

She didn't bother with hello. "Tell me Jag is there."

"No," Karen said. "What's wrong?"

Five minutes later, Sarah hung up the line, discouraged. Jag's next call-in time was almost an hour away. A lot could happen in an hour. Max could be dead in an hour. Sarah didn't know what to do but go after him herself. At least, she could tell Jag exactly where he was when he called. Doing nothing wasn't an option, because she wasn't sitting back and waiting while Max got himself killed.

So she did the only thing she could. She took off running—back to the nightclub. Back to Max.

Chapter 20

Allen stood in the corner of the ritual room, naked, without his prior reservations about being a part of what went on here—about the sexual explorations required by Caden. His duty to contribute to the power of the stones could not be questioned—not when Kate would be the reward for his actions. Two women clung to him, touching him, kissing him. For days now, he'd shoved aside guilt, promising himself this was for Kate, that it did not betray his love for her. This was to bring her back. To bring her home.

Murmurs filled the room, and Allen pried one woman's lips from his to see what was going on. The Shadow Masters had returned after a short rest, and they now stood center stage. The robes they wore pooled at their feet, and all eyes turned to them, all activity stilled.

Each time they returned, Caden tested the stones

with some magical spell, and so far he'd been pleased with their progress, which was ahead of schedule. That progress kept Allen going, kept him focused on the magic that could bring back Kate.

He held his breath as he awaited Caden's update… but it never came.

Without warning an alarm sounded and the sprinklers came on, raining water down on the crowd. Allen's heart slammed against his chest, and he shoved aside the two women, storming toward the stage, taking the stairs two at a time. He stopped just behind Caden, who directed the Shadow Masters to depart. "Where are they going?" Allen demanded.

Caden turned to face him. "The same place you are. Away from here. We are compromised."

"It's a fire alarm. It might not even be real."

Irritation touched Caden's eyes. "You fool," he spat.

"The sprinklers are on. That means smoke."

"That can quickly be dealt with," Allen countered.

"We are exposed," Caden reiterated. "We leave, and we do it now."

Allen wasn't accepting that answer. "We can't leave. The ritual can't be delayed. The full moon is coming. And what if this is a ruse? What if someone is trying to use the fire to get us out of here?"

"We are leaving," Caden said, the bite to his words telling of his growing impatience. "We have escape tunnels. Vars didn't choose a fool in me. You, though, I am beginning to wonder about."

Panic formed and Allen exploded. He couldn't let this happen. Not with Kate's future on the line. "I am the one who controls this vial." His fist closed around the glass that hung from a string around his neck—the vial that would hold the souls of the Shadow Masters once the stones had enough power to make it happen. "I am the one who can give Vars what he wants. Without me Vars cannot be a part of this ceremony. He speaks through me. And I say we stay and finish the ritual. I say—"

Caden waved his hand and Allen's words were magically lodged in his throat. "*You* say nothing, and if you aren't careful, I'll silence you permanently. You are nothing but a useful puppet that Vars needs right now to free himself. A tool to aid my efforts in this ritual. I, however, am bound to Vars, his eternal blood servant, gifted with abilities that would make you wet your prissy little pants." He pointed to the end of the stage. "Now walk. We are leaving. Before we find trouble I can't fix."

Hatred crept into Allen's heart in that moment, and it scared him. He'd never been one to feel such things, but he did now. He hated this man for claiming his control. This was his journey, his path, launched for Kate, not this man. Stiffly, he turned and walked to the edge of the stage, wishing he had the magic to make Caden eat his words. And just as he'd never been a man full of hatred, Allen had never sought vengeance on anyone. But if Caden failed to perform this ritual properly, if he cost Allen his Kate, he would deliver vengeance against Caden.

The air crackled with Adrian's fury a second before he appeared on the stairwell of the club in front of U2— or William as he was once known. Adrian pointed at U2 and the Beast flew against the wall, back plastered to the concrete with magic, feet dangling in the air.

"How much pain your future holds is up to you," Adrian snarled between his clenched teeth. Irritation wracked his nerves, the sound of the fire alarm screeching with warning and reminding him of U2's stupidity. If Vars didn't escape his prison, Adrian couldn't claim his demon army. Vars had to be freed, yet the ritual to aid that escape was now being interrupted and he had U2 to thank for that. "If this fire destroys my plans, you will wish you were dead. And make no mistake—I am allowing you to continue for only one reason. I want what is Salvador's and your brother is his. I suggest you deliver him to me."

Adrian sliced his hand through the air and U2 fell to the ground. "Don't make me come to you again. Next time you will not get off so easily."

He shot a dart of electricity through U2's body. The Beast shook with the jolt, his eyes rolling back in his head. Adrian inhaled with pleasure; U2's fear and pain were almost as sweet as sex. Yes. He felt calmer now.

But what he wanted was not calm—it was power. The power he would soon take from Vars. With his own army and that of Vars, Adrian would be unstoppable. He would destroy The Knights of White with ease, ridding himself of the hindrance they had become in his quest for power. His power would allow him to overtake Cain, and Adrian would then be king in his place. He would finally find his position within the royalty of the Underworld. And then, one by one, he would overtake and destroy the other leaders—until he ruled all of hell.

Chapter 21

Max sprinted toward the club, determined to get there before Allen took flight. He found the front door as the fire trucks pulled up. Flames flickered through the front entrance, energized now, spreading through the structure. Searching for a discreet entry point, Max darted around to the back of the building.

Even as he scouted for trouble, on alert as his senses picked up the presence of Beasts, his thoughts were dimly fixed on Sarah. Leaving her worried him. Towing her along with him worried him more. Protecting her from an army of Beasts—which could well be the case—would be damn near impossible. Not to mention his present state of internal struggle. He'd barely reined in his beast after that last battle. He was clinging to a proverbial limb, barely holding on to reality. Days ago, he'd wanted to scare her away. Now, he was terrified he might really do it. He couldn't let her see him like this. Not if he wanted her in his life. And he did. More than anything he'd ever wanted in four centuries of living.

Kneeling by a window, Max yanked up his pant leg and removed the gun he had strapped to his calf. The compact Glock wasn't his preferred weapon considering it wouldn't kill a Beast. At least a few well-placed bullets would stun his enemy long enough for Max to steal a real weapon. Using the butt of the gun, Max broke the glass that blocked his entry into the building and then cleared the opening of the remaining jagged pieces. He slid through the tight space and found himself on a smoky industrial stairwell. Sucking in the thick air, he adjusted his breathing, appreciative that he was far less affected by such things than a normal human.

Not wasting any time, Max charged down one flight of concrete stairs and found a closed door in his path. Cautiously, he opened it, finding no resistance and no enemies. Just another set of stairs. These were narrow and winding in a snakelike path. He trotted down their distance and found himself at the edge of a dark, empty auditorium, with a stage overlooking the room.

Using his exceptional night vision, Max assessed his surroundings. Chairs were folded at the sides of the room; silk blankets and cushions were covered in water from the spray of overhead sprinklers. The scent of sex and perfume lingered in the air, telling of how recently the occupants had fled.

"Damn," Max murmured, his instincts flaring with the warning of Beasts. He surveyed the room, finding no movement, but that didn't fool him.

Max went into action—the idea of being a sitting

duck holding no appeal. He plowed across the room, the water soaking his already damp clothing. Somehow, this room had another exit, different from the way Max had come in. The fire up above would have stopped their departure.

A search turned up no departure points, but Max knew, damn good and well, there was another exit somewhere. Obviously high-tech and well-hidden. And the darkness wasn't helping matters.

A low sound had Max whirling around, his weapon in front of him.

"Max." It was Sarah. He saw her the same moment he heard her voice, and she immediately started running toward him. "Thank God, you're okay."

His heart lurched at the idea of her being here, at the epicenter of danger. "Damn it, Sarah, it's not safe here."

"For either of us," she countered, leaping across an overturned chair in her path. "You're one against many. I couldn't leave you alone."

Alone. He was used to alone, though he didn't like it. Softening with her words, Max motioned her forward, wanting her by his side so he could protect her. He couldn't quite get used to someone looking out for him, but if that someone was Sarah, he'd easily adapt.

Still, she needed to learn to listen. He almost laughed at that. She would never listen. Neither Jag's nor Des's mate did. Why would Sarah? The Knights drew strong-willed mates.

"I should have known you wouldn't go back to the hotel," he commented, moving to meet her halfway.

"I don't generally take orders well," she said. "Especially when someone I care about is in danger. I—"

The rest of her words faded as Max saw William dart across the stage and leap off the edge. He was after Sarah and he was well-armed.

"Run!" Max screamed at Sarah as he launched himself forward, a bull after his target. His body collided with William's not a second too soon, because Sarah was almost in his brother's grasp. Max and William went into a clench hold, arms locked with arms, and Max's gun landed in a splash on the wet floor. The two brothers rotated around in circles as each tried to get the upper hand. A battle of wills and strength ensued, the floor slick beneath their feet, leftover chairs crashing around them as they became obstacles.

With each shove, each push, the idea of his brother hurting his mate became the ultimate betrayal for Max. It fed his anger, and he managed to rip himself free of William's hold and throw several hard blows. He took some, too, but he didn't feel them. He was driven, angry, in primal fighting mode. And when opportunity presented itself, he seized one of the blades at William's hip. That same instant, William drew the other blade he wore.

The two brothers sliced the weapons through the air, blades held at each other's throats. William laughed and dropped his weapon, fearless of Max. "You can't do it and you know it."

"Don't count on that," Max growled, his hand shaking, his fingers clutching the sword's handle.

"I'm your brother. If you can kill me, maybe you're more like me than I gave you credit for. That's it, isn't it?" William smiled. "You're more like me, Maxwell, than you want to admit. Accept it. Seize what you are. The time to accept your true calling has come."

Max's gut clenched at those words. He felt dark, he felt dangerous. He felt every bit like the beast who pressed him now to take William's head for trying to hurt Sarah. He didn't see his brother. He saw only red, saw only the Beast who wanted to kill his mate. He drew a deep, calming breath. Yet… Damn it! Why? Why had he stopped when he could have killed this Beast and ended this? Dimly, he saw the truth. His beast didn't have as much control as he had thought. The control that he would have sworn was gone, remained loosely in place. And his human side recognized William, his brother, as the only piece of his past that still lived.

He reached for reason, for rationale. This wasn't William. This was a Beast who killed humans without concern, smashing them as if they were mere flies. He couldn't let this Beast live just because it looked like his long gone brother. He had to end this. He had to do this—and not as the beast. He had to do this as Max, as the man who understood good versus evil. Salvador wouldn't save William. The truth was hard to swallow, but deep down, Max understood why. As a human, William hadn't known right from wrong. He would never be a Knight. He would always be a Beast.

"You're thinking about it." William dropped to his knees, daring Max with his actions. "Do it! Kill me or join me!"

Painfully, Max lifted his sword, preparing to do what he'd always known he'd have to do one day—just accept that William was gone. He would have acted, would have swung his sword, but voices echoed in the hall. Close. Too close. Damn it. They couldn't do this in front of humans.

Laughter bubbled from William's lips, and he pushed to his feet, backing away. "Think about what I've said." And then he turned away, taking long strides and jumping up on the stage with agility and ease before detouring to an exit behind the stage.

Sarah swiped at the tears streaming down her cheeks. Emotion welled inside her for Max; she was riveted by the torment she'd witnessed him endure as he'd faced killing his brother. But there was more to what she felt, so much more. As she'd watched Max's face, the fierce, primal desire to kill contorted into raw human agony. She'd known the minute he'd accepted the loss of his brother. And she'd had a flashback to the day her parents had died. The demon hadn't spared Sarah's life. Her friend had. He'd fought that demon possessing him and killed himself rather than Sarah. Her friend had beaten that demon, and he'd deserved the trust she'd questioned all these years. The trust she'd denied everyone around her since that day—including Max. But he had it now. He had her trust, and he had her.

Sarah walked to Max's side, where she belonged. She touched his arm and his gaze found hers. The angst in his eyes was almost too much to bear. God, how she ached to ease his hurt. To tell him that what he felt made him human.

Instead, she said, "I love you, Max. There was an empty spot in my life that I've never understood. Now I do. I was waiting for you. I don't want to do any of this alone anymore."

Shock registered in his face before he pulled her close and kissed her. His forehead rested against hers, his arms wrapping around her waist. "You have no idea how much I needed to hear that right now."

Her hands went to his face, her surroundings forgotten, her heart and body warm with the moment, with the emotion that this man, her mate, drew from her. "I believe in you. Just make sure you believe in you."

"You won't ever be alone again, Sarah. I promise. I *will* conquer this test, so we can be together. I love you and I need you. So damn much. You have no idea."

Sarah never got to tell him how much *she* had needed to hear those words. Firemen charged through the door. They were rescued.

Near sunrise, Sarah and Max returned to the town of Nowhere with the aid of Jag's travel abilities. Hours of searching the tunnels discovered beneath the club had delivered no results. A standoff at the cabin appeared more and more likely.

Sarah walked into the deserted lobby of the inn. Cathy flew down the stairs, obviously aware of their arrival. It took only a moment for Sarah to find herself wrapped in a big hug.

"I've been worried about you," Cathy said, easing back and looking them both over, her gaze taking in their muddy, damp clothing. "You two are a mess. You should clean up and get some rest."

Max stepped closer, by Sarah's side. "Any news on Edward?"

Cathy crossed her arms in front of her chest, instantly tense. She wore no makeup. Only faded jeans, a T-shirt and Keds tennis shoes. Dark circles tinted the pale skin under her eyes. "No change. I'm headed over to the doctor's office now. I took a shower and slept for an hour. Or tried to at least."

"What happened to you and Marisol trying to combine your magic to expel the demon?" Max asked.

Cathy's tone went flat. "Nothing. This stuff about me having the ability to use magic beyond what I've learned from books isn't flying. So far, I got nothing."

"You've been focused on expelling the demon from Edward, right?"

"Right," Cathy agreed.

Sarah continued, "I think we need to give Edward the power to defeat the demon himself. Somehow, focus the magic to empower Edward. Let the man defeat the demon. Don't use the magic ourselves. Direct it to Edward."

"Let the man defeat the demon," Cathy said, repeating the words. "That's actually quite brilliant. I have to go." She sidestepped Sarah and Max and reached for the door.

Sarah turned to Max, their eyes locked, warmth spreading through her limbs at the connection they shared. They didn't speak. They didn't have to. They knew tonight had been life changing. Each of them had faced their pasts and it had brought them closer. Their fingers linked, and Max eased them into motion, up the stairs. Neither questioned whose room they were going to. That they would be together was simply expected.

The minute the door shut to Max's room and the lights were on, he and Sarah turned to each other, bodies joined in an embrace, eyes locked. There was no doubt in her expression, no fear. Only love, passion, hope. He bent his head, his cheek brushing hers, the contact soft, perfect. His body heated, limbs fired with a burn for Sarah. *Pull away,* he told himself. She meant more to him than one night. Than this night. *You can't have her yet.* Pass the test first.

As good as his intentions were, when her lips brushed his jaw and then his lips, her fingers caressing his neck, he somehow lost himself in the moment. He pressed Sarah against the door and kissed her. Kissed her as if there was no tomorrow because there might not be. She tasted like honey and felt like heaven. His version of heaven. Possessiveness rose from within Max, intense, sudden. Somehow, he reined in the heat spreading through his body, shoved aside the haze of passion threatening to claim control of him. Her tongue slid against his in delicious hungry strokes, her arms wrapping his neck, her breasts pressed to his chest, soft curves melting into him.

"Max," she whispered, her lips dissolving into his again, her hands pushing his shirt off his shoulders.

When had she unbuttoned it? He let the material fall to the floor, her soft touch pulling him into a seductive spell. He had to stop. Why? He had to remember why. His body defined his mind, his groin tight, cock thickening with the promise of Sarah's slick, wet heat.

He ached for his mate. To be inside her again, this time with acceptance…but the test. He reached for honor, for reason. He tried to pull away. "Sarah—"

Her hands went to his cheeks, her teeth nipped his lip, tongue tracing it, delving into his mouth and stroking. "Don't tell me we can't do this," she ordered in a raspy reply, answering his unspoken objection. "I need you. I need you so much, Max."

Urgency resonated in her voice and her hands were everywhere. His nostrils flared with the scent of her desire, with his own desire. She leaned back to look at him, a dare flashing in her eyes an instant before she peeled her shirt off. Immediately, her bra followed. His gaze dropped, eyes devouring the sight of her high breasts and perfect red nipples. He reached out and brushed the peaks with his fingers, watching them respond before rolling them with his thumbs. The shuddered breath she drew told of her pleasure, fueling his actions, begging him for more without words.

He kissed her, filling his hands with her breasts, hard peaks of her nipples pressed against his palms. He bent at the knees, fitting his hips against the V of her body. They fit together perfectly, their limbs molded together, promising pleasure beyond anything either had imagined before now. She arched into the touch of his hands, her hips sliding against his.

She tore her mouth from his. "There's no reason to wait," she whispered.

No reason. No reason to wait. A jolt of reality rocked Max. Calling on every ounce of willpower he owned, he leaned back, forcing his hands from the woman he burned to touch, pressing them against the door behind her. His chest heaved with the effort to contain his urges, his burn for Sarah.

"The test, Sarah." The words came out a tormented hiss. "We aren't doing this. Not yet."

"You are going to pass the test," she said. "Maybe you already have. Maybe that's what happened tonight with your brother." Her finger brushed his bottom lip. "We need each other."

It would be so easy to listen to her, but Max had to love her enough to wait. "It's not time yet."

"What if something happens to one of us? I want to know we had one time together without anything between us."

"Nothing's going to happen to you, damn it," he said. "I won't let it. And there is something between us now."

Seconds ticked, Sarah's gaze searching his. "This is what you want." Her voice held defeat.

"No, but it's how it has to be. It's killing me, baby, I swear. But I want us to do this right. I want to make love to you. I want you to choose an eternity with me without regret. You should see the ranch, see my life. Know you want what I can offer you. To be my mate, my wife."

Emotion rushed into her eyes and she wrapped her arms around him, her nipples pressed into his chest. Her lips brushed his. "I don't need to see the ranch. Just pass this test and let's get on with eternity."

His heart warmed with her words, his hands sliding up her bare back. He kissed her, torturing himself with the sweet taste of her. Knowing a very long, cold shower was as much his destiny as Sarah.

Hours later Sarah lay with her head on Max's chest. They'd been talking for hours, and she'd told him about how her memory of the night of her parent's death had sparked the idea to save Edward. How it had given her new perspective on life, on her future.

When finally they fell silent, each trying to sleep, the comfort his arms delivered did nothing to deliver peace of mind. As perfect as lying with Max had become, she couldn't fight the ominous foreboding that rested heavily in her thoughts. The fact that they had fully dressed after showering, ready for trouble, only added to the darkness clinging to her mood.

She was so close to finding her way in this world again. Would the rug get pulled out from under her? No matter how much she tried to control the outcome of the next few days' events, she couldn't. Would she lose Max before she truly found him? No, she promised herself. They would get through this. They had to.

But as soon as she said the words in her head, pounding started on the door. "Sarah!" It was Cathy's voice.

Sarah and Max darted from the bed at the same time. Sarah rushed to door, Max for a weapon.

Flinging open the door, Sarah could barely believe what she saw. Cathy wasn't alone. Edward stood by her side. He was okay. She smiled and hugged him. She was taking this as a sign. She'd started to have faith again and she wasn't going to stop now.

They were winning one demon at a time. Her chest tightened. Too bad it sounded as if an entire army was on the way.

A message from the Underworld had reached Salvador. Innocents would die if Salvador did not meet Adrian immediately. The location of the meeting—a residential home in Nowhere, Texas. In other words, Salvador was being led into a trap. After great consideration, he refused the meeting, with the support of those he answered to. But when the pain of a young child began to play in his mind, Salvador reconsidered.

Salvador appeared on the front lawn of the home designated for the meeting, a child's cry sounding in his mind. Eager to act, but not foolish, he took a moment to allow the home to speak to him.

The history of the people who lived there automatically came to him. It was his gift of sight, the ability to see the past and the present—though at times, the higher powers withheld information. He didn't question why. It wasn't his place to question.

The information flowed freely now. A young couple lived within these walls. They'd lost their youngest child to cancer, and their eldest child, a daughter now ten, became a treasure they feared would also be taken from them. Each night they had prayed for her safety.

Sensing Adrian was at the rear of the house, Salvador disappeared from the front lawn and reappeared in the backyard beside a whirlpool. The child was inside the tub, her face contorted in pain, her body submerged in the Water of the Damned—water that would create such pain in a human, it would rip their hearts to shreds.

The parents were tied to chairs and gagged; a Beast was standing guard, ready to kill. The woman cried, tears streaming down her cheeks. Without hesitation, he pointed at the Beast and sent it flying across the lawn. A wave of his hands and the parents were untied. He waved his hands and flashed them across town, where they couldn't do anything foolish.

Fire singed the air and Adrian appeared a few feet from Salvador. "If you don't go in and save her, she will die."

"You know the rules. You are not to touch a human." Long ago, the Laws of Existence had been established. The higher powers allowed evil to exist within limits. It served a purpose well beyond human comprehension. And for those who had crossed over, who no longer held a human essence, there were severe penalties for breaking those laws.

Adrian smiled. Evil. Pleased with himself. "I didn't. My Beast did."

Salvador had latitude to undo the injustice done to humans by the evil that visited this realm. But that latitude came with strict guidelines. To abuse his power would come with a penalty.

"Semantics," Salvador said. "And we both know it. You did this. I can undo it."

"Feel free," Adrian offered, motioning to the child. "Save her."

Salvador showed no outward signs of reaction, though the decision before him tore him up inside.

If he went in after that child, into the water, his powers would temporarily be stripped. He'd be able to transport himself to safety, before Adrian could attack him, but nothing more. The Water of the Damned was the opposite of holy water, a hazard to all those of the higher realm, and this wasn't his first experience with it. Salvador had worked to build immunity to the water, expecting it would be used as a weapon against him again. There had been a time when the water would have ensured that he was useless for a week. But not now. Now, he would recover rapidly. He might even be ready in time for the full moon. Might. There was always the risk he would not. Not that he would interfere. The rules were clear. He kept the balance of power in proper alignment. He acted to protect the balance and enforce the rules.

Just his presence alone in Nowhere would ensure Adrian didn't break their laws. He knew it and so did

Adrian. Which was why Adrian wanted Salvador out of the picture.

The child cried out, screaming with a sharp pain; the sound wrapped around Salvador and stabbed his heart. He could not let the child die. Salvador fixed Adrian in a hard stare.

"If I find out you have violated the laws of our kind, I will ensure you pay and pay well." He said nothing more, accepting what had to be done. Salvador waded into the water.

It was time for the final Stone ceremony.

Adrian laughed as Salvador waded into the water before reluctantly flashing away from the scene of his enemy's demise, and into one of the many caverns Caden had prepared as the possible ceremonial location. Once again, Adrian became an observer, standing in the back of the lust-laden room filled with naked humans, candles flickering across bare skin. Everywhere he looked, bodies were pressed together in pleasure. Only one man stood without a partner, and that man was Allen. He sat in a corner, rocking back and forth. Adrian could feel guilt coming off the man. How pathetic. He'd come this far to bring his wife back, and now he felt guilty for the three lives that would be lost to empower the stones.

Disgusted at the sight of such weakness, Adrian jerked his gaze away, focusing on the podium in the center of the room, several feel above the collage of bodies. The three robed Stone Masters stood center stage on top of it, waiting, even welcoming, their final moments of life in this realm. A stone lay at each man's feet.

Excitement flared inside Adrian as Caden weaved his way through the crowd and stopped at the bottom of the stairs leading to the podium. Adrian was so close to embracing Vars's powers he could almost taste the pleasure of it. Caden spoke into a small microphone and began an underworld chant that Adrian knew well. It was meant to taint the souls of humans, meant to hypnotize. And it worked. It always worked. The humans quickly joined the chant, repeating his words, their desire for one another lost as they walked toward the podium, joining hands and forming a circle. The Stone Masters disrobed, giving their bodies to their cause, as they would soon give their souls. Caden began a slow walk up the stairs, the magic within already called to life, crackling in the air.

Adrian watched as Caden stepped to the center of the podium, watched as blue lightning shot from one stone to its master. Seconds passed, and the master crumbled to the ground. The two others quickly followed. The stones crackled with electricity, glowing blue.

Pleasure filled Adrian. Things were going his way. With the ceremony complete and Salvador out of the way, nothing would stop Adrian from claiming Vars's magic and his rightful place in the Underworld. Pleasure filled Adrian. Things were going his way.

Chapter 22

For two days the town had been silent, almost normal. A facade that no one believed. And now, the night of the full moon had arrived.

Max stood on the porch of the inn, Des by his side. "You don't have to do this," Max reminded Des. "You have a mate now to think about. Go back to the ranch and take care of her."

Des snorted. "Right. Like me leaving is really going to happen." His hand went to Max's shoulder before he leaned on the railing. "Jessica would kick my ass if I deserted you in your time of need. Not to mention I'd never miss a fight like this one." He sobered. "You helped me save Jessica's life, man. I am in your debt for eternity."

"If I have an eternity left," Max said, his gaze traveling the dark horizon where lightning struck, searching for the trouble, his senses raw with warning.

"You still don't remember what happened that day, do you?" Des asked.

Max's gaze shot to Des. "Do you?"

"I was freaking out over Jessica being stabbed. I didn't see what happened. I wish I had because, man, I don't believe you went all dark and just killed that man. Not for a minute. You believed in me when I thought I couldn't be saved. Back at you, *brother.*" He emphasized the last word, letting Max know he had a new brother, he had Des. "I choose to believe in you now, too."

His eyes lifted, searched, and he pushed off the railing, tense and alert. "You getting that vibe I'm getting?"

Before Max could say, "Hell yes," an army of Beasts appeared in the far distance. Jag orbed onto the porch. Rinehart and Rock rushed through the door of the inn. The Knights stood side by side, swords drawn. They all knew a team of their own army would close in from behind the Beasts. Just as they had Knights at the outskirts of the cabin, waiting, ready.

Cathy, Sarah and Edward appeared on the porch. Sarah stepped to Max's side. "Oh, my God," she whispered. "There are so many of them."

"They're early," Cathy said. "They shouldn't be able to do the ritual until midnight. It's not even nightfall."

"Apparently, they have other ideas," Edward commented dryly, back to his normal form.

"Max," Jag said, his tone clipped, short. "The minute our men attack, you and Des hit the road. Take Sarah and the others to the cabin."

Max nodded. As much as he didn't want Sarah at the cabin, her team could stop Allen and Caden from liberating Vars if they worked together with Marisol to counter the magic.

Jag turned to Rinehart and Rock. "Get the humans under cover. I'll come back for you, with Marisol in tow."

Black rain began to fall. Hell was calling. Max and Des looked at each other, their shared look saying they were ready to answer that call; they were ready to fight.

And they planned to win.

The van hit a pothole and flew into the air, crashing down to the road with a heavy thud that threw Sarah against Max. Des reached for a handle on the door; Max grabbed Sarah, righting her before she hit the wall of the van. His gut wrenched. He wasn't going to be able to protect her so easily. Her eyes lifted to his and her hand went to his where it rested on her shoulder. She laced her fingers with his. This was it and they both knew it. Live or die, eternally together, or forever separated. This town, their lives, their futures were on the line. Somehow, Max was certain his test ended here, today, along with this battle to stop Vars—both outcomes uncertain.

"Holy shit!" Edward yelled from the driver's seat.

Cathy shouted a similar proclamation from beside him. Max pulled away from Sarah to look out the front window, the cabin in their sights. Knights and Beasts were heavy in combat. A Mercedes sat beside the cabin.

Sarah pushed to Max's side. "They're here already. Please don't let us be too late."

Jag and Marisol appeared in the van. "Stop the van," Jag ordered.

Edward slammed on the brakes. Marisol moved

between Cathy and Edward and took their hands. Jag did the same with Max and Sarah and issued a warning. "We have no idea what we're headed into. Be ready for anything."

Marisol offered a grave reminder. "Take your positions around the triangle where Vars will appear, and let Max and Jag deal with Caden and Allen."

"Right," Max said. "We'll break the magic circle and end the ceremony."

"And get the vial," Jag added.

"But if they fail," Marisol said, "we have to be ready to send Vars back to his prison."

"Looks like I'm the fifth wheel," Des said. "I'll be outside kicking ass." His gaze settled on Max. "I've got your back, man. Nothing is getting inside that isn't already there. Be safe, brother."

Jag eyed the group. "Ready?"

Sarah and Max stared at each other. "Ready," they said at once.

Max had barely set foot in the cabin before things spun out of control. The pure evil lacing the air damn near stole his breath, and he knew Vars was stronger now, ready for the freedom they'd come to prevent him from receiving. Caden and Allen were both there already, both wearing black robes, both holding knives. And they were not without protection.

Four Beasts stepped between their team and the ritual area. The drawings on the floor were ready for use. Max wasn't surprised to find William was one of those Beasts; he'd expected another confrontation. Even welcomed it. Well-armed, the Beasts wore their vinyl-looking armored suits. There was no facade of humanity; the Beasts bared their fangs as quickly as they did their swords. Max wrestled down his fear for Sarah, willing himself to stay focused on the battle. There was no turning back now.

He and Jag placed themselves in front of their group, both drawing their weapons. The Beasts charged forward. With practiced precision, Max and Jag took on two enemies each, both quickly beheading the first of their foes. The heads tumbled to the ground in flames that quickly turned to ash.

As Jag dealt with his second opponent, William darted toward Sarah. Edward grabbed her and shoved her behind him. William growled and yanked Edward forward, his fangs sinking into his neck, Edward's feet dangling from the ground.

Sarah screamed, and the sound sent guilt rocketing through Max's body. He should have killed William while he had the chance. Rage ripped through him, and Max attacked William's back. Jag appeared in front of William, pulling Edward from his grip. Max threw William with all his might, and William stumbled, a loud angry sound erupting from his throat. He turned to face Max at the same moment that Max's sword cut through the air. William's head tumbled to the ground, turning to ash within seconds.

Without warning, wind erupted in the room, throwing things everywhere, hissing with evil bliss. You could feel its menacing quality, its impatience for the demon prince to be freed.

"The ritual has started!" Cathy yelled over the chaos from where she leaned over Edward's limp body. "Break the circle."

Max turned to see Caden and Allen slice their palms, bleeding into the circle. Vars appeared inside the triangle, one step closer to freedom. His deep, evil laugh resonated eerily through the room.

Before Max could stop her, Sarah dashed toward the circle, brave, without hesitation. Max's heart kicked into double time, concern for Sarah pushing him forward. She crossed the line of the circle before he could get to her and Vars roared with anger.

"Adrian!" he shouted, and then faded away, back into his hell hole.

The circle broken, the ritual had temporarily come to a halt. But they needed the vial to stop it permanently and Sarah grabbed it from Allen's neck and yanked. Max appeared at the edge of the circle and ripped Sarah from its confines an instant before Caden's blade would have claimed her. She stumbled backward onto the ground. Max stripped Caden of his knife, and shoved him far out of the circle, his peripheral vision catching Allen diving for Sarah and the vial.

Sarah. He had to save Sarah.

Max turned to find her on her back, Allen crouched over her as they struggled for the vial. Max bent over Allen and grabbed his shirt, the blade he'd just removed from Caden in his hand—throwing it down would be handing it over to Caden again. Before he could get a good grip on Allen, Caden pounced on his back. Max tried to hold the weight, fearful of all three men falling on top of Sarah. He saw Jag's boots, knew he was going after Caden. But Allen panicked and shoved upward. To Max's horror the blade he held ripped through Allen's back.

Everything seemed to fade into slow motion. Memories assailed Max. Memories of the day he killed the human. The man had turned into his blade much as Allen had now. The entire scene replayed in his mind with brilliant clarity. Max squeezed his eyes shut, realizing for the first time that killing the human had indeed been an accident. He hadn't lost control, hadn't allowed his dark side to kill.

Feeling the weight of Caden yanked off his back, Max rolled off Allen. Briefly, his gaze flicked to Jag as he shoved Caden out the front door, into the mix of the battle still raging beyond these walls. Then Max's attention returned to Allen.

Max lifted Allen off of Sarah. The knife was deep in his back. Max's eyes locked with Sarah's and relief flooded him when he noted she was unhurt. The vial remained in her hand, crushed, glass splintered in her palm.

Assured of Sarah's safety, his concerns returned to Allen. *Please, God. Don't let him die. Not again. Not Allen.* "Marisol!" he shouted, bending down over Allen, desperate to somehow make this right.

Sarah tossed the vial aside, scrambling to her knees, ignoring any pain she might feel as she crouched next to Max.

Her good hand went to Max's back. "It was an accident Max. An accident." She called out as he had. "Marisol!"

Marisol was finally there kneeling beside Allen. She touched his head as if she would find answers there. Max held his breath as he waited for her conclusion and he sensed Sarah did the same.

She glanced up at Max. "Remove the knife."

He nodded and did as she said. "Please tell me you can fix him."

"I can."

Max exhaled, relief washing over him. Relief that lasted only a minute as Adrian appeared beside the ritual circle, four Beasts by his side. "You will pay for interfering in my plans," he said. "The Knights will lose their leader this day. Jag will die." Two more Beasts appeared in the room. Then two more.

Max shoved to his feet, stepping to Jag's side. Neither Knight looked at the other, both ready for battle.

Sarah took in the sight of the man who'd promised Jag's death. He wore black leather, his long blond hair and muscular body making him look more Sex God than demon. But there was no mistaking the pure evil surrounding him. She pushed to her feet, sick to her stomach, certain that death would follow.

In astonishment, she watched another man appear in front of Jag and Max; his presence was like a shield. She could see only his back, his long black hair, his simple clothing of jeans and T-shirt. But just as there was no mistaking the other man's evil, there was no mistaking this man's power. "Hello, Adrian," the newcomer said. "Sorry I'm late. Did I miss anything?"

The man, Adrian, contorted into a beastly image. "Salvador! You can't be here. I stripped your powers."

"You should never underestimate me, Adrian. Your Water of the Damned was nothing but a temporary thorn in my side. Consequently, I've sealed Vars's prison. He won't be coming out anytime soon. And I believe one of your Beasts already dealt with Caden. You seem to be the only loose end. I'd suggest you and your Beasts retreat before I send you to join Vars. I filled him in on your plan to steal his demon legions. I'm certain he'd welcome a visit from you right about now."

Adrian pointed at Salvador, the act ominous, threatening. A laugh bubbled from Salvador's throat. Rich. Pure. It rippled down Sarah's spine. *Was he an angel?* Sarah wondered.

"Please do give me a reason to strike back," Salvador challenged, his voice laced with a taunt. Adrian hesitated before his hands balled by his sides. A second later, he thrust his fist forward and fire shot at Salvador. Palm up, Salvador received the fire, throwing it back at Adrian. A wild eruption of fireballs went back and forth, one after the other until Salvador and Adrian stood in a face-off, neither a victor nor a failure. With red, blazing eyes, Adrian glared at Salvador, the entire room crackling with his menace. There was no doubt a vicious battle could evolve from this confrontation, no doubt the danger of just that was but a hair from conception.

Abruptly, Adrian thrust his head back in the air and roared, the entire building shaking with the impact. When he finally calmed, his chin tilted downward and his stare fixed once again on Salvador. "This isn't over. Mark my words—in the not-so-distant future your Knights will fall to my Beasts. And I will revel in watching you suffer through their pain."

Fire erupted around him, and he and his Beasts disappeared. Max turned to Sarah and pulled her close. She clung to him, seeing the tension in his face. The worry in his eyes spoke volumes. He thought this was it. His final moments.

Salvador rotated around to face those who observed him but he appeared to see only Max and Sarah. That's when she saw his eyes. Green, serene, devastating in their impact. His features were not handsome, yet he was beautiful beyond belief. She shook as he approached, but not from fear.

"Hello, Sarah. I'm Salvador."

"Hello," she replied, at a loss for anything more brilliant to say.

"You've done well," he said. "Your parents are proud. They want you to know they are always with you."

Tears came instantly, because Sarah knew, absolutely knew, he had spoken to them. She collapsed against Max, shaken to the core.

"Max," Salvador said. "You, too, have done well. You selflessly refused to find the peace Sarah would have given you. You put her first. Over and over, I have watched you fight your darkness. Even when you thought you had no hope of survival, you fought to help Des find his. You had faith in everyone but yourself, and I couldn't allow that. Ultimately, it weakened you and it would have led to your destruction."

He smiled. "Now you have Sarah. I'm quite certain you have another four centuries to give me, don't you?"

"As long as you will have me," Max said, his voice cracking.

"I'd say an eternity should do," Salvador said, smiling. Sarah's heart swelled and she hugged Max tighter than she'd ever hugged anyone.

He kissed her, his hands framing her face, his finger wiping the tears from her cheeks. "And as long as you will have me."

"An eternity should do," she whispered.

"One more thing," Salvador said, drawing their attention. "Cathy is the mate of a future Knight. I'd like you both to look out for her, though I've arranged a big brother of sorts for her." His gaze shifted to Sarah. "Edward will be joining the Knights. I trust you can deal with mediating Cathy and Edward's arguments a little longer?"

Sarah smiled, laughter bubbling from her throat. "Oh, yes. I believe I can."

"Good. Good. And don't worry about Allen. Marisol will wipe his memories and he will live a long life. How he spends the afterlife comes down to how he lives that long life. But he still has hope of seeing his wife again one day." He winked at Sarah. "Kate is quite appreciative by the way." He motioned Jag forward. "Jag and I will ease the town back into their comfort zone. I thought the two of you might enjoy heading to the ranch and settling in."

Sarah looked up at Max, happiness shining in his eyes. "Yes," they said together.

Salvador touched them both, filling them with warmth. Sarah and Max disappeared and reappeared on the front lawn of a house.

Max smiled down at her. "Welcome to the ranch. The home of The Knights of White, and your home— our home together—if you decide to make it so." He pressed his fingers to her lips before she could respond. "And don't say you've already decided. I've waited four centuries for you, Sarah. I can wait a little longer. I need to know you come to me not out of duress, not out of the heat of danger. Be here. Be with me. Then make your choice."

"Max," she whispered, her hand brushing his cheek. She loved him so much in that moment. He was a man of honor, unwilling to take what wasn't his. But she was his. She always had been. She'd been waiting for him all her life.

Epilogue

Two weeks later

Breakfast at the ranch was a big event and it drew a crowd that had now finally thinned. Sarah and Max sat across from each other, at the kitchen table. In some corner of her mind, she was aware of Edward and Cathy arguing. Again. But Sarah had no idea about what. Nor did she care. The two of them were happy here. Cathy was already planning ways their operation could aid the Knights' work. No. Cathy and Edward were not her concern right now. She and Max were.

Sarah stared at her plate, afraid to look at Max for fear she might explode into flames—that's how damn aroused and on edge she was these days. She and Max had been getting to know each other for far too long now. She understood why he'd wanted to wait, why he wanted her full acceptance of his life, his world, but he had that. The ranch was wonderful. The little cottage to the east of the main house that Jag had offered to make theirs was perfect. But so far they were still staying in an upstairs bedroom—together, but not quite. It was time to solidify their mating.

She shoved her chair back and stood, her eyes lifting to Max's. "Can I see you a moment?" Heat curled in her stomach the instant their eyes connected, no doubt desire flared in her eyes. She hoped so. Hoped he saw what she felt. Hoped he knew what she wanted.

Slowly, he rose from his seat, a primal edge clinging to him. He burned for her as much as she did for him. He had to know they could wait no longer. "Of course," he said.

Sarah didn't say anything to Cathy or Edward. She rounded the table and Max followed. In silence they climbed the stairs to the second level of the house, the air crackling with sexual tension.

The minute they were in the guest bedroom they'd been occupying, Sarah whirled on Max. "Do you want to spend forever with me?"

Instantly, he reached for her. Her hands settled on his chest, the heat of his body pressed to her. His voice was low, husky, laced with fire and desire, with love. "I love you more than I could ever express and, yes, I want you forever, Sarah. I want you to be my wife, my mate. You're already my everything."

"Then make it so, Max." Her voice lowered to a soft plea. "Make it so."

He kissed her then, a long deep kiss full of tenderness. Kissed her until a firestorm of passion erupted between them.

Long minutes later, they were in the bed, clothing piled on the floor. Sarah was on top of Max, straddling him, their bodies intimately connected. She lay on top of him, their lips joined, her breasts pressed to his chest. Their hips rocked, their movements a sensual sway. The pleasure almost more than she could bear yet it still wasn't enough.

When she thought she might cry out for him, Max sat up, his arms around her back, holding her. Yellow tinged his eyes and she smiled. For she saw the beast in him—her beast.

Her lips brushed his. "Max," she whispered.

"I love you, Sarah." And with those precious words he bent his head, his teeth claiming her shoulder. Sarah gasped with the contact, a sigh quickly following, the pleasure of the moment darting straight to her core. The happiness filling her heart.

Now she was home.

SPECIAL EDITION

Kate's Boys

A late-night walk on the beach resulted in Trevor Marlowe's heroic rescue of a drowning woman. He took the amnesia victim in and dubbed her Venus, for the goddess who'd emerged from the sea. It looked as if she might be his goddess of love, too…until her former fiancé showed up on Trevor's doorstep.

Don't miss

THE BRIDE WITH NO NAME

by *USA TODAY* bestselling author

MARIE FERRARELLA

Available August
wherever you buy books.

Silhouette®

Romantic
SUSPENSE

**Sparked by Danger,
Fueled by Passion.**

Cindy Dees
Killer Affair

SEDUCTION SUMMER

Seduction in the sand…and a killer on the beach.

Can-do girl Madeline Crummby is off to a remote
Fijian island to review an exclusive resort, and she hires
Tom Laruso, a burned-out bodyguard, to fly her there
in spite of an approaching hurricane. When their plane
crashes, they are trapped on an island with a serial killer
who stalks overaffectionate couples. When their false
attempts to lure out the killer turn all too real, Tom and
Madeline must risk their lives and their hearts….

**Look for the third installment
of this thrilling miniseries,
available August 2008
wherever books are sold.**

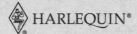

HARLEQUIN®

American ★ Romance®

CATHY McDAVID
Cowboy Dad

THE STATE OF PARENTHOOD

Natalie Forrester's job at Bear Creek Ranch
is to make everyone welcome, which is an
easy task when it comes to Aaron Reyes—the
unwelcome cowboy and part-owner. His
tenderness toward Natalie's infant daughter
melts the single mother's heart. What's not
so easy to accept is that falling for him means
giving up her job, her family and the only
home she's ever known....

**Available August
wherever books are sold.**

LOVE, HOME & HAPPINESS

www.eHarlequin.com   HAR75225

nocturne™

COMING NEXT MONTH

#45 DANCE OF THE WOLF • Karen Whiddon
The Pack

On a mission to find his best friend, who's disappeared, Dr. Jared Gies's search leads him not only to Elena Cabrera—the woman he recognizes as his one true mate—but also straight into danger. And although Elena wants nothing to do with shifters, their very lives—and those of Jared's fellow wolves—now depend on him winning her trust.

#46 SON OF THE SHADOWS • Nancy Holder
The Gifted

War would erupt before the House of the Shadows—unless its Guardian, Jean-Marc de Devereaux, could turn his back on his forbidden love with Isabelle of the House of Flames. But what surprises had their union already wrought in this world of powerful magic and age-old vendettas?

SNCNM0708